The Sand

Copyright ©

Celia Micklefield hereby asserts the moral right to be identified as the author of this work of fiction.

All rights reserved.

No part of this publication may be reproduced, stored in a retrieval system, or transmitted, in any form or by any means, electronic, mechanical, photocopying, recording or otherwise, without the prior permission of the author.

ISBN-13:978-1544779027
ISBN-10:154477902X

All characters in this publication are fictitious and any resemblance to real persons, living or dead is coincidental.

DEDICATION

For my sister who adopted Wiltshire as her home.

ACKNOWLEDGEMENTS

The Sandman and Mrs Carter takes place in the beautiful county of Wiltshire, England. I love it very much and each time I visit I find new favourite places. I wanted a quiet village for the setting of this story, a peaceful location, the kind of place where you'd never imagine life could ever be anything other than idyllic.

I've used the name *Compton* for my village. There are various Comptons in Wiltshire. They usually come with a suffix or a prefix such as Little or Greater. My setting is an amalgamation of all the Comptons I've visited over the years and I know the good people of the Comptons will forgive my messing about with their geography.

They *are* friendly people in Wiltshire. As a visiting Yorkshire lass I have always been made most welcome. They like to chat the way I do. They are interested in you the way I am interested in meeting new people. They are happy to break off what they're doing to stand and have that little conversation with you.

Their beer's not bad, either!

The Sandman and Mrs Carter

Part One

1

Listen. Don't be afraid. I'd like a soothing word in your ear before we begin. A moment of your time. If you please, a quiet start whispered in the dark. Soft breath against your neck - a hint of me. Tender touch of mystery - a clue. Let me kiss you with my voice. Let my words caress.

These chapters are like gospels. In its own way each tells the truth. Each speaks for one who believes it. Only viewpoint changes. The truth is always the truth. Their chapters are not *my* truth. Mine is complete and when we reach the end you'll see the sense in what I'm saying now.

Have faith in the narrators when they tell you what they know. They do not mean to deceive. Accept what they say. They may see things from different perspectives but it is still only and always the truth. Trust all of the narrators. Especially me. There are no liars here.

Forget you can't see me. Many things you cannot see affect your lives. Take emotions. You can't hold a piece in your hands and say, *Look. Here is a bite of fear. And here is a budding pulse of anger.* Show me a quiver of desire, an overwhelming disappointment. Where do these things go when the feeling dies?

This is Mrs Wendy Carter's story. Others' stories intertwine as is the way with people. One truth's weft weaves in another's warp to make the finished fabric. I will be your escort. My real name? Hush. Not yet.

Listen to my temperate voice. I'll make it questioning or else I'll bring you balm. I reserve the right of free expression as do all the narrators. I am your guide, here to ease your journey. Let me murmur in your ear of things to be imagined. Let me embrace your reasoning and show you what to think.

Only I can stroke away the shadows and lead you through the dark.

Hush, now. Listen. Mrs Wendy Carter is indisposed and will not speak for herself. The others speak of her and for her.

And remember, there are no liars here.

2

Marcus

I knew who Wendy Carter was, of course. Everybody in Compton had heard of the Carters: Wendy, her husband Rob and her mother, Jenny.

It's a small market town, not much bigger than a village. Some might call it a satellite town with easy access to motorways, towns and cities like Swindon or Bath, but far enough away to remain unaffected by city ways. Compton sits in a pleasant valley surrounded by hills so smooth and green in summer they look like brushed velvet. Driving is a pleasure here. Up and over those hills on country lanes and you're in another little market town and then another, each with its own church and picturesque cottages, some with thatched roofs.

People in Compton tend to know rather more of each other's business than is the case in larger places. You can see them swapping stories, standing together in the car parking each side of the main street. The tight spaces somehow call for an extra degree of intimacy with people parked next to you. It's all very polite.

Wiltshire people are friendly, relaxed, easy-going. It's as if it would be too much trouble to feel anxious about anything. Even behind the wheel they are polite. When I moved here with my wife and family five years ago we were amused by what we called the Wiltshire Stand-Off at roundabouts. Nobody wanted to be rude enough to go first. We found the whole place charming and settled quickly on a stone cottage with a view towards Marlborough and the hill with the white horse.

Compton doesn't have problems. It has good schools, a swimming pool in the leisure centre and a library behind a parade of shops on the main street. There's street entertainment in summer and flower and vegetable shows in autumn. Children take dustbin liners and slide down the white horse hill on winter snows. Twinkling lights dress all the trees at Christmas; banks of bright crocuses fill spring borders. It rains or it shines and the people of Compton take it in their stride, bolstered by that polite friendliness. When something unusual happens everybody knows about it. Wendy Carter's mother became a local celebrity.

I'd been involved, to some small degree, in the mother's case. All the Carter family was registered with us at the new joint practice. Not with me personally but from time to time we see our colleagues' patients. That's the way we deal with appointment waiting lists.

I first met Wendy Carter at the surgery in April this year after the inquest into her mother's death. She was thin, unkempt. Her open coat revealed jeans that hung on her hips, a shapeless sweater draped across a flat chest. She had her hands stuffed inside her pockets. Her eyes darted around my office. I asked her to take a seat. She kept up that furtive flitting as if she couldn't decide which seat to take. I looked in her notes. She was forty-five but looked older. Stress can do that.

"Doctor Dalton has been called away," I said. I asked what I could do for her. She was shaking. She looked extremely uncomfortable as if she might run back out the door.

"If you'd rather not see me we can book another appointment for you," I said. "Doctor Dalton will be back in next week."

She sat, took her hands out of her pockets and began twisting her wedding ring. She wouldn't meet my eyes. I waited.

"I need something to help me sleep," she said. She told me she hadn't slept properly for months and it was easy to believe her. There were dark circles under those flickering eyes. Her trembling fingers continued twisting away at her wedding band.

I asked her to explain further but she would say no more than that she'd been having problems sleeping since her mother died. I made my decision. She was grieving. No doubt she was still in shock from the manner of Jenny's death and the implications that arose out of it. I knew she'd also had difficulties with her husband. She looked exhausted. I wrote the prescription.

My daughter is a student at the sixth form college where Wendy's husband, Rob Carter works. Head of the English department. Sophie likes him. Says he's a great teacher. Through all that other business when he was suspended she kept track of developments. My wife passed it all on to me. I didn't pay much attention to it at the time.

Wendy was the first to admit she was no academic. She'd done little reading and left school with few qualifications. She told Sophie as much in the supermarket canteen where Sophie had her weekend job. Wendy had two part-time jobs, one in a charity shop and the other at the Asda supermarket in town. The girls in the canteen were having a discussion about the derivation of the brand name Nike. Wendy had never heard of the Greek goddess of victory. Afterwards they chatted while they filled shelves and so on. Sophie couldn't believe it when she found out who Wendy's husband was.

"They are so not a couple," she told me one evening after dinner. "I mean, I like her and everything but she's so . . . ordinary."

Sophie said it like it was the worst thing to be. Rob Carter was too much of a catch for ordinary Wendy according to Sophie. She thought he was brilliant. All the girls at the sixth form college rated Rob Carter, she said.

"How old is he?" I said.

"Not much older than you."

"Older?"

"Not much. Wendy's about ten years younger than him, I think. But you'd never tell. He's got one of those kinds of faces that stay looking young. He's got wrinkles and everything but they kind of look right on him. You know. It's not so surprising. Look how Mum always fancied Sean Connery."

I stopped listening at that point. My wife always coped better with Sophie's teenage opinions. I can't get excited about Sophie's choice of music or who is seeing who. Sarah handles all that better than I do. I left them making evening drinks and went to my study.

Whether or not Wendy Carter was a good match for her husband Rob was a question I didn't feel qualified to attempt. On the other hand, the questions over Wendy's mother intrigued me. The events surrounding the miraculous cure of Jenny Carter made the headlines and baffled the medical profession. Her subsequent and sudden demise was noted in the Compton Mercury and ensured the Carter name would lodge forever in local gossip.

When Wendy came in for that April appointment I made a professional decision based on what she told me. It's easy, with hindsight, to say there was something different one should have done. Maybe I should have looked beyond her wavering gaze as she sat, tapping her feet, waiting for me to sign off on her medication. When I recall it now it's true to say it did seem as if she wasn't telling me everything. Hiding something. Maybe even lying. I suppose you could say she looked shifty. Too alert to be sleep deprived. But I had no reason to disbelieve her. I had a long list that morning and home visits to make in the afternoon. I explained the dosage to her and gave her the usual warnings. I slid the prescription across the desk to her. She gave me a hurried thank you and went. I didn't give it another thought. Not then.

As a matter of interest I always thought that J.M.Barrie had invented the name in Peter Pan. Not so. Census records show much earlier use of the name Wendy but it's Barrie's version that endures. Or Disney's interpretation of her. My image of a Wendy is fixed in my own past, in my own early memories. It's strange the way we carry parts of our childhood into our adult lives and things such as your idea of what a Wendy should be like can stay the same all through your life. If challenged, our adult reasoning takes back control and we realise what nonsense it is. But when the challenge is removed we reverse our thinking. We want to. We like to hang onto the child within us. There's no harm in that. Where it's appropriate.

In my imagination Wendy is trapped forever in a demure nightgown, not quite a woman not still a child. Everyone is familiar with the story. Lost Boys. Jealous fairy. It's a child fantasy. Wendy Carter's fantasy, it turned out, was something quite different.

3

Listen. Thanks are due to Doctor Marcus Harding. I'm sure the authorities appreciate his input. People trust him. He has letters after his name. But there are things he could never know about the Carters. I'm the only one who knows the whole truth. If I told you who I am you wouldn't believe me so there's no point. I might as well be Rumpelstiltskin. Or Captain Hook. Eventually you will think you know and then you can go question your own sanity.

Wendy Carter had had a lot of disappointments. She should have married somebody with a different surname. Her maiden name was Carter. She moved from maidenhood to marriage and stayed just the same. Miss Wendy Carter had lived in a solid old semi-detached bungalow with her widowed mother. Mrs Wendy Carter lived in an identical bungalow with her schoolteacher husband.

Who can tell how much the details of her early life shaped the woman she became? I can. Wait, though. False impressions are so easily formed. Like the doctor's daughter, Sophie said, Wendy Carter was ordinary. She did what she had to do. She grew up. Got married. Kept house. Had twin boys who grew up with their father's brains and went to university a whole year before their age group. It wasn't until she hit her forties that she stopped being ordinary. I was watching just over a year ago when it began.

It was a typical evening in the Carter household. Television on. Tiffany lamps on the side tables giving out a subdued light. Dinner dishes washed and neatly stacked on the drainer. The smell of lemon cream cleaner on the worktops. There should have been a cosy glow: two boys settled and doing well at university; trimmed lawns, nice car in the garage.

But Rob was looking bored. After a few minutes Wendy sensed the movement of his right hand. She didn't see it but was aware of the slight shift in his position. Her stomach sank. They used separate sofas now at right angles to one another and with a coffee table in between but from where she sat, out of the corner of her eye she could see his head begin to loll against his shoulder. She knew it wouldn't be long before his chin fell onto the heel of that hand.

She could rouse him if she chose. She could warn him that he was going to miss *Question Time* and she knew he'd say *I wasn't asleep.* In seconds his head would be back on his hand and he'd miss the rest of the news and she'd have to rouse him again to tell him she was going to bed. They never went to bed together any more. She used to make little jokes about taking other men with her.

"Lee Child's coming with me tonight," she might say. Or, "I've got a date under the covers with Jack Reacher."

"I'll be along in a minute," he'd say and the minute would turn into hours before he flopped onto the mattress beside her at two or three in the morning or disturb her with his shuffling in the dark.

She'd tried to broach the subject with her mother.

"Well, they do go off it," her mother had said. "After a certain age. It's to be expected."

"He's only fifty three, Mum."

"Is he? I forget. He acts older than that."

Wendy's face fell. Her mother had quickly tried to make amends.

"Is he working too hard? Have you both thought about early retirement?"

Wendy rolled her eyes.

"Mum, I work longer hours than he does. Anyway, we can't afford early retirement. The twins have only just started university."

Mother had put on the kettle and brought out cake and the subject had been abandoned.

High-pitched whistling noises were coming down Rob's nose. Wendy cringed as she watched him. She couldn't remember when the rot had first shown signs of setting in but once the boys were gone, instead of rediscovering one another like her magazines said would happen, she and Rob had become like polite strangers. It wasn't only about the lack of intimacy. She thought that sometimes just to be held would be nice. Or a kind word. Or a look. Or a touch of the hand. Something. *Anything* to feel loved again. It didn't seem too much to ask.

She jumped up and left him where he was. His mouth was open and he was making choking noises at the back of his throat. She switched everything off and closed the door behind her so she couldn't hear him. She cleansed her face and brushed her teeth. Forty four, she thought, and it felt as though her life was over.

In bed she lay staring at the ceiling wondering about her friends' marriages. But they were Rob's friends really, all of them. Rob didn't count the few friends Wendy made at the supermarket as people he'd want to share an evening with. He liked to keep the circle small. He felt more comfortable in the company of other teachers. She couldn't go to any of them with her problem. None of them ever talked about personal things, let alone about sex. It was as if middle age had flicked off a switch. The subject was closed. You weren't supposed to want it more than on high days and anniversaries.

When they went to barbecues or met friends at the pub the women talked about holidays or how much their children were earning. They looked forward to being grandparents. That made Wendy's stomach flip. Wendy couldn't imagine looking forward to being a grandmother and starting the whole rigmarole over again. She wasn't ready. She hadn't stopped thinking about her own boys as children. They hadn't finished growing up yet.

There was Joan at the charity shop. She thought about talking to her. Joan was a nice person. Maybe she would understand.

Rob slept in the living room till four in the morning. He woke needing the toilet and afterwards slumped onto the bed beside her. In seconds he was snoring again. Wendy felt his weight on the mattress. She wanted his weight on her. She lay for a while, trying to remember what it felt like to have him. She got up. She turned on a news channel and sat in the place where Rob had slept. The cushions were still warm from his body heat. She could feel it rising through her thin nightdress, creeping along the back of her thighs. The thought of it made her long for the touch of his skin.

I knew it couldn't go on like that much longer, even if she didn't. I felt her need. I was sure it wouldn't be long before Mrs Wendy Carter and I became more closely acquainted.

4

Joan

I always felt a bit sorry for Wendy. She was a sweet thing, really, but you know, sometimes I thought she wasn't quite all there. Bless. Heart of gold, she had. She'd do anything for you. She never used to say much, at first, not about her home life. Well, she's a lot younger than us. She was quite shy when she first came to work here but then she blossomed. We soon brought her out of her shell. Norma and me might be old girls now but we still know how to have some fun. We like a bit of banter, a bit of harmless teasing. Sometimes even the customers join in with us.

We get a lot of regulars in here, dear. Looking for bargains. They like to browse the bookshelves, flick through the clothing racks. They poke about in the baskets of odds and sods for ages. Some of them peep through into the back room trying to see if we've put anything on one side. They think they might find something worth a fortune. They'll be lucky. We like to keep up to date, Norma and me. We like to find out how much things are worth. We've got our own copy of Miller's Guide under the counter and we watch Antiques Roadshow every week. We check everything that comes in just to make sure we're not selling something for fifty pence when it might be worth hundreds of pounds.

Wendy came in on Tuesdays and Thursdays. Sometimes the odd Saturday afternoon as well if she wasn't at Asdas. You know, if she'd done an early shift over there she'd come here in the afternoon. She always brought in cream cakes. Always. See, that's what I mean about her being kind-hearted. I'd say to her, "Wendy, my lovely," I'd say, "there's no need to go spending your money on us old trouts."

She'd look at me and say, "I don't need your permission, Joan Spencer, to do something nice."

Oh, we loved Wendy. We did, really.

She used to say some strange things, though. Ask odd questions. Personal, like. You know, the sort of things you'd only discuss with your closest friend. All I can say is, she must have been lonely. Very lonely to come asking me questions like that.

It got a bit embarrassing talking about sexual relations. I'm from a different generation, dear. We weren't brought up to discuss those things. I'd never heard of the word orgasm till some character said it on the telly. I'd had three kiddies by then.

Wendy wanted to know how old my husband was when he went off sex. Do you know, I didn't know where to put myself. I could hardly look her in the eye.

"Wendy!" I said to her. "What a thing to ask."

But she was really serious about it. She said something about an article she'd been reading in a women's magazine. Honestly, the things they put in them these days. It seems to me as if it's got to be sex with everything. Well, I could see she really wanted an answer, so I told her. Oh, I was honest with her. There's no point in trying to cover up how you really feel about something, is there?

"Not soon enough," I said. "I wished he'd put a stop to all that business a lot sooner. The sooner the better for me. The great lump."

Well, I had to laugh thinking about those days. Puffing and sweating. I used to think the old feller would bust a gut just with the effort of trying. But Wendy wasn't laughing. No. She looked really upset.

I said to her, I said, "Look, my lovely. I'm sorry to say this to you, but do you think he might be having an affair?"

"Who?" she said.

"Well," I said, "it's obvious why you want to know. You're talking about your husband, aren't you, Wendy?"

Do you see what I mean about her not being quite with it? She seemed surprised I'd worked out she was talking about herself and her own situation.

You have to wonder, sometimes, what it is that brings couples together in the first place. Wendy's husband works at the sixth form college, you know. He's a clever man. He went to one of the big universities. You'd think he'd have chosen a girl from a similar background, someone who could have serious conversations with him. As I said, Wendy's a lovely girl with a kind heart and everything but I did wonder what the attraction was.

It was fairly obvious to me what Wendy saw in him. As soon as she told me she'd lost her father when she was only a youngster I could see she must have been looking for a father figure. Not consciously, if you understand what I mean. I don't think she deliberately went out of her way to find that sort of man. These things just happen without you being aware of them, don't they?

Her husband came here once looking for her. I don't know what he wanted but he stood right there in the doorway by the card rack and wouldn't come in properly. He peered over the top of his glasses and made a sort of gesture with his head. Sideways. Like he was saying 'Come here'. Wendy had to go outside to talk to him. He's quite a bit taller than her and he stood over her with his hands clasped behind his back like he was talking to a child in school. Wendy stood there, looking up at him, and every now and then she pulled on her hair and fiddled with the collar on her shirt. He never popped his head in to say goodbye to either of us. He just walked off like he was Prince Charles, striding off into the arcade with his hands flapping behind him.

When Wendy came back in she was blushing. He'd embarrassed her. She rushed off to the toilet in the back room and I heard her blowing her nose. She'd had a little cry, I think. Norma went out to get some doughnuts and I put the kettle on. We didn't ask her what the matter was and she didn't offer to tell so we never found out what that was about. But I could guess from the way she fell into that hair-pulling habit it wasn't the first time he'd acted that way.

Oh, yes. I think you could safely say he was the one wearing the trousers at home, dear. And there was one other thing I noticed about the two of them standing there together. They didn't look like a couple that belonged to one another.

They weren't *together* together. It's funny, but somehow they both looked lonely. They stood apart like people in a bus queue not wanting to brush up against each other. I mean, even after the sex bit has gone out of a relationship there ought to be some sort of closeness left, shouldn't there? Or else what's the point of still being man and wife? I know I go on about my old feller but I'd back him in an argument with the council or something like that. You bet I would. We don't see eye to eye on everything but when it comes down to the serious things in life we're singing from the same hymn sheet.

Not Wendy and her husband. They stood in that doorway like cold statues, something you'd see in a museum, him with his chin nearly on his chest as he looked down at her and her like that cat in Shrek, eyes all big and wide. I know she'd more or less admitted they were no longer, you know, . . . doing it. But there was more to it than that, I thought. It's hard to put my finger on how I knew but it struck me then there was a whole lot of other business going on in the background that Wendy hadn't told us about.

5

Marcus

I keep a Carter file in my study. I call it my study but actually it's only the spare bedroom lined with bookshelves and a couple of filing cabinets underneath a work table where I keep my mainframe computer. From the chair by the window there's a clear view across the valley to the white horse on the hill. It's a good place to empty my mind and take some time out.

In a simple manila file are all the notes I made during Wendy's mother's case, some clippings from the newspaper, photographs. At the practice, as well as the usual correspondence between the different agencies involved in Jenny's case, we had copies of reports from the Firs care home. Dalton had especially requested them and I made my own copies. There's nothing underhand about that although some might consider it unusual to go to such lengths over a patient not technically your own. But it was such an extraordinary case. We all wanted to know what was happening to Jenny Carter.

I took out the file and began adding to my notes after I'd seen Wendy in April. I can't explain why I felt it necessary but now I'm glad I did. I suppose there was something at the back of my mind telling me the whole affair wasn't yet finished.

Wendy had first brought her mother to see Dalton in February last year. She showed the usual symptoms: short term memory loss; forgetting the names of commonplace objects; repeating herself, asking the same questions. Dalton mentioned it to me. We considered a referral.

"It could be normal signs of ageing," I remember saying to him. "Hell's bells, I'm getting there myself. I can never remember where I put down my glasses. If Sarah asks me to pick up some milk on the way home I'll forget."

"Let's hope you're right," he said. He raised those black eyebrows of his and his forehead scrunched. The rest of Seamus Dalton's hair is white as . . . I was going to say snow but that wouldn't get it. I think he uses a special shampoo and sometimes there's a definite hint of violet going on in a certain light. He might not be aware of it. His eyesight isn't as good as it used to be. He's not far from retirement and knows he's slowing down. But his patients love and respect his gentle ways. To my knowledge nobody at the surgery, neither staff nor patients, has ever mentioned the colour of his hair.

Sarah and I were out to dinner that February night. Sophie was busy with homework and although we pressed her to come along, she declined.

"It'll be good for you two to have a romantic evening together," she said. "All girls need a high-heels night out with their man once in a while. Don't they, Mum?"

Sophie can be very thoughtful like that. She's turning into a lovely young lady. We're very proud of her. Performing Arts is her thing. Sarah used to hope Sophie would follow me into medicine but the lure of the spotlights won that battle. We've seen her in a number of productions and she does have talent. She hopes to make it into television one day.

I would have been happier to settle for home-delivery Chinese and stay indoors by the fire but Sarah had her heart set on her favourite country pub restaurant. It was bitterly cold. The car was already frosting over as we left. There'd been rain on top of what was left of the snow so I kept to the main roads rather than the cross country route I'd normally take. Before long I was muttering obscenities under my breath. I caught myself commenting on the lack of gritters, cursing poor street lighting. I drove slowly, the rear wheel drive of my BMW playing up on the icy surface. When we reached the car park I was glad the landlord had scattered fresh ash from the fires over his paths. I helped Sarah from the car in her tight dress and high-heeled spaghetti strap shoes, inappropriate for the weather, I thought, although I'd never dream of actually saying that to her. I took her arm and we trod carefully as we went inside.

There's an unpretentious conviviality about the Kennet Keep, an old coaching inn along the banks of the canal. In summer it's a popular venue for its beer garden. Great food and log fires in winter keep the regulars coming back. Sarah took a high stool up at the bar. The slim fitting dress and high shoes suddenly looked more alluring. She noticed my appraising look and smiled.

"Have you settled down now?" she said.

"What do you mean?"

"Coming over in the car. You were not quite yourself."

"Very astute, darling," I said.

She is. Never misses a trick. I told her what had been bothering me.

"I was concerned about driving on icy roads," I said. "Then I got concerned about being concerned. Sarah, am I turning into my father?"

She laughed and reached out to stroke my arm. "I'll let you know if it happens."

She would, too. If you could rely on Sarah for anything, it would be her honesty. I trust her implicitly. I looked at her sitting there smiling at me and thought she wore her forty-three years well. Dark, shiny hair. Happy face. If anything, she just kept getting better. But nothing lasts forever.

"What's on your mind?" she asked.

Perceptive. Never misses a facial expression either.

An unsettled feeling had been building since morning surgery and my conversation with Dalton. Nervous, like stage fright.

"Old age, Sarah. I was thinking about old age," I said. "Not ours. I don't mean that. I was thinking about ageing parents and illness. I can't help thinking it's coming our way very soon."

She put her head on one side and gave me the sort of smile my mother used to do when I came home from school with a tear in my uniform. Sarah's parents went to live abroad in their retirement. A place in the sun. It works for them. We visit them in Cyprus and we know that, at present, they're fine. They have a full social life, lots of friends. *My parents, though* . . .

"We'll cross that bridge . . ." Sarah said. She knew my concerns. "Marcus, it's my birthday. Please let's leave that conversation for another time."

I agreed. It wasn't the right time. We picked up menus and made our choices. But the niggling thoughts wouldn't go away. At the back of my mind a nasty little voice persisted.

It could happen to any of us. Without warning.

I'd been aware for some time that the number of dementia sufferers continues to grow. There's a projected increase over the next twenty years of forty per cent in Europe alone. Elsewhere in the world the numbers are staggering. The logistics of caring for that number of people are terrifying. It's a global catastrophe waiting to happen.

Dalton's fears about Jenny Carter's condition proved correct. Practice records show that she became very confused very quickly. Surprisingly fast. Dalton saw her throughout the spring of last year and made several home visits. He told me she became abusive toward him. Accused him of trying to hurt her. Wendy also reported her mother had begun to accuse her of stealing things. Ornaments were missing, Jenny said. Strangers were coming into the house to take things from her. She could hear them when they got in through the loft. Once she'd seen them running away down the garden and jumping over the fence into next door's.

6

Nobody asks me what I think. But, listen, I'm going to say it anyway. When you're not sure who you can trust somebody has to open your eyes. Wendy Carter had a lot to put up with. Nobody else but me knows to what extent. Doctors can say this and that happened but they don't know how it feels until it happens to them.

Through the spring before Jenny went into care Rob came home from work each day complaining about feeling stressed and looking for sympathy. He paid no attention to the fact that Wendy had been running around all day trying to fit in visits to her mother in between her two jobs. When she explained to him how upsetting it was to see her mother in such a confused state he said he had enough on his plate. Then he asked what was for his dinner.

"He never sees the ninety-nine out of a hundred things I *have* done," she once told me. "He picks up on the one thing I haven't had time to do and complains about that."

She went alone to see her mother at Easter. The weather was kind and daffodils by Jenny's front door bobbed and curtseyed as if everything was normal. Wendy let herself in and found her mother sitting by the patio doors at the back of the house, staring out into the garden. Wendy put on a cheerful face before she spoke.

"Hello, Mum. How are you today?"

Jenny didn't turn around. She sat, fixed. Then she pointed at something outside.

"What's that?" she said.

"What's what, Mum?"

"*That*, stupid. Are you blind, or what?"

Wendy looked out. There was nothing to see. The garden was as it should be. A square patch of grass and Dad's old shed down the bottom corner. The ornamental cherry tree was full of fat buds. By the fence next door's forsythia was still in full flower. After recent warmer weather the grass was growing thick and long.

"I must have missed it," Wendy said and put her hand on her mother's shoulder.

"Don't you touch me," Jenny screamed. "I know what you're after."

It took over half an hour for Jenny to calm down. Wendy made tea and found half a packet of chocolate biscuits. When she went back into the living room Jenny was sitting up at the table, waiting, as if nothing had happened. Wendy put out the plates and her mother clapped her hands like a little girl. She bounced in her seat. Her eyes lit up and she devoured all the chocolate biscuits one after the other. Wendy could hardly bear to look at her mother. A blank expression had worked its way onto Jenny's face, the way an infant looks when it doesn't understand much about the way the world works.

As Wendy washed the cups and put them away she saw the hob was recently cleaned, the kitchen floor swept. In the fridge, as well as shopping Wendy had brought in, there were the usual supplies. Mother's favourite juice, salads, chicken breasts. Cans of soup in the cupboard, cereal, flour and sugar. Spare bread in the freezer. Wendy took comfort from these small things. She thought everything might be all right if only her mother could look after herself at home.

Jenny came into the kitchen behind her.

"Shall we have some tea and biscuits?" she said.

"They've all gone, Mum."

"Who's eaten them? Was it you? I *know* there were some chocolate biscuits. Was it you?"

Her face twisted and her mouth grew slack. She pushed past Wendy to get to the wall cupboard where she kept the biscuit tin and dragged it from the shelf.

"Where are they?" Her voice was loud and threatening. "What have you done with them? Let me see your hands."

She grabbed Wendy's hands and twisted them over looking for telltale crumbs. Wendy turned her face away to avoid the hand that came whipping across. The blow caught the back of her head and she stumbled against the sink.

"You make me sick," her mother snarled. "All of you. You all make me sick."

Jenny rushed out of the kitchen. Wendy heard her stomping down the hallway to her bedroom. The door slammed shut. When Wendy looked in a few minutes later her mother had wrapped herself in the duvet on top of the bed and was asleep.

Wendy went outside to pull some weeds. She got out the lawnmower. She hoped to catch sight of somebody from next door to ask them to keep an eye out. Maybe they'd take Wendy's number and give her a call if they thought anything was amiss with her mother. It would make her feel easier to know there was somebody else on hand. But there was nobody in. It was Easter, after all. They were probably having a day out, down to the coast maybe, or a nice run out into the country. Her throat tightened and she fought off the need to weep.

At home she prepared a special dinner for her boys. She wanted to feel as though the old times had come back when they were little and dependent on her. When they needed her love. But she didn't voice her feelings. They wouldn't understand. She made light of the tears in her eyes and blamed the onions she was peeling.

They gobbled the meal like starving animals and she couldn't help feeling disappointed they were in such a rush to finish and go out again. Wendy had work next day. She said she was happy for them to go to the pub without her.

"No, of course I don't mind," she said to Rafe when he asked. "Off you go. Have a good time. It'll be nice for you and Richie to spend time with your dad."

"There's live music tonight," Rafe told her. "They've got an extension. It'll be late."

"Well, that's it then," Wendy said. She stroked her son's face. "I'll enjoy a nice long bath and a bit of peace and quiet."

She said she was sure when he asked again and after they'd left she wept over the dishes as she cleared them away. No matter how hard she'd tried to be happy, to bring back those old feelings of contentment from when the boys were little, she carried a pain inside that wouldn't go away. Like nausea, a sour ache gnawed at her. She cut short the time she'd planned to linger in the bath. Her perfumed candles lacked something. Their pale flicker of cloying sweetness irritated her. The hot water made her feel drowsy and her head was heavy with thoughts. She got into bed with that unsettled, sickly feeling still churning inside and was only dimly aware of the boys and Rob coming home later.

She had her first encounter with her secret visitor that night. Wendy was unsure at first and thought she'd been dreaming. She put it down to fatigue. The handsome face that buried into her neck and attentive hands stroking her into arousal were fabrications of her exhaustion, she thought. She turned to her husband thinking he had reached out for her in the night. Rob was asleep on his side away from her.

But she could feel the warmth of soft lips on her neck and shoulders, moist breath on her skin. Shivers of desire surged from her head to her feet. Searching fingers at her thighs brought flickers of pleasure. She knew then it was no dream. She gave in to the sensations and, afterwards, slept without stirring once.

7

Rafe

We don't always do things together just because we're twins but that Easter most of our group had gone off skiing and we were both kinda stuck. We were up to the limit on our overdrafts and neither of us fancied eating beans on toast in the flat on our own so we went home. Mum doesn't mind us showing up with bags full of washing and enormous appetites. Dad gets embarrassed about the cost of things when stuff like that happens.

"Don't worry about it, Dad," I said. "We didn't fancy going skiing anyway, did we, Richie?"

Richie was messing about on the Wii. Skiing. I noticed Dad's sorry face.

"Listen, son," Dad said, "I can't run to it. I wish I could."

I don't know how much a Head of Department brings home. My parents never discussed specifics in front of us but I guess if there'd been only one of us it might have been different. University costs. I mean, it really costs a lot. At least we won't have huge overdrafts to come out to. Mum and Dad see to that. You can't have everything.

We're not identical. We just arrived on the same day. We're not much like each other at all. Richie's the outgoing one. He's the one with crazy hair and weird taste in clothes. Baggy circus pants and waistcoats. Me, I stick to boring jeans. Richie's the one with all the popular mates as well. He can outdo me on most things. Beer. Women. And on the Wii.

We knew there was something weird going on with Mum. It was like she was in a dream most of the time. When you talked to her it was as if she wasn't there. Then you felt as though you weren't there because she'd look straight through you as if you were invisible. Her eyes were glassy and empty, like dark holes in her head.

Dad told us to ignore it. He said Mum was under a lot of stress and was best left alone. We knew about Grandma and expected Mum to be upset and worried, not this dreamy, floaty person we'd never seen before. Dad said she had been worried at first when Grandma started going funny but by the time we saw her Mum was always tired and went to bed early. Sometimes she went for a lie down in the afternoon after she'd come back from visiting Gran.

Richie didn't want to see our grandma. I did, though. I offered to go with Mum but she said Grandma might not remember who I was and that it upset her to have too many people around.

I didn't know much about Alzheimer's. You don't think about things that can happen to people in their old age unless you have to. So I Googled it. It's heavy, scary stuff. I couldn't get my head round not being able to recognise your own next of kin. Too weird. No wonder Mum was acting odd. After I'd read about how someone with dementia can completely change personality I could understand why Mum didn't want us to see Grandma like that. I read there's evidence of hereditary links and that scared the shit out of me. The propensity to develop Alzheimer's can run in families, this article said, although there's no hard proof. What use is half-arsed information like that? Why don't they know? Dad and Richie didn't want to talk about it so I let it be.

Just before Easter I went one morning by myself when Mum and Dad were at work. Richie was still in bed. I really wanted to see my grandmother. She'd always been happy to see us. She used to bake cakes especially for us when we were little. We never knew our grandfather on Mum's side. He died when she was about nine. The grandma my brother and I knew had always lived alone. I always thought she was a bit scatty. She used to get in a muddle over paying bills and stuff like that. Dad sorted her out at the bank with direct debits. When I was at sixth form college I gave her my old computer and tried to show her how to use the internet. It took ages to get as far as M&S shopping online.

When I got to the house the curtains were closed. I knocked on the door but couldn't get an answer so I went round the back. The patio doors were open but there was no sign of her. I went inside, pulled back the curtains and sat down to wait. I could hear the shower running in the bathroom. When I heard her coming along the hallway I called out. I didn't want to startle her.

"Rafe!" she said as soon as she heard my voice. "Sweetheart, come here, you lovely boy."

We met in the doorway and she hugged me hard. It felt good, that hug from my grandma. We don't do a lot of hugging at home like we used to. I don't know why. It just sort of stopped as me and Richie grew up. It was nice to have my grandma hold me the way she did when I was a kid.

"How did you get in?" she said.

"Grandma, you left the patio doors open."

"No, I didn't. I haven't been outside yet today. Somebody else must have done it."

She breezed off into the kitchen like it didn't matter and left me standing there looking stupid. I couldn't believe she didn't think it was important. I mean, anybody could have got into her house. She brushed it aside. I followed her not knowing what to say next. She got out a packet of pills and took one with a glass of water. She saw me watching.

"Nothing to worry about," she said. "Just anti-inflammatory. I gave my back a tweak the other day moving heavy plant pots. And I've been clearing some things out."

She showed me a tray filled with some of her old bits and pieces. You know, the sorts of stuff grandmothers put in window sills, on the mantelpiece and on top of the telly. She picked up a black glass Scotty dog.

"I remember that one," I said. "I won it on a stall at the fair when I was seven and gave it to you for your collection."

"That was you, was it? I forget. Well, that was very kind of you. Would you like to have it back?"

She didn't wait for my answer. She tore off a piece of kitchen paper and wrapped it up.

"There you are," she said. "When you get a place of your own you can start your own collection."

She chattered on about how the spring weather had made her want to do things in the house. It never looked any different to me. The patterned wallpaper in her living room was so old it had come back into fashion. Big flowers on a contrasting background but instead of on one feature wall, the way they do it on DIY designer programmes, it was everywhere. Mum said it used to give her a headache. But Grandma didn't want to change anything. Dad had offered to redecorate but she'd always refused. I stuffed the glass animal in my pocket.

We took mugs of tea and a plate of chocolate biscuits into the living room.

"Will you do something for me?" she said. "Will you bring something down from the loft?"

I asked her what she wanted and she stood at the base of the ladder while I inched through the trapdoor. I had to use the torch on my mobile phone to see. There wasn't a lot up there, just a couple of cardboard boxes and a few black bin bags.

"They're in one of the boxes," she called up.

I found the album she wanted and an old shoebox full of loose photographs. I brought them down and went back to push up the ladder and close the trapdoor. When I went back to the living room she was sitting on the sofa looking through the photos.

"Look what I just found in the sideboard," she said, holding up the album.

I didn't know what to say. My face went cold. Grandma was smiling at the pictures, turning the pages and running her fingers over each glossy print. She looked so happy. She really thought she'd found the album in the sideboard. I felt completely spaced, like something in my head was spinning around. She looked at me and patted the space on the sofa beside her. She wanted me to sit with her. I did as she asked for a while but she kept on saying strange things.

"That's cousin, Fred," she said, tapping at a photo of someone in military uniform. "You two used to get into such trouble."

I'd no idea who cousin Fred was. I don't know whose cousin he was.

"That was taken just after he came back from Korea," she said. "He was too young to go. Only sixteen when he went. You two told such lies."

She started chuckling to herself and I didn't know whether to laugh along with her, ask some questions or keep my mouth shut. She turned over another page.

"Do you remember, Gordon, that holiday in the Lakes? There you are, look, sitting on a dry stone wall."

My ears grew hot. A wave of heat spread across my face and down my neck as I realised what was happening. There was a heavy feeling in the pit of my stomach as if I'd swallowed a stone. She leaned back on the sofa and smiled at me. She patted her hair and smiled some more. Then she put her head on one side and kept looking me up and down. The expression on her face made me feel sick. She looked like she was flirting with me. Jesus, she was running her tongue across her teeth and licking at the corners of her mouth. My insides twisted and my mouth went dry. When she reached out to touch my leg, I flipped. I jumped up and, like a dirty coward, I ran out the patio doors, down the garden and hopped over the fence. I didn't stop running till I reached home.

I didn't tell my parents where I'd been. I didn't tell anybody. It was too embarrassing. All I wanted to do was forget it ever happened. Richie would have made a huge, unfunny joke about it. I didn't want him to know and go passing it around the people at uni. How could you explain to your mates that your own grandmother was coming on to you? I don't know how I should have handled it. It made me feel so fucking useless.

8

Listen. Boys will be boys. Some would say that so will most men. They'd say you have to remember they're simple creatures underneath all their bluster. Easily pleased. They don't ask for much. They like everything to run smoothly so that everybody can be happy. They do not change, my darlings. Not after they are eight years old.

The best of them will work hard to provide for their families. Give them a good dinner and a willing partner in the bedroom when they're up for it and everything in their garden comes up rosy sweet. Most of them will turn a blind eye to an unmade bed or an un-vacuumed carpet. Some of the dear creatures will even make the bed themselves and bring out the vacuum, especially if it's one of the newest gadgets with clever add-ons. They like the way all the little attachments slot in and are fascinated with the way the whole thing clips together. When it goes wrong the man of the house will be happy to take the thing apart and even watch a video on YouTube to find out how to install a new motor or post motor filter.

Of course, while he's fixing it he will take up all the kitchen floor and your table and worktops and spill dust everywhere. It takes a surprising amount of tools and boxes he might need. It's a major operation and you must give him his head. You must not move anything and you must carefully stride over the mess on your kitchen floor and ignore the deep gouges that have suddenly appeared on your worktop surface.

And when he's finished with it and all the little pieces have been put back together again he will invite you to come and admire his handiwork. My darlings, you must drop at once whatever you are doing and rush to his side to gasp in excited delight your unbounded appreciation. It's such a small thing to ask of you, this expression of pleasure at the things he does for you. It makes him feel so happy, you see, that it is well worth the effort of forgetting all the other things he does which annoy you so much.

Men know what they like and they want their lives to stay as simple as when they were those eight year old boys. They want a partner who can be mummy and nurse, hostess and helpmeet, housekeeper and assistant plumber, lover and slut. You know you're all Goddesses, ladies. You surely realise you have all these qualities within you. All you have to do is express them. In the right place, it goes without saying. Horses for courses, darlings.

But the one thing you must not do is bring home hassle. Anything to do with emotions comes under the masculine definition of hassle. It is a dreaded word. It is their greatest fear. Hassle includes any form of nagging, clinging, whining or neediness. Anything to do with the disturbance of the smooth running of their lives is unwelcome and they will avoid it at all costs.

I speak from my own observations of what people say and do. I deliberately exaggerate to make my point. Didn't I tell you earlier that I would make you question yourself? But you get my point. There are patterns in people's behaviour. I see them so often.

If Rob didn't want to deal with his mother-in-law's dementia you could hardly expect his sons to do any better. So they all left it to Wendy. Women know best what to do in these situations. Wendy would be able to deal with Jenny. Her own mother, after all. Blood is thicker than water and all that. You couldn't expect the men of the family to take it on. They'd be like little Lost Boys, wouldn't they? Not knowing the right thing to do and frightened of making things worse. Emotional upsets are like crocodiles to little Lost Boys. Dangerous things, lurking in dark waters, waiting to get them. Wendy Carter had to fight all the crocodiles herself.

The morning after her first visit from her secret lover she rose to greet the day with a surge of energy. A good night's sleep is a wonderful remedy, my darlings, and can go a long way toward making yesterday's problems seem less severe. And this is what she told herself as she moved about her house.

When all's said and done, I'm used to doing things by myself.

Her head felt clear and light. It was as if she'd lost a burden of weight from her back and shoulders. She remembered how, when she was a child, she'd been aware whenever she'd had a growth spurt when she got up in the morning and the furniture seemed lower, further from her reach. It had given her a sense of herself. She'd become aware of her own physical presence. She could see more of herself in the mirror her mother kept over the fireplace and she enjoyed the novelty of growing, developing. As if she'd been endowed with extra powers.

Now here was that feeling again. A lovely, confident, fit and healthy, *powerful* feeling. There was purpose in her stride as she began her household chores. For a moment her heart wanted to sing. But the vitality that coursed through her had nowhere to go other than on her daily tasks. She made breakfast and set out plates and she floated from table to cupboards to sink. Her feet didn't touch. Her mind was miles away and she couldn't focus. Thoughts ebbed and flowed. Her boys were home for Easter and that made her happy. Her mother had treated her cruelly and that made her sad.

The other thing had made her feel wonderful. She couldn't name it. Dare not name it. If it had been only her imagination, well then, she wouldn't think about it. She pushed away that particular thought. She didn't want him to be a dream. Asleep or awake she wanted him to be real. He had to be real. How could he have done those things to her, made her feel the way she did if he wasn't a real person? But if he was real how could he have slipped into the house and into her bed with Rob lying right there next to her? Shouldn't she be afraid?

She searched inside herself for a feeling she could make sense of. There was the happiness about the boys. This was an easy one, weightless like a silent laugh or a child's soap bubble. Alongside the happy thoughts she found mixed up anger and sadness at her mother's condition and Jenny's cruel words and actions. That was more complicated like the other side of a balance scale holding strange-smelling mysteries and exotic fears.

She put a lid on the feelings she couldn't name. Like Pandora's box. Better to close it off and lock it away. There was enough on the dark side of the balance scale without worrying about new things. So when she reassessed her position in the middle of all these thoughts there was only some sadness and some happiness. Nothing more. There were no other feelings so there was nothing to fear. Everything was going to be all right.

But her certainty wavered. She struggled with the lid on the forbidden thought box. It was hard to keep it fastened tight. She couldn't resist another little peep and, when she allowed herself to venture in its direction, she came to acknowledge that more than anything she hoped for *his* return. It was too wonderful to happen only once. But still, forbidden. She replaced the lid quickly before too much came tumbling out. And so her mind slipped away again and she floated back into the kitchen to make coffee.

"Mum, is there any more bacon?" Richie said without looking up, his eyes firmly fixed on his plate of food.

Wendy set down two mugs of coffee and drifted out of the kitchen into the hall.

"Mum!" he shouted after her. "Is there any more bacon?"

He looked at his brother and shrugged. Rafe shook his head and silently mouthed, *Leave it.*

Wendy came back wearing her coat and carrying her handbag.

"I've got to go now," she said. "Have a nice day, you two. Your father will be back at the usual time."

Rafe got up to see her out and said, "Are you all right, Mum?" He put his arm around her shoulder.

She said she was fine and stroked his cheek. She smiled at him but she missed the concern in his eyes, the knot in his brow.

"See you later," she said and went out.

It was Thursday and she decided to walk into town to work her shift at the charity shop. The day was crisp and fresh with a sweet smell of newly cut grass. With airy steps she slipped along the avenue. Spring flowers burst from tubs on people's doorsteps. Pansies and primroses. Pretty grape hyacinths pushed their bright blue heads between all the yellows and purples. Narcissi exploded through flowerbeds, hyacinths in more sheltered spots, their perfume sweet and succulent. As she passed by her neighbours' houses she suppressed a smile.

Life goes on, she thought. *Look at those neat gardens and sparkling windows. Look at those carefully pruned specimen plants and waxed cars on the driveways. Look how clean it all is.*

In estate agent speak it was a much sought after area. What would the neighbours think if they knew she'd taken a lover?

And then she felt remorse. It struck at her mood with a crushing blow. The air turned sour and in her mind's eye she could see her sons at the breakfast table enjoying their food, glad to be in their own home. It pained her that she'd paid so little attention to them. A sharp stab of regret obliterated forbidden thoughts of secret lovers. She resolved to make the most of her boys while she had them, spoil them a little, spend more time with them. She shouldn't be so selfish. She must make it right with them. It wasn't their fault her life was so difficult. *Make it up to them*, she thought. *And while you're at it, make it up to Rob as well. Pay him more attention. Be more patient with him. It's not his fault, either.*

Joan was already hard at work when Wendy walked into the shop. The pungent smell of lavender all- purpose cleaner met her at the door. There was stock all over the counter and Joan was on her knees washing down the shelving units. Wendy could hear the slop-slop of a wet cloth. Joan had her head down and her backside in the air. It wobbled from side to side as she swept her arm in an arc across the surfaces.

Wendy called out, "It's only me."

Joan continued wobbling. "Just going round with a damp cloth," she said from under the counter. "Put the kettle on, my lovely."

Wendy took off her coat. When she went back with the tea Joan had finished and was wringing out the cloth in a plastic bowl on the counter.

"Wendy," she said. "Look at you! All dressed up and nowhere to go but this old place. Is that a new top? What a pretty colour. Wendy, you look lovely."

Wendy looked down to check what she'd put on. She said a quiet thank you and helped Joan up from her knees. Norma came in from off her bus and put a greasy bag on the counter top.

"Pasties," Norma said. "One cheese and onion, one regular and one chicken and mushroom. Take your pick, girls. We'll zap 'em in the microwave later for lunch."

Norma looked up and Joan winked at her. When Wendy took the pasties into the back room Norma raised her eyebrows and pursed her lips.

Joan said, "Somebody's feeling better this morning."

9

Marcus

People tend to confuse what the word dementia means. They're often surprised to hear there is no disease with that name. Rather, it's the name of a range of symptoms which diseases cause. Alzheimer's is one such. There are other conditions that produce very similar behaviours.

There's no one test to prove a person has Alzheimer's. We can say with near certainty that a person has dementia but it can be difficult to determine the exact cause. Diagnostic tests are more to do with eliminating possibilities of those other conditions which might cause the symptoms of dementia. These are conducted over time. It's virtually impossible to reach a conclusion quickly. In Jenny Carter's case the psychologist conducted tests into her concentration skills, her problem solving, language and other mental functions. The MMSE, mini mental state examination showed Jenny scored only thirteen out of a maximum score of thirty which indicated moderate dementia.

Dalton came looking for me at the end of morning surgery. His eyebrows shot skyward as he showed me Jenny Carter's results.

"Look at this," he said, rapping the report with his knuckles. "I've never seen such a rapid decline. You'd expect a two to four point drop per year. At this rate . . ." His voice tailed off and he wandered back into his own office rubbing at his lilac hair.

Our practice held Jenny's full medical history. She was not on any medication. At sixty seven she took nothing more then the occasional paracetamol. She had her winter flu injections and, generally, had always looked after her health. She didn't drink to excess. She'd never smoked, there was no kidney or liver disease nor thyroid abnormalities. Blood tests showed no evidence of anaemia. There were no problems with her heart or lungs. Tests for diabetes came back negative. She'd had a slight fall during the previous six months and strained her intercostal muscles as she'd twisted. She said it was tender but as it was soft tissue damage only Dalton had prescribed painkillers stronger than proprietary brands and the problem cleared up without further complications. That was it. Physically, Jenny Carter looked good for her age.

Jenny stayed in her own home to begin with. She coped better in familiar surroundings according to her daughter and was still able to shop and cook for herself. Weeks passed with little more to report. For a time it looked as if we might expect her decline to follow the usual, steadily progressive path. Each case is different, of course, and some progress more rapidly than others but the general rule is often as simple as wait and see.

An episode with her car marked a further turning point. Apparently, she marched into the Compton police station one afternoon to report her car had been stolen. She told the desk sergeant she'd seen who took it and described Seamus Dalton so well the officer knew immediately who she meant. Her interpretation of the combination of his hair and eyebrows did it. She was in an agitated state and demanded action be taken to apprehend the criminal. She said she could lead the police to where he worked. A phone call to the surgery soon made the situation clear. Jenny took a ride home in a patrol car and Wendy later found her mother's vehicle in the supermarket car park where Jenny had left it. I believe the car was put up for sale very soon afterwards. Dalton and I both felt Jenny was no longer safe to drive.

After that she began to wander. Dalton took worried phone calls from Wendy after the first few times when Jenny had disappeared from her home in the early evening at the time Wendy usually called in on her. The first time, Jenny was discovered standing in a primary school playground staring at the walls. The caretaker had been just about to call for an ambulance as when he'd asked her what she was looking for Jenny hadn't been able to answer. She couldn't give her name either. When the caretaker had asked, Jenny had replied, *I'm me.*

On the second occasion Jenny had walked to the centre of Compton. The shops were closed in the arcade that leads off the main street but Jenny was pushing at the door of the charity shop where Wendy worked. She'd seen something in the window and wanted to buy it, she said. She couldn't understand why nobody would let her in. Wendy said afterwards she believed her mother didn't know how to find her way back. In fact, Wendy told Dalton, Jenny seemed to have no idea where she was nor how she'd got there.

The third time, after neighbours found her sitting in the middle of the road in her dressing gown, Dalton called Wendy to tell her the multi-disciplinary team had secured a place for her mother where Jenny would be safe and comfortable.

10

Listen. Here's what really happened. Outsiders, you'll remember, don't know the whole truth. They don't know what goes on in other people's houses. Authorities make their decisions and say things like, *it's for the best.* Maybe that's the case. Maybe it isn't always. Maybe they made a mistake. But they step in and intervene and then they leave. The decision has been made. There is nothing more for them to do so they go back to where they were before, pull out somebody else's file and get ready to make another decision that affects other people's lives and families. They're never there to witness the aftermath.

In June Jenny went berserk when Wendy told her they'd had to take her car away from her. She screamed and lashed out. She knocked a cup out of Wendy's hands and hot coffee scalded the back of Wendy's fingers. Then Jenny threw herself on the floor and sobbed into the carpet. She balled her fists and thrashed at the furniture. She rolled onto her back in the damp patch of spilled drink and kicked at the gas fire.

Wendy removed her mother's ornaments from around the fireplace and went to the kitchen to run her hand under cold water. She waited until her mother had calmed down enough to watch television then began to prepare a light salad for Jenny's meal. Jenny had sent the home-delivery meal people away again.

"Who are you?" she'd asked them at the door.

"We've brought you a nice lunch, Mrs Carter. Shall we pop it on the table for you?"

"You can't come in here," Jenny told them. "I don't know who you are. I don't want strangers in my house. Go away."

From the kitchen Wendy could hear the strident voice of Judge Judy telling some hare-brained idiot to stop interrupting or she'd have him removed from court. Jenny was laughing loudly and clapping her hands. She'd forgotten about her car.

"Would you like your lunch now, Mum?" Wendy said from the doorway.

"No."

"You've got to eat something . . ."

"Shut up, can't you? I'm watching this. I can't hear what they're saying if you keep talking over the top of them."

"I've made you a nice salad, Mum."

"If I have to tell you again you'll feel the back of my hand, girl. Shut up!"

Wendy covered the plate in cling film and set it on the table. Her mother would find it later. She said goodbye and let herself out.

The summer streets were busy. In the park children played on swings under a sky sprinkled with fluffy, marshmallow clouds. Flowerbeds teemed with pink roses and deep violet fuchsias, pure and faultless, eye-catching and playful as a tin of boiled sweets in bright shiny wrappers. By the ice cream van a queue of excited little people hopped about from one leg to the other in anticipation. Wendy stopped to look for a moment. Such a joyful, innocent scene. Watching small children used to make her feel nostalgic. Not any more.

Since Easter Wendy had had other things to think about. Her boys had gone back to university and left a huge hole in the house. Sometimes Rafe would remember to give her a call and let her know what he and Richie were getting up to. They had a field trip planned somewhere in Scotland and they'd decided to extend the trip into the summer break so they wouldn't be returning home till later. Rafe always remembered to ask about his grandma and made a point of stressing that he hoped Wendy was well too. Then the conversation would come to an end. Rafe would say something nice about looking forward to sleeping in his own comfortable bed or eating his mother's Sunday roast. Then he'd be gone and Wendy would put the phone back in its cradle slowly as if holding onto it could keep her son with her that moment longer. She'd run her fingers across the handset as though his voice was still inside it.

Rob was busy as usual. He came home with stacks of examination papers to mark and, sometimes, the second plate she laid for dinner was the only way she could be certain he was actually in the house. Rob seemed content with everything just the way it was. So what, she thought, if he fell asleep on the sofa at ten each night? After all, he had an important job with a lot of responsibilities. She felt the need of his touch much less. Truth is, she'd almost stopped thinking about him in that way.

But she had her little secret. It made her feel warm inside and just a little bit naughty. Her husband might have sensed there was something making Wendy act differently but he didn't know what it was.

I do. I know. She had her own lovely world to live in. A place where there were no troubles. It was a place where her thoughts could wander and she didn't have to feel sad or upset, or remorseful, or lacking in any way whatsoever. She could simply be.

She'd found her escape in the arms of her tender visitor who knew exactly how she like to be touched. She had rediscovered the joys of afternoon delight on cool sheets with the window open and fresh air blowing over her skin. In the warm glow of their daylight lovemaking she melted when he turned those eyes on her. Her favourite kind of eyes, so dark and deep and soft they made the back of her neck shiver and her stomach thrill. Her lover's eyes were bottomless. Fathoms of feelings, liquid caverns of dark desire drew her into their mysterious depths. She burned under his gaze. Drowned in those eyes. Fire and water. Searing and quenching at the same time. Her lover was everything she'd ever needed. Each time he brought her to the heights of ecstasy and afterwards she slept like a baby.

11

Marcus

Jenny's first assessment at the Firs residential care home where she was admitted at the beginning of August showed further deterioration in her capabilities. The speed with which she was falling into decline startled and concerned her carers. Disorientation at her unfamiliar surroundings threw her into panics.

On her first night staff reported a commotion coming from her room. They said it sounded like she was trying to move the furniture around. When they opened the door they discovered her in the dark, hanging onto the wall and wailing. Jenny believed she was trapped. She began to scream. One of her carers switched on the bedside light. Jenny said she'd been locked in. They showed her the open door. She said somebody was trying to capture her. They switched on the main light but Jenny was insistent that the door had been moved onto a different wall so that she couldn't find it in the dark and someone had removed the light switch. They made her a cup of tea. Jenny said everything that had happened had been a deliberate plan to frighten her. The report emphasises her extreme distress. She could hardly speak through her tears.

"You don't understand," she'd said. "This has happened before. Somebody is trying to kill me."

The following conversation is taken directly from the Firs' report.

"Let's get you back into bed, Mrs Carter."

"It's frightening me."

"What's frightening you, Jenny?"

"This place. I want to go home."

"When you're better. You can go home when you're better."

"Is that why I'm here? What's the matter with me?"

"That's what we're going to find out."

On another occasion she wandered into the staffroom fully dressed at three am., asking to go out into the snow. It was a clear August night. They told her there was no snow but she grew angry, adamant that she had seen it. She said they were all lying to her, trying to make her look foolish. She went to the window, pulled back the curtains and pointed outside.

"Look," she said. "Everything's white."

"It's just moonlight," they told her.

She stopped caring about personal hygiene. She didn't notice if her clothes were covered in food stains where she'd spilt. She had to be reminded to change her undergarments, too. Staff coaxed her into the shower and she screamed at the touch of water on her skin. She asked for her dinner straight after she'd eaten it and threw a tantrum when she wanted another biscuit or piece of cake.

Wendy visited regularly. She always went alone and, according to staff, spent a long time in her mother's room with the door closed. Staff said this was unusual. Noticeable. Most visitors would take the opportunity for a gentle stroll with their loved ones, out in the fresh air, perhaps sit in the rose garden. That sort of thing helped to pass the time. It sounds heartless, this desire to wish visiting time away but I imagine it's difficult to hold a conversation with someone who doesn't respond. Not everybody has the skill to keep up a one-sided conversation. I suppose some are too tired and worried and the lack of response would only add to the visitor's own anxieties. It must be even harder when patients don't recognise the visitor is their own son or daughter. It must be heartbreaking trying to explain to your parent who you are.

Staff had all noticed that whenever Wendy visited, whatever the weather, she and her mother never came out of Jenny's room. They could hear voices when they listened at the door but couldn't make out what was being said, or by whom. If they took a cup of tea in to them the conversation stopped immediately and if they left the door open as they came out, Wendy would get up and close it tight again.

12

Hush. Listen. Wendy didn't want anybody to hear what she was telling her mother. She was afraid they'd think her mad. Stories about a mystery visitor behaving like a fantasy lover? They'd say it was rubbish straight from the pages of some paperback romance. They might even laugh. Wendy kept her feelings about him locked away in her private thought box until it was safe to let them out.

She knew other people wouldn't believe in his sexy eyes that made her stomach tie itself in knots. His dark hair with a hint of curl at his neck when he got hot. When he got hot for her. Tall. Oh, so tall, like Jack Reacher in the novels she read with long, firm legs and a back that went on for ever from slim, lithe hips to wide, straight shoulders. And strong. Yet gentle. Perfect. Wendy loved the manly smell of him. She couldn't get enough of everything about him and she couldn't stop talking about him whenever she had the chance.

If anyone heard what she was saying to her mother, Wendy thought, they'd have her committed. But, sometimes people have an overwhelming need to talk, my darlings. They feel they must burst if they don't tell *somebody.* When Wendy went to visit her mother at the Firs care home there was no point in trying to hold a normal conversation. Staff had advised her this would happen and the many pamphlets she'd been given confirmed it.

There are information leaflets put out by the Alzheimer's association or some such, designed to help family members come to terms with what is happening to their loved ones. Just like all medical information pamphlets they are matter of fact, impersonal. They give you bullet point ideas of what you might expect so you can be forewarned. They are glossy and smooth, these leaflets. Like flyers at the tourist information office for theme parks and what's- on- next -at- the -theatre brochures only not so colourful. They are bland. Innocuous to the touch. They rise in slotted ranks in holders on the walls of doctors' waiting rooms. The dreaded words are printed plain and clean and crisp. Cancer. Alzheimer's. Multiple Sclerosis. Parkinson's. Wholesome and commonplace as liquorice all sorts, simple black words in plain font so you can get used to reading it, *saying* it.

My darlings, it can be very difficult to continue thinking in terms of *loved one*. The loved one has changed beyond all recognition in some cases. Family members find it hard to love this impostor, this creature that has taken over mother's body and makes her behave in abnormal ways. They want their mother back and they have to learn that's never going to happen. Mother has left and each time they see her she will have slipped further and further away until the day comes when she doesn't know who they are.

Information pamphlets don't tell you how you should respond when mother tells you the wrap she wears around her shoulders was knitted by Colonel Gadaffi's grandmother. They don't make it clear how you should play it when mother believes her room is a railway carriage and you are all hurtling through France on your way to a holiday in Italy. When she asks you how you are going to manage carrying all the suitcases, how are you supposed to reply? When she tells you next door's dog is learning to be a car mechanic, how do you stop your heart from breaking?

She won't understand if you tell her about the things that are happening to you. She will look at you with those empty eyes and the blank expression that stabs you in the stomach. She won't remember anything you say so you can tell her how his mouth feels on your breasts. You can describe in detail the shape of his erection and how it excites you to have a man want you again. Mothers are supposed to be there for their daughters. Through thick and thin a daughter should feel she can tell her mother everything and still be loved. So Wendy told Jenny all of it.

"Who, dear?" Jenny said.

"I don't know his name."

"Whose name?"

"My lover."

"Is he kind, Wendy? It's so important to find a man who is kind."

Her mother's question opened the forbidden thought box. Wendy launched herself through the opening and her thoughts rushed at the opportunity to be out in the open.

"He's wonderful, Mum. He's patient and gentle. Just like when I was a little and I had a secret friend. Do you remember when I was a little girl and I couldn't go to sleep?"

Jenny had no answer.

Wendy continued. "Do you remember when it started?

"When what started?"

"It was just after Dad died. It was a terrible time and I was frightened. I was afraid of everything and for ages I couldn't let you out of my sight in case something happened to you as well. I didn't want to go to school because you might not be there when I got back."

"I used to take you to school."

"Yes, Mum. You did."

"My father never came to my school."

Jenny looked away as if she was trying to find the answer to something that was just out of reach. And then she found it.

"Parkwood," she said. "That was the name of my school. My father never came there. Did you go to Parkwood school?"

Wendy sighed and said, "No, Mum. I went to a different school. My dad did come to meet me sometimes and whenever there was a school concert he came to that when he could."

"Is he coming here?"

Wendy couldn't speak. The words wouldn't come. She couldn't think of a way to explain to her mother that her husband had been dead for more than thirty years. Then Jenny's face brightened as she remembered something else.

"You liked stories," she said. "I used to tell you stories."

"Oh, that's right, Mum. You did. And when Dad died and I was afraid to close my eyes, you used to sit on the edge of my bed and make up stories of your own. Do you remember you used to tell me about the Sandman? I've never forgotten. You made him kind and gentle not some kind of bogeyman like in the comics. *My* Sandman was someone special just for me. I loved those stories. He was my secret friend who would always be there to look after me. I thought he was beautiful magic especially for me. He made me feel better and I always fell asleep while you were talking. I never heard the end of those stories."

A flicker of understanding made Jenny put her hand to her lips.

"Now my lover helps me to sleep, Mum. He knows just what I need."

"Who, dear?"

"It's all right if I tell you, isn't it? You won't tell anybody will you?"

"Is it Gordon?"

"No, Mum. I'm talking about me."

"I remember Gordon."

"Yes, Mum."

Jenny went to her bedside cabinet. She rummaged in the drawer and said, "I have a picture somewhere."

She rustled papers and found her purse. "Is this what I was looking for?"

"Mum, come and sit down here," Wendy said and pulled out the easy chair by the window. Her mother sat and let out a sigh. Wendy sat on the edge of the bed.

"It was Gordon, wasn't it?" Jenny said. "Do you know him?"

"Yes, Mum. I knew him."

"Have you got a lovely man?"

"Oh, yes," Wendy said, still filled with desire to talk about him. "He knows when to wait and when to move. He knows how to keep me just at that point where you nearly tip over the edge. And his kisses. Oh, his kisses. I never knew kisses could be so erotic. Just the touch of his skin is enough to make me want him."

"Who dear?"

With the door to her mother's room firmly closed Wendy delighted in repeating luscious words of loving. She recalled them slowly and with each word she relived the sensations. She could almost feel his body pressing against her. She could smell almonds in his hair and taste the salt of his skin.

Her pupils widened, soft and black, as she imagined his warm breath on her neck. She heard his moans of desire as he pleasured her. She leaned back on her mother's bed and closed her eyes. She dreamed of the times they shared as his fingers stroked her, flicked her, gently rubbed and nudged her to fulfilment.

Jenny was busy watching the grass outside moving in the breeze.

13

Marcus

My parents came to stay with us last summer. Dad pulled up outside the house and before he'd opened the car door I could hear him complaining. Sarah touched my arm as we stood in the drive to greet them.

"Smile," she said. "Don't forget to look as if you're pleased to see him."

I went to help mother out of the passenger seat while my father lifted their things from the boot. Mother took my arm and when she'd straightened up she hugged me. She was a little unsteady and when I put my arms around her there was less of her to hold than the last time I'd seen her.

"Marcus," she said. "And Sarah, it's lovely to see you." She embraced Sarah and began looking around for Sophie. "Where is she? Where's my favourite granddaughter?"

Father poked his head round the back of the car.

"Margaret. Go inside," he said.

"Sophie is on a theatre trip, Mum," Sarah said, linking arms with my mother. "Let's go in and have a cup of tea, shall we? Marcus will help bring in the bags."

Sarah took mother indoors and I waited for instructions.

"Don't touch anything," Dad said as he leaned into the boot. "I know where everything is."

I can't remember the last time my father and I said hello and greeted one another properly. I used to make the first move but I could tell he felt so awkward, so uncomfortable that I stopped doing it. I waited till he'd lifted out their bags and placed them on the drive, precisely, like soldiers on parade in the order he wanted them. I carried in the load he designated to me. Mother was sitting at the kitchen table with Sarah who was keeping the conversation going. I took my parents' things to their room in the sequence Dad said. Then he went upstairs to check.

"He likes to know exactly where everything is," Mother said when he'd left the room.

"Even your personal stuff?" I asked her.

"Oh, yes, dear," she said. "He likes to take charge of everything in case I forget."

Her smile didn't reach her eyes. Father came in from upstairs and Sarah sent me one of her looks.

"You should cut back that wisteria," Dad said as he came into the kitchen to join us. "It'll get in the guttering if you don't."

Dinner that night was awkward. My father dominated the conversation around the table. He interrupted my mother, finishing off her sentences and did the same to Sarah. By the time we'd had dessert both women had stopped participating. Later, when we were in bed I asked Sarah what she thought.

"I'm worried about my mother," I said. "Don't you think she's kind of getting smaller?"

"I'm not surprised," Sarah said. "It's your father. He's so bombastic. He just takes over."

"Well, you know he's always been a bit like that. Mother always handled it before. She could give as good as she got."

Sarah sighed. "Maybe she's fed up of having to do that," she said.

My father came with me next morning to the DIY centre in Chippenham. I'd promised Sarah I'd fix the washing line. It's one of those parasol-shaped gadgets that spins in the wind. It was leaning at a precarious angle and I thought I could sink a piece of pipe into the ground and set it in place with concrete. Dad was a total embarrassment in the store, arguing with an assistant about the best way to tackle the job.

"I assure you, sir," the young man said, "this is the best material for the job."

"And how many washing lines have you fixed?" Dad said.

"I've done similar things on my training course."

The assistant tried his best but my father had his face set. Eventually the poor guy gave up trying and walked off. My father grumbled and threatened to speak with the manager.

"Young kid like that trying to tell me what to do," he said. "He looks like he's only just out of nappies."

"Dad, I'm going to take his advice. I'm sure he knows what he's talking about."

"And I don't? Is that what you're saying?"

"No, that isn't what I meant and you know it."

"I'm putting in a formal complaint," he said but I persuaded him to come away.

"Fancy calling in for a pint on the way home?" I asked him.

We went through the checkout in silence. I paid at the cash desk and ignored the grim set of his face as I loaded the boot.

I drove the country route back to Compton along narrow lanes threading between hedgerows, passing through tiny hamlets, Dad grousing all the way. I always enjoy looking over hedges into other people's gardens but Dad made no response when I commented on a spectacular display of sunflowers or a pretty cottage. He stared ahead and grumbled about sharp bends and awkward junctions.

"I don't know how you put up with these roads," he said, hanging onto the support handle above the passenger window.

I pulled in at a pub Sarah and I were keen to take a look at. As we crossed the car park Dad said,

"We'll never be served in here, Marcus. Are you sure this is the best place? Look how many cars there are."

I kept on walking. "We'll see."

He followed me inside like a truculent child. Judging by the number of customers in the bar there was one per car outside, I thought. Two men sat at one of the tables nearest the door and I nodded at a face I thought familiar. Service was quick and friendly but I made no mention of the fact and neither did my father. We both chose a pint of best bitter and moved towards a window table near the empty fireplace.

Outside the sun climbed into a hot, clear sky. When Dad and I took our seats I heard the two men discussing me.

"That's Doctor Harding," one of them said in a tone of voice that made it sound as if he was surprised I should be in a pub.

Dad lifted his glass.

"Your mother's getting worse," he said after his first taste, as plainly as that, as though he was commenting on the beer.

"In what way?"

He looked around and lowered his voice.

"I think she's losing it."

I looked at him. His expression was far from caring. There was no tenderness in his face. No nuance of regret in the tone of his words. He looked accusatory, almost spiteful. His eyes narrowed and his mouth was set in a thin line. He leaned forward and brought his head closer to mine.

"If it gets much worse I don't know how I'm going to cope with her." The corners of his mouth turned downward as he shook his head.

"Dad," I said. "You can't expect Mum to be like she was when you were younger. Everybody slows down as they get older."

He took a swig of his beer and set down his glass on the table with a thud.

"Well, I don't suppose I should have expected much support from you," he said. "You always were your mother's favourite."

"That's not true," I argued. "I was just nearer. I was able to come visit more often."

I tried to convince him but he wouldn't listen. He had made up his mind. When he spoke, his words were wrapped in such anger. He'd wanted to pick a fight all morning and wherever the conversation moved, whatever subject came up, he laid down the law according to Anthony Harding. I retreated from the battlefield. I didn't offer to buy another drink.

When we returned to the house he went into the sitting room, switched on the television and sat with his arms folded, watching the midday news by himself. Mother was in the garden, reading. Sarah was in the kitchen preparing lunch.

"Has something happened?" Sarah asked me.

"No. Not really. Just Dad being Dad. You know."

"Ah," she said.

We took my parents out to dinner that night. It was a beautiful evening. It had been one of those rare days when temperatures in England are higher than on the continent and, next day, all the newspapers feature photographs of sunbathers on crowded beaches and children and dogs sharing ice creams. Some diners had bright red faces with white eye creases. We took a table in the orangery, an oversized conservatory tacked onto the back of a village pub one of Sarah's friends had recommended.

"What a lovely place," my mother said, admiring the view across open fields.

"Yes," Sarah agreed. "I'm glad you like it."

"Tell me about Sophie's theatre trip."

"She told you last night, Margaret!" my father snapped.

Mother kind of grew in her seat. That's the only way I can describe it. One minute she was just my mother, smiling and quietly enjoying herself and the next thing her whole presence expanded.

"Anthony," she said, "I know that Sophie has gone to New York. I know that while she's there she's going to see a Broadway show and be fortunate enough to take part in a master class with the director. If I have forgotten the name of the show it's only because I'm unfamiliar with what is currently fashionable."

My father snorted.

"And you can stop doing that," my mother continued. She turned away from him. "Sarah," she said, "tell me about where they're staying and what other activities they've planned."

Eventually the atmosphere settled and we had our meal. But that was the mother I remembered from when I was a boy. Patient, but firm when she needed to be. It was good to see she hadn't forgotten how.

There was a small craft show in Compton next day. Sarah and my mother browsed the stalls while father and I went to the beer tent to taste real ale. We regrouped by the hog roast for lunch. Sarah and Mum had bought cakes for tea later. I had evening surgery and when I returned to the house my parents' car was no longer in the drive. Sarah took me by the hand and led me to the kitchen where she put some coffee and a measure of brandy on the table for me.

Mum and Dad had left to go home a day early. I immediately assumed something had happened with my mother.

"What's the matter?" I said. "Was she feeling ill?"

"Marcus, your mother isn't the problem," she said.

"But she does seem frail at times, wouldn't you say?"

"Marcus," she said. She put her hand on my shoulder. "I think you should know what your mother has told me."

My stomach lurched. I expected the worst. "What is it? What did she tell you?"

She pulled up a chair and sat beside me.

"You mother is very unhappy."

"Yes. I could see that."

"She wants to leave him."

"What?"

"She doesn't want to spend the rest of her life with him. She's had enough."

"That's ridiculous," I said. "She's seventy four."

"It isn't ridiculous, Marcus. I'm only telling you what she said. She mentioned her age. I'm seventy four, Sarah, she said. Who knows how long I have left? All I know is I don't want to spend another moment with him."

I gulped at my cognac.

"Have you told her she can come to us?"

"She doesn't want to do that. She wants a little place of her own. I've offered to go with her to view a sheltered apartment."

"My mother in sheltered accommodation? Don't be silly."

Sarah took my hands.

"Don't speak like that," she said. "That's the sort of thing your father would say. I'm not being silly and neither is your mother."

It's not the kind of conversation you expect to have when your parents are in their seventies. I couldn't shake off the idea it was absurd they should consider separating at their age.

"Marcus" Sarah pulled me out of my thinking. "Your father doesn't know."

"You mean she hasn't told him anything?"

She gave me a funny little smile and said, "You can understand why, can't you?"

Of course I knew what she meant. He would try to browbeat her into giving in. He would go on and on until she lost confidence in her plans. He would make her believe she couldn't do it. And yet, I'd seen her rise to the occasion the night before. Perhaps Sarah was right that mother had simply had enough of Dad's domineering ways.

"You're asking me not to tell him," I said.

She nodded.

"Is that the right thing to do?" I said.

She breathed in deeply and puffed it out.

"I don't know, darling. I've never been in this situation before."

14

Through late summer when her mother was in care Wendy Carter looked forward to visits from her secret lover. I saw how she wore a girlish smile when she thought of him. I watched how the words *dream lover* played across her lips. That's the name she'd given him, not because she was asleep when it happened because she wasn't. She was fully awake and enjoying every minute of it. She struggled not to cry out the first time he brought her to orgasm with his body rather than his fingers. She had to put her hand over her mouth to stifle her whimpering. She wrapped her legs around him to hold him there, to keep him there inside her. Then she slept deeply.

In the morning she had more vigour. Her legs felt weightless and there were happy thoughts swimming around in her head. From top to toes she felt as though she'd been given a new body. She laid out the breakfast things for Rob and went to her early shift at the supermarket. Her eyes were clear and sparkling. Colours seemed brighter to her. The world was a friendlier place. She felt she could cope with anything life threw at her. With her dream lover, her perfect lover to comfort her the problems with her mother seemed less severe. She would manage. She could enjoy life again.

Fresh energy renewed her interest in other things. She was excited about planning something different for dinner. She thought about it as she wheeled out fresh bread trolleys from the warehouse. Humming a tune she stacked shelves, feeling like a new bride. When she took her turn at the cash till she had a pleasantry to offer customers. She cooed at babies and sympathised with harassed young mums. She passed goods over the scanner more slowly for elderly customers so they could organise their packing, or she helped with it, separating light weights from heavy, fresh from frozen. When customers thanked her she felt special.

She cooked Kung Po chicken that night. She'd put out a fresh tablecloth in the dining room and found placemats in the sideboard drawer. Rob said nothing. Not about the food nor her efforts. When she asked him about his day he shook his head.

"You wouldn't understand," he said.

"The boys will be home soon," she said. "Maybe we could all do something together like we used to."

She looked at him with a hopeful expression but her suggestion annoyed him.

"For God's sake, Wendy. Those days have gone. When will you get it into your head they're not boys any more? Stop calling them that. Why should they want to do anything with us? They've had a great time with their friends in Scotland. Why would they want to do anything with us for the rest of the summer?"

Her face crumpled. She choked back tears.

"Oh, grow up," he said.

She waited up that night until he made a move to go to bed. Maybe there was still something between them that could be saved. Perhaps if she could find a way to bring him comfort they could get through all of this and come out the other side with a new understanding of one another. She still felt it was her duty to try.

He apologised for the way he'd spoken to her. He said he had a lot on his mind preparing for a new course of study at work. Something to do with a different examination system and it had to be in place by the time the new academic year began. He was tired. Worn out, he said. He kissed her on the cheek and his face felt surprisingly warm and soft. She smiled at him and he brought his hand to her chin and smiled back. She thought he might be waiting for her after she'd brushed her teeth. The idea was not entirely unpleasant. She used to long for him. Pine for his attention. Not so long since. Her secret lover had shown her she could still respond to a man. It would feel odd to have Rob's body again.

But the bedroom was in darkness. He'd turned out the light and was already on his side with the covers pulled up to his ears. She slipped into bed beside him and her feelings turned to stone. She told herself she'd been a fool to think she could change things by herself. When Rob began to snore there was an ache inside her, a pitiful yearning for the life she had lost.

That was the last time Wendy had thoughts like that about Rob. From that moment they ceased as easily as turning the last page in a novel and closing the book. You know how it is. You might regret the passing of your enjoyment of reading that book. You might suffer a minute's bereavement when you know you won't pick it up again to settle into another session of following the plot to see where it takes the characters you've come to care about. But you won't spend the rest of your life thinking about them, wanting them still to be a part of your everyday life. You will let them go. They will drop from your consciousness. There will be no irreparable hole in your psyche. You will still be you.

Wendy knew now that Rob couldn't give her what she needed. The realisation that this nothingness between them was where their relationship had delivered them had no more effect on her than reading a train timetable. It was simply a matter of fact. Nothing more. From that very moment, whenever she looked at him there was a dull hollow where once there had been longing. It was no more disappointing than a missed train.

She searched inside herself for the yearning feelings, wondering how she could have changed so abruptly, but the desire for Rob's attentions had disappeared. Her heart was a finished novel, a discarded timetable. It was a relief to be free of the pain. She stopped wanting him to want her.

She welcomed instead the warm mouth moist against her neck and his searching, stroking fingers. She gazed into his soft eyes and nestled in his arms. She arched to meet her lover's thrusts and marvelled at the way he took her beyond herself, out of time and place, into another world where nothing else mattered. She opened to her dream lover and took him to that empty place in her heart. He told her his name.

She wasn't surprised. She felt she'd know it all along. The sound of his name pleased her. She repeated it over and over in her mind. Of course. It had to be. Who else could have brought such peace and contentment into her life? He had been waiting for her call. Listening out for her need of him. Gently he had reawakened her and brought her back to womanhood. He loved her. He had always loved her.

The Sandman gave her what she needed how she needed it. And then he gave her sleep. I believe it was on that particular occasion that Wendy Carter knew she loved me.

15

Marcus

From the beginning of Jenny's time at the Firs it was clear she wouldn't be able to return to an independent life. It wasn't safe for her to do so. She was a danger, not only to herself, but to others too. Her rapid decline and the level of her aggression took everybody by surprise.

She lashed out at her carers verbally and physically. Physically, of course, she was fit and well and her strength was remarkable. She could land a hefty blow. She threw her dinner at the wall if it wasn't one of her favourites. She cursed at everybody when she couldn't get her own way. She took off her clothes if she felt too hot regardless of who could see her. It was obvious to all the staff that Jenny Carter was no longer the mother and grandmother her family knew. Records show that it became necessary to administer anti-anxiety medication to treat her agitation and aggression, to calm her down and prevent her from hurting herself and others. Only a matter of months later, after the 2011 National Institute for Health and Clinical Excellence N.I.C.E. published guidelines, Jenny Carter would have had access to the cholinesterase inhibitors we now know can help stabilise the symptoms of Alzheimer's disease. The promised vaccine is still years away.

Social Services looked at Jenny's care package and, in consultation with her daughter and son-in-law, a reluctant decision was made to sell Jenny's house. It all happened very quickly. This must have caused further stress for Wendy. I can only imagine what it must feel like to come to terms with the fact that the family home is at risk. It's always unfortunate when a patient has to lose their home but that's the way the system works, I'm afraid. As medical practitioners we don't get involved with that side of things however unfair it might seem. If Wendy's father had been alive and living in the house the question wouldn't have arisen. But Jenny was a widow and the assets tied up in the property were all hers alone.

The way that Alzheimer's is classified, strange though it may seem, excludes the sufferer from totally free NHS care. Frailty and other age-related conditions are not clinical concerns. I can fully understand why families are outraged. I've heard the arguments. The end result is always the same when it comes to care packages.

In Jenny's case, here was a woman who had never had serious illness, had never taken up hospital care other than when her daughter was born and yet in her hour of need there was no support for her unless it was paid for. She needed round the clock specialist care at a cost of over thirty thousand pounds per year. There was no other way round it. Cuts in local government had decimated the deferred payments scheme so Jenny's daughter and her husband opted to sell before the end of the twelve weeks assessment period. They put the bungalow on the market before house prices fell further. I saw the For Sale signs outside. The property is only one street away from our practice. A retired couple from Lincolnshire bought it, I understand. I drove past some weeks later and saw the sign had been removed and the new people had already moved in. I thought it cruel such change could happen so quickly.

I continued taking that route over the next few days and saw a skip in the driveway, full of broken up kitchen units and ripped carpets. There was a tangled heap of flowered wallpaper and black bin bags. Another time there was a plumber's van outside and I saw two men carrying radiators inside. Weeks later all the windows had been replaced and there was work going on in the garden. I stopped passing by after that.

I've no idea what Jenny's family did with her belongings. What do you do with a lifetime's possessions? You sell the furniture, I suppose. Get what you can for things that once held great sentimental value. Hold car boot sales. I don't know. Maybe Wendy gave some of it to the charity shop. I only hope I never find myself and Sarah in a similar position. It must seem like the person is already dead before they die. It's a shameful way to treat people.

I thought about what Sarah had told me. There were going to be radical changes in my own family. Sarah had made arrangements to meet my mother and view some properties and, still, my father hadn't a clue what Mum was planning. I didn't like being party to that kind of deceit but I hoped that afterwards, when things had settled, I'd be able to smooth the waters a little. Compared with what was happening in the Carter family it didn't seem so bad. I emailed my brother Niall. He's in West Africa with an oil company. I told him what our mother was planning and his response surprised me.

She should have done it sooner, he wrote. What took her so long?

I thought long and hard about his question. Why had she left it till she was in her seventies?

16

Was that a shock, my darlings, when I told you who I am? Ah, you had your suspicions but couldn't be sure. It's true but only in part. It's Wendy's truth. It's what *she* called me. I have as many faces as there are people in the world.

Is there something else you think you know? Don't be embarrassed. Listen. Accept. There are no liars here. Wendy accepted gladly. She'd known the Sandman from childhood and trusted his care. Didn't the Sandman love her and bring her peace? What's so wrong about that? It wasn't hurting anybody.

As August rolled towards its end the skies settled into a pattern of high pressure and warm, sultry days. But still Wendy closed the door to her mother's room at the Firs. Thunderstorms broke the heat and wind brought rain from the west lashing against Wendy's car as she drove from home to work and from work to the Firs and from the Firs back home again. All the while, whenever Wendy was with her mother, that door stayed firmly closed. The storms passed and afterwards the air was fresh and smelled of green things. When the sun came out again flowers raised their heads and glowed with clean, bright faces. Cooler winds swirled through the valleys.

Wendy was visiting alone again. Rafe had offered to come but Wendy had persuaded him against it. Jenny was sitting in the chair beside the open window staring at the view of the garden. Lawns were freshly trimmed and that delicious summer smell wafted through. The voile drapes puffed and sucked in the breeze. Someone had put a throw around Jenny's shoulders and she was wearing somebody else's white knee socks with her slippers.

Wendy kept her voice soothing and gentle.

"Hello, Mum. How are you feeling today?"

Jenny turned her head. She had that look on her face, the one that pulverised Wendy's insides. Her mother's eyes were those of an innocent child, open and trusting. Puppy eyes, beseeching. Jenny's mouth was partly open, her tongue peeping out between her teeth.

Jenny cocked her head and said, " Have you brought me some chocolate?"

Wendy reached into her bag and brought out the caramel bar. Her mother snatched it and tore off the wrapper. She twisted around on her chair so that she had her back to her daughter and sat, hunched over the chocolate bar, shielding it between taking bites as if she expected it to be taken from her. She sucked at it and made slurping noises then, when she was finished, she wiped the back of her hand across her mouth.

Wendy took a baby wipe to remove her mother's chocolate moustache but Jenny wouldn't be touched. She flapped her arms and circled them like the blades of a windmill, faster and faster. Wendy couldn't come near. When Wendy backed away Jenny got up and moved her chair square on in front of the window so she could turn her back completely. Wendy sat on the edge of the bed aching to talk.

At the window, Jenny began to sway. Left. Right. She rocked from side to side slowly. From her position on the bed Wendy watched the game. Her mother was oblivious to anything other than the movement of her own body. When the drapes blew into the room Jenny swayed left; when they were sucked back to the window she leaned to the right.

"The Sandman came to me again last night," Wendy said as Jenny continued swaying and once Wendy had begun she couldn't stop. "Oh, God, it was wonderful. I excite him so much, you know."

Jenny stopped rocking and pointed at something outside.

"I've never known such passion," Wendy said. "Sometimes he cries out because he loves me so much. My God, Wendy, he says, what are you doing to me? And when he's finished he wants to do it again. Straight away. Just like that. *And* he's ready for it. He makes me want to scream with happiness. Actually, sometimes I think I do."

Jenny pulled a lopsided smile and put her head on one side like dogs do when they're listening.

"Rob never notices anything," Wendy went on. "He hasn't noticed me for years, anyway. Well, it doesn't matter any more. Not now. I don't care now. He can do what he likes as far as I'm concerned."

A knock on the door. Wendy jumped up from her mother's bed and let in the ladies with the tea trolley. They rattled into the room. Volunteers with tight perms and pearl necklaces.

"Here we are," they announced. "I bet you're ready for this, aren't you?"

They took turns speaking in a well-rehearsed litany of small talk while cups clattered against saucers.

"One with and one without. That's right isn't it? No need to ask about biscuits, is there Mrs Carter? We know what we like. Don't we Mrs Carter? Oh, Mrs Carter you *are* a naughty girl. You've already got chocolate all round your mouth."

Wendy hung back and let one of the women take hold of Jenny's head to wipe her clean. The other poured strong tea and put out biscuits on a pretty china plate. Then they reversed the trolley back through the doorway with a cheery *see you later*. Wendy closed the door behind them. When she turned back her mother had her mouth stuffed full and was trying to pack more in while crumbs escaped and dropped on the carpet. Jenny ate all the biscuits, shoving them into her mouth one after the other, gulping and whimpering. She wore a sly look with narrowed, deceitful eyes as if she knew she'd deliberately allowed the tea lady to touch her while keeping her daughter at arm's length, like it was a punishment. Her smirk was as good as saying I'm having all these biscuits and there's nothing you can do about it. She sloshed and spattered and continued her gasping, drowning noises but her eyes stayed fixed on her daughter's face. Wendy ignored her mother's cold gaze. Her mother's eyes were like Rob's. Empty.

17

Sarah

The September sun was hazy but still warm as I waited to meet my mother-in-law off the train in Swindon. My nerves fluttered. I was apprehensive about how the day would turn out. It was a huge thing Margaret was planning to do at her age. I wanted to be calm, to be steady and comforting for her. I thought she would need that. I tried to concentrate on the beautiful day, the lovely autumn colours beginning to appear and that quiet glow that comes sometimes at the end of summer when all the fields and hedges look glazed with buttery yellow. Inside I was anything but quiet.

Margaret strode with purpose along the platform. She looked like a headmistress full of the sense of important things to do. She had on a smart, short-sleeved dress and carried a wrap over her arm. She was fresh-faced and seemed happy. My nerves subsided a little.

"Come here and give me another hug," she said when we reached the car park.

I did. She held onto me afterwards and stared into my eyes.

"Now, you're not to worry about a thing," she said. "This is what I want, Sarah. This is what I've wanted for a long time now."

"I know, It's just that . . ."

"Yes," she said. "I know it's sad after all these years and I'm sorry I've involved you in keeping the truth from him. You do realise that this is the only way, don't you?" I nodded. "You must trust me to tell him when I judge the time is right."

I helped her into my car and got in beside her. She was bright and perky and much more in control of herself than I was. "I shall be nearer to you and Marcus," she said, "and although I don't want you to feel that I'm becoming dependent on you, it will be good to have someone close who actually cares."

I took her hand. "We would never think of you as a burden," I said.

She put her finger to my lips. "Shush," she said and shrugged her shoulders. "I am getting forgetful. I know I am. There's no point in denying it. I'm supposed to be a bit forgetful at my age. So is Anthony. He forgets things all the time and then blames me. He says I never told him. That's the difference between us. He denies it."

"You're a remarkable woman," I said.

"Not really," she said. "Quite ordinary, in fact. Women have to be strong, don't we dear? Anthony can't bear to have me around reminding him we're both old people now. That he might be losing it, too. I don't want to put up with his silly moods any longer. I shall be much happier in my own place. Now, where are we going first?"

She fastened her seat belt and turned to look out the passenger window. I put on the radio and as we moved off I kept glancing at her. She was absolutely fine with all of it. No question. She looked as though she was setting out on an adventure, eagerly anticipating new sights, fresh happenings.

We didn't need to look any further than the first place. As soon as Margaret saw the pretty gardens and lovely view of rolling hills she was sold. The gated community was built in local stone, the single storey buildings sited in an attractive arrangement around various small gardens and water features. Birds twittered around feeders and fussed in the bird bath. Gentle paths crossed the different plots and there were benches and tables set here and there amid shrubs and under trees. It looked very welcoming.

One of the caretakers showed us around. Each small house had its own kitchen and bathroom, one bedroom and a sitting room just large enough to take a small dining table. There were alarm pulls strategically placed throughout. Outside, each bungalow had a small terrace beneath the overhang which could make a lovely garden room. In the main building there were communal rooms, too, a small meeting room and a larger hall with a small stage at one end. A notice board in the porch advertised tea dances and visiting speakers. In another block were shops: a unisex hairdresser, launderette, a café and a small grocery store run by volunteers.

"Would you like to meet any of our residents?" the caretaker asked. "You know, get a feel of the place?"

"No need," Margaret said. "All in good time."

We went to the main office to deal with the paperwork. I thought there might be some small print and was ready to point out possible pitfalls in the contract but there were none.

We found a place for lunch in nearby Devizes. The bookshop at the front gave onto a sweet bistro with tasty-looking pastries and hot dishes. We chose a table next to an open window which overlooked a small courtyard at the rear, neatly paved and with urns filled with late geraniums.

Margaret said, "I'm going to love it here." She hadn't stopped smiling since we'd seen the house at Barleycroft. "So many new places to visit. Things to buy for my new home. What do you think about a patio table and a couple of chairs for my terrace?"

"Perfect," I said. "I know just the right garden centre."

The waitress arrived with our food and Margaret ate with appetite.

"It seemed a straightforward rental agreement," I said.

"Yes. Very easy. And there's no need for you to be concerned about finances. I have a good pension of my own. It should be more than enough."

She went on to tell me about other financial arrangements she'd already put in place. She had it all worked out. I was amazed at her strength of purpose, her determination. She sat talking in between mouths full, taking sips of her glass of wine, as excited and happy as if she was on holiday. I was afraid for her. I thought her expectations were too high, that she would come to realise, all too soon, that her life wasn't going to be as easy as she thought. She'd been with Anthony for more than fifty years. I would have been terrified striking out alone at her age.

"What about your lovely house in Kent?" I asked.

"What about it?"

"Won't you miss having all that space? Your gardens?"

"Good heavens, no," she said. "Why would I miss all that cleaning?"

"Will you sell, do you think?"

She laid down her knife and fork. She leaned forward and lowered her voice.

"My dear Sarah," she said. "I shall have no say in the matter."

"What do you mean?"

"The house is in Anthony's name only."

"What?"

"That's how he wanted it. That's how we started out together and that's how it stayed."

"But you could have had your name added to the deeds later," I said.

"I asked him once about that but he can be very stubborn as you know. His need to be in control of everything grew stronger over the years. I didn't think it would ever matter." She let go a sigh. "It's a good thing I went back into the Civil Service when the children were older and built up my own pension pot. From now on it will be paid into my own bank account and there's nothing he can do about that."

She spooned up a piece of cheesecake and munched in satisfaction. I searched her face for clues to how she must feel having just revealed all that about her relationship with Anthony. There was no sign of anger nor regret. Her face was peaceful, content. She smiled at me and took my hand across the table.

"Everything's going to be all right," she said. "Don't worry. You'll see. You can tell Marcus what I've just told you if you like."

Her quiet manner and gentle words made me wonder how she could be so serene. I had thought I'd be the one doing the comforting but it had been the other way round. I knew I'd do everything I could to help her settle into her new life.

18

The warm, late September afternoon session with the Sandman had left Wendy feeling sated. She showered and used all the creams and lotions she usually had little time for. She styled her hair, put on a clean outfit and she was still floating around the house playing at being young and beautiful when Rob came home unexpectedly early. Surprised at the change in his routine she didn't at first notice how stooped over and worried he appeared. He walked through to the living room, dropped his bag on the floor and flopped onto a sofa. She followed behind.

"You're early today," she said. "Don't you usually have staff meetings after classes on Wednesdays?"

He didn't say anything. His head dropped into his hands. "Rob, is something wrong? What's happened?"

She knelt in front of him and when he looked up she could see tears in his eyes. "Rob, what's going on?"

She feared the worst. There'd been an accident. The boys were hurt on their way back to university. The national Express coach had overturned in a ditch. They were lying in hospital somewhere with tubes coming out of them and drips, and drains, heart monitors and all manner of other instruments packed and beeping around their beds.

"I can't believe it," Rob said.

"Believe what? Rob, speak to me."

It wasn't the boys then. She could tell by the way he was looking at her. If it had been the boys he wouldn't look like he did now, wearing the sulky pout that told her the trouble was about *him.* He reminded her of the way her mother stared at her. Needy. Those questioning eyes. The slack mouth. Her stomach twisted. She didn't want Rob to need anything from her.

"I've been suspended," he said.

"Suspended?" It took her a moment to take it in. Suspended was a word usually associated with student behaviour. "What for?"

"I'm being investigated."

She watched him struggling to find the right way to say the rest of it. He kept biting at his lower lip and clearing his throat as if his words were getting stuck there.

"I've been accused of inappropriate behaviour," he said. "with one of my students."

Is that it? she thought. It was hardly likely. Rob couldn't stay awake long enough.

"That's rubbish," she said. "Who is it? Tell them it's nonsense."

He shrugged and said, "I don't know who it is. They don't tell you."

"You mean you don't get a chance to defend yourself?"

"Not yet. No. That comes later. After they're satisfied there's a case to answer."

She thought it a stupid arrangement. She could go up to college herself and tell them what an idiotic mistake they were making. Rob held out his arms looking for comfort from her and her stomach twisted again. She let him rest his head against her chest and she put her arm around his shoulders but she turned her head to one side in an effort to distance herself. After a minute she said she had to see to dinner and left him staring into space as though the answers to his questions were written on the living room walls or somewhere just beyond them, through them, somewhere in a different dimension.

At dinner he wanted to talk, to go over the events of the day. It was an effort to listen to him. She had to force herself to respond.

"Rob," she said, "you haven't done anything wrong. It's just, what do they call it? Procedure. That's all it is. You've got nothing to worry about."

"I never imagined how it would feel," he said. "I never, not for one moment, thought about how wrong it is to treat a member of staff like this. How could they possibly think that I would . . . .. Dammit, don't they know me?"

He couldn't finish his plate. He said he'd lost his appetite. She saw him flicking through the television channels while she cleared away the dishes. He sat with his head in his hands or with his hand over his mouth as if he was trying to stop himself from screaming. She found it repulsive that he had fallen so quickly into despair. He sulked like a child through an episode of *Body Farm* and when she went to go to bed he decided to go with her.

In bed he wanted her to hold him but she was afraid where that might lead.

"Go to sleep, Rob," she said. "Things will look different in the morning."

"Are you going in to work tomorrow?" he said.

"I'm at the charity shop."

"Can't you take the day off?"

"Why?"

"I just thought it would be nice if you were here."

The churning sensation that rose from her stomach up to her throat was like a kind of fear. Blood drained from her face and her mouth dried. Reality seared its way in. She realised she hadn't thought through what Rob's being suspended would mean to her day. He would be here, at home. All day.

He would be in the way. The Sandman would be waiting for their afternoon delight and she wouldn't be able to go to him.

She lay quietly, waiting for Rob to sleep so she could find comfort with her lover. Despite his concerns Rob fell asleep easily, she thought. She waited a few more minutes until he had rolled on his side and his breathing had slowed. She inched her body away from his and lay close to the edge of the bed as far from Rob as she could so that not even their elbows were touching. She closed her eyes. She breathed the secret name.

Sandman. Sandman. I need you. I need you now.

She opened her eyes expecting to sense his presence but the bedroom was dark and silent. She stared into the shadows of the room hoping to feel the change in the atmosphere that signalled his approach, that rippling effect she could never see but felt against her face and at her neck but there was only the pale light from the radio alarm. She concentrated on his name again and wished for him. She projected the wish as far as she could, pushing it out of her head towards the corners of the room and beyond to where he must be waiting for her call. He didn't come.

19

Joan

We had an idea things were not going well for Wendy at home. Sometimes she'd come into work and, to tell you the truth, it looked as if she hadn't even had a wash let alone brush her hair or put on a bit of makeup. That must have been about the time her mother fell ill although Wendy never mentioned it to us at the time. I thought she must have been having some more trouble with her husband. Well, you can imagine how I might think that way after the way I'd seen them not being together on the day he came here and embarrassed her. That, and bearing in mind the sorts of questions she'd been asking me. I just put two and two together. I tried to bring her round. So did Norma. We kept having a go at bringing up some new topic of conversation and so on, but we couldn't get through to her. Couldn't even get her to pass comment about the weather.

Norma came in one morning soaked to the skin. Absolutely dripping, she was. She stood in the middle of the shop and shook herself like a dog that's been in the river. Her hair looked like she'd been dragged through a hedge. We'd had one of those summer downpours where the heavens open and throw everything at you. I'd just missed it. I'm usually first into work and Wendy wasn't far behind me. We'd had to switch all the lights on. It got darker and darker like an eclipse of the sun. We'd been watching from the doorway, Wendy and me, then there'd been one almighty clap of thunder that made the windows rattle and we shot back inside. Well, anyway, Norma said she'd been waiting at the bus stop when a car came speeding past and ran through a deep puddle right by the pavement. She said it was like being at one of them aqua parks in Florida or somewhere where they get a whale to soak the spectators. This great wave of water flew up from under the car's wheels, she said, and drenched the whole queue. Some of them were furious, she said, but Norma was laughing her socks off. She came in here and could hardly stand up straight from howling with laughter.

She said, "Joan, think how much money I've just saved."

"How do you mean?" I said.

"Well," she said. "How much does it cost to go to Florida?"

We picked out a skirt and top from the racks for her to put on while her clothes dried over a chair in the back room. Wendy was the only one of us not laughing. She stood staring and never said a thing.

Well, a few weeks went by. I think it was a few weeks. I can't be sure just how long but, anyway, Wendy seemed to perk up. It was good to see her looking brighter and happier. She was like a different person. I mean, so different that even her face looked younger, somehow. She did her hair up nice and wore prettier clothes like she'd started taking an interest again just in being alive. She offered to bring things in from the bakery or pop down the dry cleaners for us. That sort of thing. More like her old self. She wanted the radio on while she washed down the shelves and rearranged the china bits and pieces. We all sang along. Radio two. They play a lot of oldies, dear. Ones we know the words to.

So, I felt I could ask her what had been bothering her before. She told us all about her mother then. But she said she thought everything was going to be all right in the end. She just had a feeling, she said.

"I can cope, Joan," she said and carried on singing. She didn't want to say any more so I left it alone.

Then when her mother went into the care home I thought Wendy was going to have a breakdown. I did really. Everything went backwards again. She'd pulled herself up out of the dumps and now, here she was looking worse than ever. She looked terrible. You could tell she'd been crying, poor thing. Every time she came into work there'd be dark rings under her eyes and her eyelids would be all puffed up. I don't think she was eating properly, either. She got way too thin.

I told her to try not to worry. I said her mother probably wasn't aware of what was happening to her. Our Sid went like that. A cousin on my mother's side. He got so as he didn't even know his own face in the mirror. Can you imagine that? Bloody frightening. I think if it gets as bad as that you're better off not knowing. But at least Wendy was talking to us about it. I always think it does you good to get things off your chest even if there's nothing anybody can do to help. I think just talking things through helps to ease the burden.

But that wasn't all. Poor thing. As if she hadn't got enough to deal with. How many problems can a body cope with? I don't know. It was like one thing on top of another. So when she had that trouble with her husband up at the college she did go very quiet for a while.

We didn't like to mention it in front of her but we knew it was something to do with a girl because my granddaughter, our Louise told me. She's in her first year at sixth form college. Clever girl is our Louise. Wants to study business law whatever that is. Oh, she's got some big ideas. She wants to live and work abroad somewhere. Her mother worries about Louise leaving home but I told her, I said,

"Let the girl go if that's what she wants to do. It's a different world out there now."

Well, you can't hang on to them forever, can you?

Anyway, it can't have been easy for Wendy when all that extra trouble blew up. You know what people are like. What they think and say behind your back. There's no smoke without fire. You know what I mean? It's a small town is Compton. News travels fast. Wendy must have known people would be whispering. She didn't need any more trouble piling up on her, poor girl. She must have been going out of her mind with worry, what with one thing and another.

20

Listen. Wendy felt as if nobody paid any attention to her and how she was feeling. Nobody could understand how much she had lost.

During the time he was off work in September Rob became very needy. With his hands clasped behind his back he wandered from room to room staring at the furniture. He switched on the television news. He switched it off again. He followed Wendy about the house watching her at her morning tasks like an extra shadow clinging on her back.

The college was taking its time investigating the accusations against him. They said they wanted to be certain. One of his female students had brought a very serious complaint against him and they wanted to proceed steadily. Do it all by the book. They had the reputation of the college to consider.. Surely he could understand what a difficult position they were in. They must be seen to be doing things properly. The girl in question was off sick but as soon as she was back in college they would interview her again, with her parents, and they would let him know the outcome.

He sent in a work schedule for his students and set their assignments. A supply teacher acted as go-between and called at the house from time to time. His name was Jonathan Palmer and his face was as fresh and white as his new diploma. Inexplicably he chose to wear Bermuda shorts over his thin legs, a vivid Hawaiian shirt covered in a sickly yellow hibiscus pattern and no socks with his slip on shoes. He breezed into the house and wafted out again on a current of brand new enthusiasm for the job, keen to assure Rob his students were in good hands. Rob wished he could be a fly on the wall last period on Thursday afternoons. The Public

Services and Physical Education groups doing their G.C.S.E. resits would make mincemeat of young Mr Palmer.

The whole situation galled him. When he grew tired of watching news channels he picked up one of his favourite books. Then he paced the house again looking for something to do. There were plenty of small jobs he could have done if he'd put his mind to it. A shelf to fix. A loose hinge on a kitchen unit door. He could have gone up in the loft and laid the extra insulation he was always saying they needed. He could have offered to cook dinner but instead he drifted through the rooms like another Lost Boy.

When Wendy came home from work he hovered around her. He told her about his morning. He described Jonathan Palmer and his Bermuda shorts. He hovered and paced until Wendy asked him to leave her alone to get on with what she had to.

"I'm leaving something in the oven for tonight," she told him. "It'll be ready when I get back."

"Get back?" he said. "You've only just got in."

"Rob, I'm going to see my mother."

"I'll come with you," he said.

"There's no point," she said as she put the casserole in the oven and adjusted the timer.

Rob had no idea how his wife was feeling. He didn't ask. He had very little space left in his thinking to consider anything outside his own problems. Isolated from his work and his colleagues, consumed by the injustice of the college's treatment of him he failed to recognise that Wendy's behaviour had shifted again. Instead of gliding around the house with a faraway expression, she moved slowly with eyes half open as if the lids were too heavy to lift. Her speech was slow. The tone of her voice dull as November.

His own body language mirrored his wife's. His shoulders drooped. His mouth was set in a permanent downturned line and there was a deep, vertical crease in his forehead above his nose. He turned away from Wendy and went back to his sofa. The cushions were crumpled and the throw was a tangle of lumps and ridges where he'd been sitting. He sat on them and picked up the TV remote. He turned up the volume when Wendy said, See you later, and let herself out.

Wendy paid no attention to the beautiful autumn colours on the drive to the care home. She parked at the rear and kept on her jacket, fully fastened. Record-breaking late September temperatures had set the countryside aglow. The people of Compton had put away their woollen knitwear and gone back into tee shirts but Wendy paid no attention. Around the Firs Lavatera shrubs were throwing out new blossoms. Petunias in hanging baskets still flourished. Residents and their visitors strolled the gardens and occupied benches. Some of them recognised Wendy and smiled as she passed but she kept her head down and made for the entrance. A care assistant came to stop her as she made her way to Jenny's room.

"She isn't there, Mrs Carter," the young woman said. "She's in the sun room. Hasn't it been a lovely day?"

Wendy said, "How is she?"

"Oh, I think she's feeling much better today, Mrs Carter. We'll send the tea trolley round shortly."

Wendy found her mother sitting watching birds feeding from grease balls hung in a birch tree. A low, reddening sun flickered through the branches backlighting papery bark and leaves already yellowed.

"Sit down," Jenny said, impatient hands motioning. "Don't disturb them. Did you know they have to eat their body weight every day?"

Wendy took one of the basket chairs and looked at the blue tits outside. "They're pretty birds," she said.

Jenny said, "Did you know they have to eat their body weight every day?"

"No. I didn't know that."

Jenny spun round to look at her daughter. Her face was severe. Her eyes were hard and scornful and her mouth curled with derision. She raised her chin and tilted her head so that she had to look down her nose.

"What?" she said. "What didn't you know?"

Each dry word of her reply choked in Wendy's throat.

"I didn't know they had to eat their body weight every day." she said.

"I know that. What are you telling me that for? Why are you telling me things I already know?"

Wendy didn't respond. Her eyes brimmed with tears. She attempted to brush them away.

Jenny tossed her head and said, "What's the matter with you now?"

Wendy brought out a tissue and blew her nose.

"He's gone."

"Who has?"

"You know. *Him*. He's stopped coming to see me. My Sandman."

"I don't know what you're talking about. What's got into you? Sandman? You're not making any sense. Have you gone stupid? I know it's not me. There's nothing the matter with me. Don't you dare say that there is."

Jenny dismissed her daughter with a flick of her wrist and turned to the window. Wendy stared at the back of her mother's head. Through aching eyes she saw the stiff pride in Jenny's shoulders, the familiar arrogance in the way her mother held her head and she could hardly contain her grief.

"I love him," she said. "I miss him."

Jenny stood and put her hands on her hips. She spun on her heels to look down at Wendy. She threw back her head and laughed.

"I wonder what makes you think you're so special," she said. "You're just a widow now like me." She strode toward the door, her head held high. Jenny Carter laughed all the way down the corridor to her room.

Wendy could hear Jenny's laughter growing louder. She tried to shut it out. The sound made her flesh crawl. It brought back memories of childhood days she would rather forget. She shivered. History was repeating itself.

Part Two

It's the morning of Wendy's ninth birthday and mother is having another one of her bad days. Mother has stayed in her bed. Mother doesn't want to do anything today. She says she'll only spoil it for other people and she's best out of the way and left alone. Her husband is taking care of breakfast and his packed lunch. The sink is full of last night's dirty dishes and the waste bin needs emptying.

"I haven't got a clean blouse, Dad," Wendy says, still in her pyjamas. She rummages through the pile of ironing in the laundry basket on the kitchen floor and pulls out a school shirt from the bottom. It's been in the basket so long underneath the weight of the mound of clothes, the cheap cotton is creased and twisted. Wendy gets out the ironing board and plugs in the iron.

"Shall I do that for you?" her father says.

"No, Dad. It's all right. I know how to do it. I only have to do the collar and cuffs. The rest doesn't show underneath my school jumper. Will you make me some toast, please?"

They sit at the table and find a place to put their plates among newspapers and mail shots. Wendy has honey on her toast. Dad has marmalade. His eyes are soft and kind when he tells his daughter what a good girl she is.

"I don't know what we'd do without you, Wendy," he says. "You're a special girl."

He clears away the plates when they've finished and Wendy dashes to brush her teeth and get dressed. When she comes back into the kitchen there's a package on the table. The wrapping paper is pretty but it hasn't been done well. There's too much sticky tape and Wendy has to tear at it instead of opening the parcel carefully and smoothing out the paper so she can use it in her scrapbook later. Inside is a copy of Charlotte's Web and some new accessories for her bike.

"We'll go into town and try on roller boots on Saturday, sweetheart," her dad says. His face looks red and he's breathing hard and she knows the reason her roller boots are not already here is because her mother has been having bad days for over a week now. Dad has been trying to do everything and Wendy can see he's tired. Sometimes he makes loud noises when he breathes.

Wendy dries the dishes her dad has washed and puts them in a pile on the worktop. She can't reach the shelves in the wall cupboard where the plates live. Gordon Carter puts on his coat and kisses his daughter as he leaves the house for work.

"Have a good day at school, sweetheart," he says. "You'll be all right walking, won't you? I don't have time to drop you off."

"I walk to school every day Dad. It's not far."

"I'll be back early tonight and we'll go to the cinema. Would you like that?"

"Is Mum coming?"

"We'll see, Wendy. We'll see."

He kisses her again and tells her she looks very grown up and beautiful now she's nine.

"Dad?"

"Don't start anything now, Wendy, please. I've got to go to work. I'm late as it is." His face looks even redder.

He hurries away and Wendy doesn't get the chance to say, *Why is Mum so often poorly? Why doesn't she go to see the doctor?*

She grabs a chocolate wafer biscuit from the tin and slides it into her schoolbag for her morning break. Then she runs along the hall to tell mother she's going to school now but through the gap in the partly open door she sees that Jenny is on her side with the covers almost over her head. Wendy creeps back. She remembers there'll be nothing for tea so she runs to the freezer and takes out a pack of sausages. She puts them near the sink to defrost. They'll be ready to cook when she comes back from school. She'll be able to eat early with her dad and then they'll be in time for the seven o' clock showing of Bugsy Malone. Everybody at school says it's great and Katie Wadsworth said her parents laughed all the way through it. It would be good to see her dad laughing again. She would like to laugh too and forget that at home there was hardly anything left to laugh about.. . . . .

Sausages lie in congealed fat in a cold frying pan. Clean plates sit on the table with clean, unused knives and forks beside them. There's a doctor in the living room with mother and a policewoman in the kitchen with Wendy and the house feels still and cold, like it's all a bad dream, but it isn't a dream. It's real and it's really bad. People are whispering and Wendy's head feels as if it belongs to somebody else.

Men Dad's age don't have heart attacks and fall down dead in the garage on their daughter's birthday. They come home from work and take their girls to the cinema and they have fish and chips afterwards if they're hungry. They keep their promises to go to town for new roller boots and then, for the rest of the year, they come home from work every day and have their tea with their families and go on summer holidays and eat too much at Christmas and laugh at Morecambe and Wise and then it's spring and birthday time again.

On their birthday, girls don't come home from school to fry sausages because mother is still in bed. They don't have to get their mother up out of her room because Dad is late home and hear someone tell her over the phone that Dad never went to work at all that day. Girls shouldn't hear their mothers screaming in the garage and shouting at them in a wild voice, *Don't come in. Don't come in. Stay away, Wendy. Stay away.*

Birthdays are supposed to be special. Birthdays are supposed to be happy.

Wendy wonders what would have happened if she hadn't gone to school. If she'd stayed home to look after her mother she might have had reason to go to the garage for something and she might have found her father before it was too late to save him. She could have phoned for an ambulance and they'd have come to take him to hospital and put him on one of those machines she'd seen on Angels on television and everything might have been all right in the end.

Jenny tries to comfort her but Wendy thinks her mother's eyes look as if she's the one who's dead. Wendy can hear sounds like words but they make no sense against the strangely cold whistling in her ears. In her thoughts she goes over all the things her father said to her that morning, trying to make time go backwards and start the day again. Maybe she should have made him take her to school. She would have been right by his side then when it happened. He wouldn't have been on his own with nobody to help him.

For days Wendy plays the same mind game with time. She remembers everything he said about being late for work, the promise about going to the cinema and choosing roller boots on Saturday. Every small detail burns so hot in her head her eyes sting. She dare not close them. She tries not to sleep. She pinches her face when her eyelids droop. Sleeping is a normal thing and you do normal things when things *are* normal. She can't allow herself to be normal. It wouldn't be right. Life will never again be normal for Wendy. Fiercely she concentrates on keeping her dad's voice in her head but as the weeks go by it gets harder to remember the sound of him. Before a year has passed Wendy needs to look at photographs to know his face. His words on that ninth birthday morning slip away bit by bit until the last thing Wendy will remember about her father, the one tiny detail about that day that will live with her forever is that he had marmalade on his toast the day he died.

22

Margaret

I first met Anthony at a summer dance. He was such a handsome man, slightly taller than me and so charming. It was in 1957 when I was nineteen. I wore a blue satin evening dress and pointed toe shoes. I don't remember how I wore my hair but it was dark brown then. We used vinegar or beer in those days to make our hair shinier. I wore *Blue Grass* or *Je Reviens*, my favourite perfumes, light and flowery and feminine.

I'd noticed this young man standing near the bar watching me and when he finally came over to ask me to dance the music changed to a Pat Boone song so we were thrown together for the first time in a slow smooch. One of the first things I noticed about him was his hands. They were graceful hands with long tapering fingers and neatly cut nails. His arms were strong and he smelled good although I remember thinking at the time he'd used too much *Brylcreem* on his hair. It looked wet and slippery.

He worked in the drawing office at an engineering firm. My parents took to him straight away and soon we became what today you'd call an item. We married in 1961 after years of hard saving for a house deposit. That's what engaged couples were expected to do. We watched every penny and hardly ever went out. Girls kept a bottom drawer where they saved things for their future home. You didn't expect personal gifts on your birthday or at Christmas. It would always be something for the bottom drawer. It took years to gather together all the household items you needed to set up home independently.

We had a nice semi at first on the outskirts of town. I remember feeling as if I was playing at house using all my own pots and pans. Decorating and deciding where to put the furniture was exciting. We had lovely neighbours and there was a real sense of community where we all looked out for each other.

Niall was born in 1962. Marcus came along three years later and Claudia just eleven months after that. That was the happiest time of my life. I was so happy it made me afraid. There were so many terrible things going on in the world I was fearful of losing what I had as though I didn't deserve to possess such happiness when so many others were struggling to survive.

I used to see harrowing reports on television of people being killed trying to get across the Berlin wall. Shot in the back. Dear God. I saw burning villages in Vietnam, starving children in Biafra. It seemed as if every year there was another crisis and yet, there I was with everything I could possibly want. I had such contentment when others had so little and I clearly remember thinking that this was the best that life was ever going to be for me. I dreaded coming to the end of it. I don't know whether other women sometimes feel this kind of sixth sense but I knew one day something was going to strike out of the blue and ruin everything.

When my daughter died it felt like the end of the world. She was attacked coming out of a night club with her boyfriend. Stabbed. They both were. He survived but poor Claudia . . .

It was a dreadful time for all of us, especially Marcus. They'd been so very close. Eleven months apart, that's all. So close. She had her whole life in front of her. She was only sixteen. Marcus was doing his A Levels at the time. I don't know how he managed to get through. Niall had already left home by then.

Life was never exactly what you would call easy with Anthony. In the early days I had my beautiful children and I felt fulfilled looking after them. Simply being a mother was such a joy. As they grew older I went back to my job in the Civil Service. I had to do some retraining to get up to speed with developments but I enjoyed the work and being with colleagues again. I managed my shifts so I was always there when the children came home from school.

Anthony didn't like the fact I was contributing financially to the household. He seemed to think it made him somehow less of a man. I told him it would mean we could have extra special holidays and so on but he still didn't like it. So I saved most of my earnings and helped out the boys when they set up on their own.

Anthony was always very particular about many things but when we lost Claudia he became very difficult, I'm afraid. We were all suffering, all of us experiencing grief in ways we could never have imagined. Grief happens to you in stages of disbelief and numbness, sorrow and weeping and then an overwhelming anger that consumes you and makes you hate the world. You grow so angry you are in danger of destroying everything else that is good in your life, but I believe it's necessary for you to go through these feelings so you can come out the other side and be on your way to some kind of healing. Anthony never expressed any of those stages of grief.

When he retired things became even worse. I think he must have been a difficult person to work for. He was such a stickler for doing things by the book. I used to say to him, Anthony, sometimes the book hasn't been written yet, but he wouldn't have it. There's always a procedure, he'd say. He truly believed that. I think if he could have his time again a career in health and safety would suit him down to the ground. Rules. Procedures. Of course, when he didn't have his job to go to he brought all his rules and regulations home.

The first week after he retired he set about changing things in the house and garden. I didn't mind to begin with. I've never been much of a gardener myself so I was perfectly happy for him to grub out some old shrubs and want new borders. It seemed to keep him happy. He needed to fill his time. He still felt that necessity to keep his body busy and his mind occupied so he didn't dwell on what had happened to Claudia. The pain never went away for Anthony.

He never cried. I've never seen him shed a tear. He threw himself into some project. That was his way of dealing with it. We never talked about Claudia's death. He couldn't. He was simply unable to talk about the pain of his grief and so, as a result of how he felt, he never asked me how I was coping. I don't remember him ever comforting me about the loss of our daughter. It was as if he had closed himself down, shut himself off.

The boys tried to help him come out of it but, in the end, even they gave up. Their father had turned into a bitter, angry man and it's such a shame. At the very time when we all needed each other more than ever Anthony made it impossible.

I don't blame Marcus for never wanting to return to Kent. He met Sarah while he was at university and they stayed together. She worked in administration. She's a lovely girl. She brings out the best in him. She's so caring and such a good mother. It's a pity they didn't have more children. Sophie is such a credit to them.

23

Rob was hanging around in the kitchen like a little Lost Boy. His presence annoyed Wendy. She hadn't been used to having him always right there under her feet, getting in the way. He'd never before shown the slightest interest in how to cook dinner and now here he was asking questions about ingredients and methods as if he would ever take it upon himself to actually produce something of his own.

"Rob, if I tell you how many eggs," Wendy said, "you'll only forget. I can write it down and pin it on the notice board if you like. Or you could find a recipe in a cookery book. You know where they are."

"I like watching you," he said.

He wore a hurt expression. His brow was creased and the corners of his mouth turned down in a sorrowful sulk. There was a time when she would have clasped him to her and her insides would have thrilled at that look in his eyes. Now, it seemed pathetic.

"I'd rather you didn't watch me," she said, looking away from his mournful gaze. "You're getting in my way. Why don't you go and find something to do?"

He said he'd walk to the corner shop for a newspaper. She resisted the temptation to tell him to take his time. As soon as she heard the front door close she rushed to their bedroom. It was the first opportunity she'd had to have the house to herself during the day since Rob's suspension from work. She needed the Sandman. With Rob at her heels all the time she'd had no space to think about her lover. Surely, she thought, he hadn't completely abandoned her. She plumped the pillows, kicked off her shoes and lay on the bed, fully clothed. If Rob came home and found her there she'd think of some explanation. He'd never suspect anything.

She couldn't settle. The room was too bright. Should she draw the curtains? No. The neighbours would notice. Should she take a shower? There was no time. She let her head sink back into the pillow and closed her eyes. The house was quiet. Only the hum of the fridge drifted along the hallway and into the bedroom and the clicking, whirring noise as it switched itself off. She forced herself not to listen to the domestic noises. She ignored the lingering aroma of aftershave coming from Rob's pillow and focused instead on imagining the manly smell of the Sandman.

"Sandman," she whispered and the sound of his name made her mouth water. "I'm waiting for you."

She stretched out on her side of the bed and let her arms relax at her sides. Her head sank deeper into her pillow. She concentrated on thinking about his last visit. How long had it been since then? Too long. She made herself thrill at his imagined touch, a shivering sensation at the back of her neck and tingling that raced down her arms right to her fingertips. Her mouth felt wet and her lips swollen. She attempted to conjure up the sensations of his mouth, his hands, his body. But thoughts of her mother's laughter kept getting in the way. She could hear her laughing all the way down the corridor at the Firs, the sound bouncing off the walls and hard flooring, echoing horribly. The tone of the laughter, that *particular* sound resonated in her head. Wendy tried to shrug off the picture of her mother standing with her hands on her hips, sneering at her with cold, cruel eyes.

And what makes you so special?

Other images from long ago rushed into her mind, crowding and milling around in her head. Her mother standing over her with that same nasty expression on her face, the head tilted to one side and her face too close. The same laugh. The same words.

"*And what makes you so special? She is saying. "Come on. Answer me. Cat got your tongue?*"

But Wendy is too young to think of an answer. They haven't got a cat and anyway, she wouldn't want one if that's what they do to your tongue. She's just a girl. She doesn't know what she's supposed to say. She thought all children were special in their parents' eyes. Wasn't that how it was meant to be?

She goes to her room to get out of her mother's way and there she curls up into a ball on her bed and hides her face under a pillow. She makes pretty thoughts come into her head of fairies and princesses, enchanted glades and handsome princes astride beautiful horses. Or, she might be a different Wendy, the one from *Peter Pan* and fly out her bedroom window, away from Compton, over the rooftops and beyond the hills out towards the sea. Peter would take her hand and fly with her through the clouds and they would be happy all the way to *Never Never Land* where she wouldn't have to worry about cats snatching her tongue ever again. There would be a magic table where delicious meals appeared all by themselves with no dirty dishes to clear afterwards. And, best of all, people's faces would be smiling and jolly. They'd be happy to see her and want to be with her as if she was somebody who really mattered in their lives. She would be beautiful and not even the tiniest bit fat. Her hair would shine like gold and her clothes would be made from princess material, shiny and very, very beautiful. There would be music and that would be beautiful, too, like magic flutes that sounded like the wind singing and bells that sounded like birds. The sun would always shine on her and inside her. It would shine out of her eyes because she was so happy and it would make her voice sparkle so that everybody loved to hear her speak.

All the bad things would not be allowed. They'd be locked up, shut away forever in a dark corner of the woods where nobody ever went because it smelled bad there. And it wouldn't matter that she didn't have a father because all the boys and girls in *Never Never Land* didn't have fathers either.

A tall grey shadow might appear by her bed and at first she'd smile and not be afraid because, if it's a ghost, it will be her father come to tell her he's still looking after her from a far off place a bit like never Never Land and he'd say,

"Don't worry. Everything's going to be all right. I love you, Wendy. My special girl."

And she'd come out from under her pillow and open her eyes. But the ghost isn't her father and it isn't a ghost either. It's her mother with her face still angry and her eyes full of something horrible.

On her marriage bed, in the solid, old semi-detached bungalow, Wendy rubbed at her eyes.

"Oh, Sandman," she said again. "Please."

Nothing. Only the room and fridge noises. Sounds of cars passing along the avenue. She rolled over again and tried to relax . . .

It's Wendy Carter's wedding day and there is nobody to give her away. It's a funny way to put it, she thinks. *Give her away* like she's an unwanted gift. But she understands the symbolic meaning of it, the handing over by a loving father to the man she loves. It's a beautiful thing, really, and it would have been wonderful to experience that feeling for herself, to know that the two most important men in her life loved her and cared about what happened to her. But it wasn't to be.

She has grown up with little masculine input. The only men in her life have been teachers. She doesn't know much about the way grown men think or the things they like. She doesn't know she's always been pretty, always had the kind of face and figure most men find attractive, rounded and curvy and soft.

It was a huge surprise when she first learned how much men wanted to *touch* her. At first, when Rob had put his hand on her breast she thought he'd made a mistake, that he'd gone to the wrong place. Surely he'd meant to hold her hand? But then he'd squeezed her and when she looked at his face it was obvious how much he was enjoying it. She didn't know she was supposed to enjoy it too. She knew about babies and how they came into the world. She knew how they got made in the first place but that wasn't anything to do with *love.* Love was holding hands and gazing into each other's eyes. Love was kissing and being together. Love was white horses and Never Never Land. Sex was something you had to do when you wanted a baby, quite a separate thing from loving somebody.

Rob has taught her how to enjoy being touched and she trusts him. He's the only man in her life now. He's dependable, like a teacher should be. Her father would have approved of him. Rob is going to make a wonderful husband just the sort any girl would be proud to call her own. Like being proud of a father who loves you enough to give you away to another man on your wedding day.

She doesn't want her mother to stand in the place of her father to give her away. She wants somebody kind and loving but there's nobody she knows. It doesn't matter. She's found the one who will care for her now and for the rest of her life.

She walks alone down the aisle to meet her fiancé. It's a small gathering. She passes by the rows quickly, paying no attention to the rhythm of the organ music, not looking at the faces in the pews. Most of all, not looking at her mother. Mother will have to take care of herself now. She's not too old to do it even though she makes out she is.

"How will I manage, Wendy?" Mother said when Wendy announced her engagement. "How will I cope on my own?"

"I won't be far away," Wendy told her. "I'll come to visit."

"Visit? Visit? What use is visit, Wendy? You know how hard it is for me when I'm having one of my bad days."

And Wendy had found the courage to look her mother in the eye and say, "It's my turn to be happy now, Mum. I hope you can be happy for me."

"He's too old for you. You should have waited to meet someone in your own age group. Don't come complaining to me when he bores the life out of you."

Wendy thinks she could never be bored with Rob as her husband. He's clever and he loves her and he understands all about difficult childhood. He still finds it hard to talk about his own. When she's with him it feels as if it's just the two of them against the world.

She looks at the two figures waiting in front of the altar. With his best man beside him, there he is, Rob Carter looking tall and very smart in his new haircut and hired suit. He turns to greet her and she takes her place by his side.

This is where I belong now, she thinks. *Always by his side. He wants me for his wife and I will love him forever.*

She gazes into his eyes and he looks happy as if he's thinking this is where he belongs too. The honeymoon in Jersey is filled with squeezing. Rob wants to touch every part of her. She enjoys the closeness of him and the way he can't stop himself from touching her again. He asks her if she's satisfied and she says she is but doesn't know what she's supposed to be satisfied about. Her heart is full of love for him and so that's all that matters. Pleasing him is the most important thing in the world. It's all she wants to do forever.

The fridge rattled at the end of its cycle. Why couldn't she keep her mind on the Sandman? Why did her mother and then Rob keep getting in the way? Her thoughts were muddled and spoiled. It wasn't fair. Nobody should be able to spoil your thoughts. Thoughts were private and they should be safe from other people. On her bed, she curled tighter. She heard the front door open.

"Wendy," Rob called from the hall. "I bought you a magazine. Where are you?"

Wendy uncurled her legs and slid from the bed. She opened the bedroom door and he was there with a sheepish grin on his face and she should have thanked him but instead said,

"Oh, it's you."

"Who did you think it was?" he said with a forced laugh and went to the kitchen. "Fancy a cup of tea? I'm just about to make some."

She put on her shoes and followed him. He was taking down cups from the wall cupboard and the kettle had started its rumble. The magazine was lying on the table. It was one of her favourites and it was the first time ever he'd thought to do something like that for her. She turned the front cover and began to read. When she looked up Rob was watching her. He looked so grateful he had pleased her with his gift it made her insides twist.

24

Marcus

The report from the Firs dated October sixteenth makes special reference to the first signs of improvement in Jenny Carter's condition. She took a morning shower and afterwards wanted to go outside to see the rose garden. Wendy wasn't due until afternoon so a member of staff accompanied Jenny and, because it was such an unusual request from a patient who had never gone outside, paid particular attention to everything Jenny said.

Apparently Jenny commented on the roses looking battered after recent high winds. She said it would be a good time to prune or the gardeners would have to wait until all risk of frost had passed the following spring. Her expression was alert, it was noted, and the tone of her voice sounded more natural. When they returned indoors Jenny ate a good breakfast then took a seat in the conservatory. She read a magazine. She wasn't simply looking at it. She was reading. She could answer questions about the article she'd read and went on to give her own opinions on the coalition government.

The episode was documented in Jenny's notes but, as we are only too aware, these sudden onsets of bouts of lucidity can occur for no apparent reason. Later that day when Wendy came to visit Jenny had retreated back into herself. After lunch she had immediately regressed and was once again confused and bewildered. She appeared extremely tired and had to be helped back to her room.

Over the next few days Jenny's episodes of coherence increased in frequency and duration such that she became able to take a walk in the gardens by herself. She dressed properly according to the weather and passed comment on conditions outside when she returned. After Seamus Dalton received a phone call from the Firs he went to see for himself.

"I've never seen anything like it," he told me. "We must keep a close watch on this, Marcus. Why don't you come with me next time?"

I accompanied him on the next visit a few days later. The Firs residential care home is an attractive building. Once a country hotel and restaurant, the annexes had been built in similar stonework and in a complimentary style so that the whole presented a welcoming face to the world at the head of a curved drive which swung around the back of the building into the car park.

We were expected and shown into a private meeting room. The manager, Lauren Mills, was waiting for us. She was a tiny woman. Her frame didn't look strong enough to take on the responsibilities of her position. She greeted us with a cheerfulness that seemed too big for her face.

"I wanted to speak to you," she said in a gush, "as this is so unusual. I honestly don't know what to do next." She rubbed her little hands together and nodded her head like a child's toy.

"Go on," Dalton said.

She pursed her mouth and made a slight sniffing noise. "Mrs Carter," she said, "seems to have made a full recovery." She quivered from top to toe. She reminded me of the dormouse in Alice, cute but annoying at the same time.

Dalton made a humming noise. "But we know that's not possible, don't we?" he said.

Lauren Mills shook her head. In fact, she shook the whole top half of her body.

"I know, Doctor Dalton, but the facts speak for themselves. You saw what she was like the last time you visited." Her words came out in a rush of excitement while her body twitched and quaked. I had to look away. The poor woman was obviously extremely perplexed.

"I did take note," Dalton said. "What changes have there been since then?"

"She sleeps a lot."

"More than before?"

"I can't say. I don't know what her habits were before she came to us." She went back to rubbing her hands, her head still nodding as though it were on a spring.

I interjected. "There's nothing in her medical notes to suggest any abnormal pattern," I said.

Dalton said, "What exactly are you referring to?"

Lauren Mills sucked in a breath and brought her hand to her mouth as if the answer were on her fingertips.

"Two or three times a day she goes to her room to sleep," she said. "Yet she still sleeps well at night. Each day, since we last saw you, her periods of lucidity have increased so that now . . . well, I think you should come and see for yourselves."

She hurried through her office door and skittered down the corridor, her rapid, short strides clicking against the flooring. We followed her into the conservatory where Jenny Carter was reading a novel. She looked perfectly peaceful. Her hair had been dressed and she had on lipstick. She wore earrings matching the colour of her blouse. She looked up when she heard us come in.

"Good afternoon, Doctor Dalton," she said. "Have you come to let me out of here?" She laughed. The tone of that laugh was melodious in a practised way. It occurred to me she knew she was under scrutiny like an ageing actress in an interview meticulously prepared and supremely in charge. "I'm only joking," she continued, "but I think you have to agree I don't really belong here, do I?"

Jenny Carter motioned with a manicured hand, fingers delicately splayed, varnish matching the lipstick. Lauren Mills fluttered about behind her, tidying a pile of magazines, rearranging the blinds. Dalton and I glanced at one another then he pointed to Jenny's book.

"What's that you're reading?"

"Oh, this is just something I found on the shelf over there. Actually, it's very exciting. One of Kathy Reich's. Have you read her Doctor?"

Dalton shook his head. He clasped her hand in both of his.

"I'm delighted to see you looking so well," he said.

She crossed one leg over the other and leaned back in her chair her arms resting casually at her sides.

"Can I go home?"

"Not just yet, Mrs Carter," Dalton said. "We don't want to rush things, do we?"

"Why don't you put me through some more tests?"

Dalton gently touched her arm.

"I think that's a very good idea," he said.

We returned to Lauren's office in silence. I was at a loss as to what to say. What I had just witnessed was phenomenal. Jenny Carter had put on a display worthy of an Oscar acceptance. What was going on? It was unthinkable that every member of Jenny Carter's medical team had made a mistake over her diagnosis. And yet, what we had observed was equally unimaginable. Lauren went to her desk, I took a seat and Dalton stared out the window. Nobody spoke for some minutes.

"We haven't told her about her home," Lauren said. "I feel awful. There's no procedure for this eventuality. Who should I speak to? I don't know what to do. What do you suggest?"

She stared up at Dalton, her head still jerking and her fingers clenching. He addressed us both.

"I think we must leave that for Mrs Carter's family to decide. This is extremely unusual but what we have here is one of those periods of remission we know can happen. It is remarkable, I agree, the extent to which Mrs Carter would seem to have recovered. It is not recovery. It can't be. In cases like Jenny's full recovery is not possible. We must keep sight of that. Sadly, Mrs Carter will relapse and continue to need your care here. As for her family, there is only the daughter. That's right, isn't it? How has she reacted to her mother's improvement?"

Lauren Mills laid her hands flat on her desk. Finally, she was still.

"I'm glad you asked," she said. "I can't give you an answer. I think she must be as shocked as we all are. She said nothing. She just accepted it, almost as if she was expecting it to happen."

25

Listen. Wendy ached for her Sandman. Her fingers tingled when she thought of him. The back of her neck thrilled when she remembered how she quivered when he licked it. He would slowly draw his tongue across her hairline and blow softly along the same line so that her skin cooled under his breath. And then he'd do it again. The memory of it made her respond with an excited shiver. Deep inside her, a dragging sensation pulled at her womb like fathomless, empty contractions.

Every night she lay in bed quietly waiting for him. She listened for the sound of Rob's breathing slowing. She willed him to roll over so she could concentrate on the darkness where her lover should appear. But the room remained still and silent. Through the curtains the street light outside the bedroom window cast a pale yellow glow that fell onto the bed at Rob's side but, beyond that, the room was full of barren darkness. There was nobody in the shadows coming to her with promises of paradise. When Rob began to snore she propped herself up against her pillows, staring into the blackness, longing to sense that first warm breath from him, to feel that first exquisite half-touch. Her eyelids drooped. She drifted into fitful sleep and then woke to watch and listen again. Nights slipped by in their cold and empty lovelessness and in the mornings she rose, exhausted, to begin her day's work.

On the day Rob was called into college Wendy's spirits lifted. When she finished her morning shift at the supermarket she hurried home to bathe and prepare herself for her lover's return. With Rob out of the house all day surely, she thought, her Sandman would come back to her. She sang a little tune as she dried her hair. She powdered and perfumed and curled her eyelashes, all the while imagining his face. He had such a beautiful, manly face with eyes full of love and passion for her. She couldn't wait to taste him. She put on a satin teddy that had been a Christmas present from Rob once in another lifetime and she varnished her toenails. She checked her reflection in the wardrobe mirror and then got on to the bed.

She heard the front door open. Rob came in, loud and boisterous. She could hear him running into the kitchen. He was shouting her name. She went after him and stood in the doorway.

"It's all over," he said. "Thank God, it's all over." Then he noticed the way she was dressed and said, "Sweetheart!"

He grabbed Wendy and swung her around. She was so surprised he'd called her sweetheart and so shocked he was holding her she didn't stop him from kissing her as he let her down to the floor. She wanted him to explain what had happened at college. She expected him to want to tell her about it. Mostly, she wanted him to take his hands off her. He pulled her close and pressed his body against her hips and his mouth came down on her face.

She wanted to scream or slap him. His mouth was dry and hungry and it wasn't supposed to be Rob kissing her. His lips felt like sandpaper on her skin. She backed away from him but he moved forward and thrust his hand under her slip.

"What are you doing?" she shouted.

"I'm loving my wife," he shouted back misinterpreting the volume of her voice for joyful exuberance. He swept her along the hall and into their bedroom and she couldn't object because his arms held her tight against him and his mouth pressed down hard on hers. She tried to move away from him as he stepped out of his pants but he held her with one arm, scratching her with his thirsty kisses. Her neck and shoulders froze at his touch. Her throat tightened and her mouth felt dry. He pressed her onto the bed. He was hot and hard and heavy and he mistook the tears in her eyes for thankful relief. He must have thought her sobs signified release from her frustration. Her cries were an expression of her need of him. She was limp beneath him. He thrusted harder and faster and exploded inside her.

Afterwards he couldn't stop grinning. He sang in the shower and shouted out that they should go out to celebrate his good news. She didn't answer.

"Where would you like to go?" he shouted louder. "Wendy! Where would you like to go?"

She lay curled on the mattress, holding her stomach, holding in the pain, fighting back tears. He'd offered no explanation of his sudden reinstatement at work. He'd marched into the house and behaved like an animal. She was disgusted at what she'd allowed. There had been no love in it, whatever he'd pretended. Rob hadn't *loved* her. All he'd wanted to do was make himself feel better. There'd been no thought of Wendy and how she was feeling. He'd had good news. He felt relieved. He must have thought he was a proper man again. It had all been about Rob Carter.

She felt soiled. Rob was repulsive. His body was an alien thing. There was no consolation at his heavy hands, no pleasure from his mechanical pushing inside her. The taste of his mouth made her feel sick. His body fluids stank.

Worse, she had betrayed her lover and she was afraid that after this the Sandman would never come back.

26

Marcus

My father stood in his drive with his arms folded against his chest watching me load the hire van. The expression on his face cut me as though he had called me traitor. I pushed the cardboard boxes of mother's things as far into the rear of the van as I could and went back into the house for the suitcases of her clothes. Mother was staying with Sarah and me until her new place was ready. Dad watched me, silently, as I packed everything in.

"Why didn't she come with you?" he said when it was done.

"She didn't say, Dad."

I waited. I expected fury from him but he unfolded his arms and said,

"Would you like a cup of tea before you go?"

The quiet kindness of his words stung worse than his anger. I sat in the kitchen while he made the drinks and wondered what he was going to say next. He sat opposite me and his expression further surprised me. His eyes were softer than I'd seen them in years.

"How is Sarah?"

"She's well, thank you. So is Sophie."

"And your work is going well?"

"Yes."

It was painful, this edging around and avoiding the subject at the heart of it all. Finally,

"I always loved her you know," he said.

"I know, Dad. She loved you too."

"How did it come to this, Marcus? How could she just walk away from me like this?"

What was I supposed to say? What could I say?

"I don't know what to say to you, Dad."

"It won't work for her," he said and his eyes hardened again. "She won't be able to see it through for long. Tell her

I'll be here when she wants to come home. I give it six months. All she has to do is ring me."

Even in his sorrow he couldn't quite give up all control. He had to put his stamp on the business.

"I don't know about that, Dad," I said. "Her mind seems made up to me."

His laugh was a hard, dry crack at the back of his throat. His eyes narrowed. He folded his arms across his chest again and crossed one leg over the other.

"She's never been on her own. Never managed anything by herself. She's always relied on me to do everything. What's going to happen the first time she needs a plumber or an electrician, huh? She wouldn't know where to begin."

"I think maintenance of the property is all part of the deal, Dad. Mother will pay a yearly . . . "

He didn't let me finish. He wasn't listening.

"Wait and see, Marcus. She'll hate it."

His chin went up as his mouth curled downwards. He was nodding his head as if he had an image of the future in his mind and he could see he was right. I wanted the conversation to stop there. His body language and the tone of his voice told me he was in denial. It sounded to me as though my father was trying to convince not me but himself that mother would struggle to live alone.

I hadn't yet seen my mother's new home but Sarah had told me about the bungalow and how much mother was looking forward to moving in. They'd been into town looking for curtain fabric. My father didn't know Mum had already placed her order for her new bed and had appointed a painter and decorator to refresh the place.

"I'm going to have colour," Mum had told me. "Beautiful bright colour all over the house. If I never see a magnolia wall again it'll be too soon."

I knew from my mother's enthusiasm that it would take a lot longer than six months for the novelty to wear off, let alone grow tired of it. My father was mistaken. He had no idea how far my mother was revitalised. She had come into her own away from his influence.

I looked around at the magnolia walls in Dad's kitchen. There were pale squares and oblongs where I'd removed pictures my mother wanted to have with her. All through the house those telltale shapes on the walls bore witness to who had put the life into their home. It was my mother who'd framed her own watercolours to brighten a dark corner, she who had made collages of family photographs to hang in the hall. She'd bought cheerful posters and prints and had a collection of greeting cards she kept because she liked the pictures. She squeezed them into photograph frames, all shapes, all sizes, all colours. Nothing matched but the display was vibrant, eye-catching. She had a way of knowing what would look good together. Now, my father's walls stood stark, the empty spaces like sightless eyes in their naked faces.

"Are you going to be all right, Dad?" I said.

He uncrossed his legs, gathered up the empty cups and took them to the sink.

"Of course I shall be all right. I've plenty to keep me busy here."

"I'll be in touch," I said and my words sounded hollow.

"Of course you will," he said as he rinsed the cups and set them on the drainer. He turned around and, for a moment, I thought he was going to reach out and hold me but he stayed where he was and said,

"Marcus, I'll be honest with you. There's a part of me that's going to enjoy this separation. Look, I've got the place to myself. I can do what I want."

"What will you do?"

"I haven't decided yet." He gestured at the kitchen. "Paint these walls for a start. I've got some paint in the garage. Yes, it'll look better with a fresh coat and without all your mother's clutter."

He picked up an ornament from the window sill. "Did you forget this?"

I remembered the onion jar, a squat green and brown ceramic container shaped like an onion with a tearful face and a pointed lid like an onion stalk. Mother used it for chutney. He held it out and I took it from him.

"I won't be making any chutney," he said. "Never could stand the stuff. Your mother might need it."

He couldn't say her name. Not once did he refer to her as Margaret. He had already begun to withdraw. Already, it seemed he was in the process of removing her from his life. He was making his own plans and made it clear that when she wanted to come back it would be on his terms. He came to the front door to wave me off and, through my rear mirror, I saw him go into the garage to look for magnolia paint.

My mother was happy and excited about her move. My father, although his pride had taken a knock, seemed resigned to life without her. As I drove across country I tried to make sense of it. At the halfway stage I broke the journey for a drink and a sandwich and made a quick call home to let Sarah know I was on my way. By the time I pulled into our drive my mother had already gone to bed.

Sarah helped me unload mother's things into our garage and drove the car to pick me up from returning the hire van. I parked it and handed the keys over to the night watchman, all the while reflecting on the things Dad had said and the surreal quality of the whole day. My thoughts were taking me round in circles and my mind felt numb. Sarah was waiting outside the gates of the van hire place. She drove us home.

"It's all happening too fast for me, Sarah," I said on the way back. "I can't fully understand what's going on in their heads."

"It might be too fast for you," she said, "but it's taken them years to reach this place."

"Why didn't they do something about it before it was too late?"

"Your mother tried, Marcus. I'm sure she did. It takes two, darling. You can't mend it by yourself."

"No, I suppose not."

"How was he?"

"Much quieter than usual. He didn't tell me how to load the van. Didn't even offer any advice. He simply stood and watched me, Sarah. At first I thought he was going to tear into me but by the time I left I had the distinct feeling that he was reasonably content."

"We can't see into other people's heads," she said. "We're too tied up in our own. Our own selves get in the way. What one person sees as his truth may be very different from the way another person sees the same truth."

I think my jaw dropped. Sarah had obviously been doing a lot of thinking of her own.

"Well, listen to you," I said. "Is that Eysenck? Jung? Freud?"

She glanced across at me and winked.

"It's just common sense, darling," she said.

27

Even the unexpected news of her mother's recovery couldn't compensate Wendy for the emptiness inside her. Rob was back at work with renewed enthusiasm and came home each day bristling with energy and purpose. She watched him, sometimes, as he worked through his students' assignments, piles of folders scattered on the sofa, coffee mug on the side table, and she remembered how the sight of him at his work used to make her feel proud to be his wife. She would watch his hands as he annotated someone's essay and admire the way he held his pen or moved his fingers. There was a time when she thought he was at his most attractive when he was unaware she was watching him. When he was completely absorbed in his work and she caught him in profile as he concentrated on his task, she used to think he was so beautiful it brought a lump to her throat. Those are the hands that make me feel like a woman, she would think. Those are the eyes that make me tingle when he smiles. She would never have disturbed him then. She was simply happy to be in the same room as the man she called husband and wait until he was ready to give her some attention.

All of those thoughts and feelings had gone. Now there was no flutter in her stomach when she looked at him. No twinge of desire for his body, for the warmth of his skin. Now she saw only a familiar figure, someone whose presence she was used to, a person she happened to share a house with.

He'd told her nothing more about the reason for his suspension from work. He wouldn't tell her anything about why the complaint against him had been dropped. Most of all he wouldn't disclose the name of the girl who had accused him.

"What good would it do you to know her name?" he'd said. "What difference would it make?"

"I feel I have a right to know. It affected me too, you know."

"Wendy, it's best left alone now."

"But you'll still have her in your classes."

"Yes."

"How can you bear that? How can you look her in the face and be nice to her?"

"Wendy, that's the reason I don't want to know who she is. I want my classes back to normal. I have work to do."

He'd refused to discuss it further.

"So she gets off scot-free. Just like that."

"I wouldn't say that."

"I would."

"Wendy, she probably feels very silly and immature right now. We need to move forward."

"Didn't the college principal punish her?"

Rob's face coloured when he said, "There'll be no recriminations. Will you leave it alone now?"

Wendy saw his embarrassment and realised, suddenly, that Rob had had his hand forced.

She said, "They've made you accept this, haven't they? They've told you what to do. They haven't allowed you to do what's right."

"That's enough. I don't think about it any more. Neither should you. *That* is the right thing to do. No point in making any more trouble. It's over. Finished."

He'd left the room.

"I know how you can find out," she'd shouted after him. She was thinking aloud and carried on although Rob couldn't hear her. "The girl was off sick, you said. Jonathan Palmer must have recorded her absence."

Now he sat among his files and his rustling papers with all that behind him and, as she watched him, she thought him weak and disappointing. He looked up briefly and she thought he was going to say something but he picked up another folder and continued with his work.

"Is there any more coffee," he said with his head in his books.

"I'll make some." She took away his used mug.

It wasn't an offer to make him fresh coffee in an effort to please him. It was an automatic response. There was no conscious thought to do something for him so he would think well of her. It was learned behaviour, what she did every day, no different from washing her hands or brushing her teeth. She took clean cups from the wall cupboard, her hands and arms moving like automatons, mindless.

Yes, she thought as she spooned instant from the jar, *It's all right for you, Rob. You can go back to being just how you were before. You might be all positive and full of yourself now you're man of the house again. Not crying on my shoulder now, are you? Not needing me now, are you, Rob?*

Her thoughts swirled like the milk she added to his drink.

Good. I'm glad. I don't want you. I won't let you near me ever again, Rob Carter. Do you think you can just pick up where you left off? You've got another think coming.

She took his coffee to him. She put it on the side table. He nodded and put his finger to his lips to let her know he was concentrating on his thoughts. It was his signal to her that he was very busy and didn't want to be further disturbed. His dismissal of her didn't bother her. She hardly noticed. She didn't care because it didn't hurt her any more. But he should have stood up for himself over the false accusation. He shouldn't have rolled over and taken it. *That* was like being dismissed. It was belittling, like they'd told him to go away as if he'd been the one to cause the trouble in the first place. It wasn't just him who'd been affected. Nobody gave a thought to how it had affected her.

The Sandman had left her on the same day Rob had been accused. He might have come back to her if Rob hadn't forced her to have sex with him. None of this mess would have happened if it hadn't been for that little witch. She had a lot to answer for, whoever she was. Something should be done. It wasn't right and it wasn't fair. She'd find out somehow. But she could wait. She was good at waiting.

28

Marcus

The Carter family asked Seamus Dalton to accompany them on the day they planned to tell Jenny about the sale of her house. They said they needed an independent figure of authority, one with whom Jenny was familiar. Someone she would trust. He agreed to help wherever he could. In our position as family practitioners we've both had to deliver worse news but I could understand that Wendy and her husband would need support through this difficult explanation.

Seamus was reluctant to tell me how the meeting went. I had to persuade him. We discussed it in his office after morning surgery. He'd met the Carters in the car park at the Firs and they went inside together. He said Wendy in particular was very nervous. Her husband said little. Lauren Mills had made her office available and there was coffee set out on a tray on her desk.

"She invited us to help ourselves," Seamus told me. "Then she went to bring Jenny in. I chatted with Wendy and her husband trying to put them at their ease. I told them I would explain the NHS system regarding residential care to Mrs Carter and the reasons why her family had made the decisions to sell. Then the door opened and in she came."

He stopped speaking and looked as if he didn't know how to continue. I urged him on.

"She glided into that meeting room, Marcus, like she was playing Cleopatra on a Nile barge. I knew immediately we were in for a peculiar episode. There we were, drinking coffee just as we are now, unaware that we were awaiting the arrival of the queen. It felt very odd. I have to tell you, the minute she came in the hairs bristled on the back of my neck."

He gulped at his drink and put down his cup.

"Go on, " I said. "What alerted you?"

"There was something about the way she held herself, Marcus. Disdainful. The expression on her face. Almost sneering, I'd say. And her eyes. I tell you now, if looks could kill, the undertaker would be painting a smile on my face right now."

"She was angry?"

"No. Not at all. She was in control of us. Powerful. She knew exactly what she was doing and when I looked into her eyes I saw something that I can describe only as . . . malevolent. It gave me the shivers."

"Who spoke first?"

"She did. As I said, she swept into the room and took centre stage. She regarded us from her position in the centre of the floor and said, Thank you all for coming, as if we were her subjects and sh'd summoned us."

"Delusional?" I said.

"Completely away with the little folk, Marcus. If it hadn't been so frightening it would have been fascinating."

"Frightening?"

Seamus took a deep breath and let it out slowly.

"I think we might have made a terrible mistake, Marcus. I don't believe we've been witnessing a remarkable period of remission. There's something else going on here."

"What happened next?"

"I pulled out a chair for her and she sat on it like it was her throne. She laid her hands in her lap and waited. Smiling with a sickly benevolence, she was. Ah, Marcus, if you could have only seen it for yourself. Her daughter told her they had something to tell her. *Yes, I know,* Jenny interrupted. *You've come to tell me that my house is ready for me now. I'll get my things.* Then Wendy's husband spoke up and said they'd had to sell the house."

I poured us both another cup. Seamus was shaking his head.

"She imploded, Marcus. My God, but it was strange to see. Her face convulsed. She sucked in her mouth and cheeks so tight her face looked like it might turn inside out. God forgive me, but it was a monstrous transformation. Her jaws tightened and she began to shudder. The tremor ran through her body from top to toe. Then she composed herself and stared at her daughter."

"Go on."

"She asked what they'd done with her laptop."

"Her laptop?"

"Yes. She didn't seem to be concerned about her furniture. Wendy told her they'd kept some of her things in the garage but as they didn't have enough space for all of it they'd had to sell some. I explained the financial situation her daughter and son-in-law had found themselves in. I watched her face as she assimilated the information. Marcus, what do you think would be a normal reaction to news like that?"

"Well, I wouldn't expect the laptop to be the first thing you'd ask about. I'd say, extreme distress. Tears. But then, I'm not sure. Has this sort of thing happened before? You'd be mortified you'd lost your home but at the same time you'd be relieved you'd recovered from . . ."

"But that's just it, isn't it, Marcus? What has she recovered from? We both know it can't be Alzheimer's." He shook his head again and bit at his bottom lip. He looked as if he wanted to say more.

"What? Seamus, what?" I said.

He put his head down and rubbed at his hair. When he raised his eyes he looked defeated.

"There wasn't ever a firm diagnosis," he said.

"But she had all the tests."

He shook his head again. "Not all, Marcus. She never had a scan. There wasn't time. She was on the waiting list but her condition progressed so rapidly. Well, you saw it for yourself. What were we to do? Her primary care became more important. What else could we have done? Her symptoms were obvious to all of us and we dealt with what we observed." He paused for a moment gathering his thoughts. "I'm afraid we've been wrong all along. I think Jenny Carter's rapid deterioration obscured the real root cause of her behaviour. Even though we ruled out all the usual suspects that mimic dementia, I think we misdiagnosed."

We stared at one another. His last word reverberated through the room and hung there like a threat.

"The Carters could bring in a complaint," I said.

He nodded and his brows knitted. "They could indeed. But that's not all. That's not what my ultimate fear is. Jenny Carter's behaviour leads me to believe that she has been ill for a long, long time. Long before her daughter brought her to me and we saw what we thought was her dementia. We simply didn't know. How could we know if the problems were not put before us?

"So what do you think?"

"I tell you, Marcus, the woman is unbalanced. I have no previous experience of the things I've seen her do today, the oddities she has exhibited. After that violent reaction to the news about her home she stood up and glared at her daughter. *Wendy,* she said, *congratulations. I expect you think you've got me where you want me now, don't you dear?*

Ah, she was scathing. Nasty. Wendy said she didn't know what her mother meant. Jenny turned away and made for the door. Then she turned and spoke over her shoulder. Hissing, she was, Marcus. Jesus, she was hissing like a snake. *He won't come back to you,* she said. *You know who I mean. The one you told me about. He'll never come back.* She walked away and left us. I'll never forget the look on her face."

"Who was she talking about?" I said. "Who would never come back?"

"I've no idea what she meant and neither did Wendy nor her husband. Wendy began to weep. She said she'd been full of hope for her mother's recovery but after this her hopes had been dashed. She said she could see her mother was still acting strangely and she was worried for the future."

"It's a mess," I said. "What did you do next?"

"Lauren Mills joined us and we discussed our options. It was clear that although Jenny's symptoms would seem to have diminished, her mental state is still erratic and unpredictable. We decided to wait until the psychologist has seen her again with a view to organising an overnight stay or weekend with her daughter. If that goes well we'll take it from there."

We left off our discussion. There was little point in second guessing what might happen next. There were fresh and more puzzling concerns for us to consider. We knew Jenny's full medical history. There had never been any sign or symptom of an underlying condition. I planned to conduct some further research, in privacy. I didn't ask what Dalton was planning but I realised this kind of controversy would not be welcome at this late stage in his career. He was looking forward to a quiet retirement. Now, we had a mystery on our hands and I couldn't forget that look of total bewilderment on Seamus's face as he related what he'd witnessed. The implications over a possible misdiagnosis became masked under cover of Jenny's newest indications of instability. Dalton wrote to request an early appointment for Jenny with a consultant neurologist and I began putting my Carter file together.

29

Towards the end of October the multi-disciplinary team suggested Jenny would benefit from a short stay with her family, pending results of recent tests. But listen. They didn't consider the effects from Wendy's point of view how the family might *not* benefit from having Jenny in their home.

On a bright, crisp day Wendy collected Jenny from the Firs to bring her home for the weekend. Jenny smiled and waved at Lauren Mills who had come to the car park to see them off. As soon as they turned out of the drive Jenny muttered something under her breath. Wendy paid no attention so Jenny said it louder.

"Little shit."

"I'm sure she means well, Mum."

"Huh. What would you know?"

Wendy bit back on a response. The weekend was going to be difficult enough without adding to it. She concentrated on driving. She forced her mouth into a smile and focused on her breathing. *Stay calm*, she thought. *Getting into a state isn't going to help. Breathe it away.* When they came to the roundabout on the approach to the town centre Jenny spoke again.

"Go straight across. I want to look at the town."

Along the high street shops displayed day-glo orange Hallowe'en lanterns. Fat plastic spiders with jolly faces and wide-mouthed grins hung from netting strung across windows. Witches' brooms leaned against shop doorways. Rubbery bats hung from lintels. Yellow leaves fluttered down from the trees and swirled by the kerb as Wendy drove past.

"It was summer when you got rid of me," Jenny said. "Now, look. It's nearly winter."

"I didn't *get rid* of you, Mum."

Jenny squirmed in the passenger seat and said, "I'll never forgive you."

They said nothing more to one another. Wendy kept her hands on the wheel and her eyes on the road but she knew exactly what kind of expression her mother was wearing. She thought the blank stare of dementia was preferable to the sneering grimace that was sitting next to her.

Wendy drew up outside the house and before she'd pulled on the handbrake Jenny was out of the car and throwing open the front gate. Wendy watched her mother swoop up the path to hug Rob who was waiting on the doorstep.

"Look at you," he said. "You look marvellous, Jenny. It's wonderful to see you looking so well," and he took her indoors while Wendy brought in her mother's weekend bag. She took it to the spare bedroom then came back to make tea.

"Doesn't she look fantastic, Wendy?" Rob said.

Wendy might have used her mother's words. *Huh. What would you know?* Rob hadn't seen Jenny at the Firs when she looked a lot less than fantastic in a crocheted granny shawl and knee socks. He'd stayed well away.

She said, "Yes, she does," and filled the kettle.

Rob walked Jenny to her room and showed her how her own furniture made it look almost exactly like it always had in her own home. She passed comment on the new curtains Wendy had chosen. She said she'd never liked blue.

"Such a cold colour, Rob," she said. "I prefer warmer shades. More feminine. Something with more *personality.*"

She laughed her actress laugh and touched Rob lightly on his arm. He patted her hand and left her to sort out her things. Jenny emptied her bag and set out her sponge bag and cosmetics purse on her old dressing table. Wendy caught glimpses of her mother through the open door as she moved around the room. She hung her coat in her own wardrobe. She glanced around the room and smiled. She joined them in the kitchen and took the seat next to Rob.

"Chocolate biscuit, Mum?" Wendy asked.

"No, thank you, dear. I don't know what they've been feeding me in that dreadful place but I need to shed a few pounds. By the way, my furniture looks fine in your spare room."

Rob hung his head. Wendy wondered why her mother had called her *dear* when she'd been so difficult in the car just minutes ago.

"Jenny, I'm so sorry," Rob said. "If we'd known this was going to happen . . . I mean, you know. Your house."

Jenny patted his shoulder.

"Rob, you mustn't blame yourself. You did what you thought was best. I've always trusted your judgement and I still do. In your position I would probably have done the same thing."

She sipped at her Earl Grey. Wendy watched her mother's latest performance.

"If only we'd known," Rob went on.

"Listen to me, Rob Carter," Jenny said. "The money is safe, isn't it? If I hadn't given you the proper power of attorney when I did the government would have appointed a deputy to manage my affairs and how much would they have charged for that?"

Rob whistled. "Two to three thousand pounds a year."

"There you are then," Jenny said. "The house would still have been sold and I'd be worse off than I am now. I've never been good at handling finances. You know that. That's why I handed all that over to you. Now, I don't want to hear any more about it."

"How did you know about the government deputy thing?" Wendy said.

"Oh, I eavesdropped on a conversation in *that* place," Jenny said. "Some poor soul hadn't made a lasting power of attorney and his son was furious that the Court of Protection didn't deem him a suitable deputy."

"The Court of what?" Wendy said.

Rob explained. But his phrasing made the system sound so complicated that Wendy wondered how her mother had remembered any of the conversation she'd overheard, let alone understand it. Jenny was sipping at her tea. Rob looked relaxed and too pleased with himself. Wendy felt nerves fluttering. Something wasn't right.

"Well, isn't this lovely?" Jenny said. "Back to normal again."

Wendy turned her face away.

Jenny said, "Are you all right, dear?"

"She's tired," Rob answered for her. "I think she's been doing too much."

"I've told her, Rob. I've told her before." Her mother swivelled in her seat to face her. "Wendy, dear, why don't you think about giving up one of your jobs. It's not as if you really need the money, is it? And, look, dear. If I'm to be staying here with you well of course I shall contribute to the household. Besides, we'll be company for each other."

Jenny sipped at her tea again and smiled at Rob.

Wendy couldn't put a name to what was making her feel uncomfortable watching the two of them but the result tasted sour.

"Have you seen Doctor Dalton recently?" she asked her mother.

"I'd like to pop in, dear, before I have to go back to that place. I want him to see me out and about. I want everybody to see me. Could we pop into town this afternoon, do you think? I'd like to pick up something new to wear. Everything I've been wearing in that place feels soiled. I'm going to put them in the bin. No. Better still, I'm going to burn them."

They went out together, the three of them, an unusual event. Wendy couldn't remember the last time such a thing had happened. Shopping was something she usually did alone. She watched her mother link arms with Rob as they walked around the town, stopping to look in a shop window here and there. Wendy followed on behind them like an afterthought.

30

Marcus

Jenny Carter came into the surgery one Monday morning at the beginning of November. I was in the outer office at the time and witnessed her supercilious stride across the room to reception. I noticed her immaculate turnout, lipstick and nails matching as I'd seen before at the care home. Her shoes and handbag were so new I could smell expensive leather. She demanded to see Dalton.

"I can't stay long. Tell him I'd like a quick word, would you?" she said to Pat, our receptionist, ignoring me.

"I'm sorry Mrs Carter. He's with a patient at the moment," Pat told her.

Jenny said, "Call him."

"I can't do that," Pat said. "Not during a consultation."

"Call him. I know he'll want to see *me.*"

I stepped forward. "Good morning, Mrs Carter. Is there anything I can do for you?"

She looked down her nose at me and said, "Have we met?"

"We have Mrs Carter. Only briefly. You might not remember."

"Are you suggesting that I forget things, young man?" she said.

"I'm Doctor Harding, Mrs Carter. I was with Doctor Dalton when he came to see you at the . . ."

"Do not mention the name of that place," she said. "That's why I'm here now. If Seamus Dalton is too busy to see me then you will kindly relay this message."

"Certainly, Mrs Carter."

"Tell him I have no intention of returning to that place to stay. My son-in-law is waiting outside for me and I shall be moving in with my family later today when I have collected my things from . ."

"I see."

"You see nothing, Doctor Harding. You have no idea."

"What is it that I don't see, Mrs Carter? I don't understand."

"Of course you don't. Well, you have my new address on your records. I'll be in touch."

She inclined her head in the most affected faux regal fashion that my intended response dried on my lips. Before I'd caught my breath she was gone and through the glass entrance doors. I saw her get into a car and the driver pulled away.

Jenny Carter left the Firs that same day. A few days later, as I came out of the surgery, two men were waiting for me in the car park at the rear of the building.

"Doctor Dalton?" one called out.

"He's not here," I told them. "I'm Marcus Harding. Can I help you?"

"*Doctor* Harding?"

"Yes, that's right."

"We have a few questions, Doctor. I wonder if . . .?"

Then I saw the camera the other one was holding.

"What is this?" I said. "Who are you?"

"We're from the Compton Mercury, Doctor Harding. We understand one of Doctor Dalton's patients has recently made a surprising recovery. We'd like to know more about it."

"I'm sorry gentlemen," I said. "Haven't you heard of patient confidentiality?"

I opened my car door and moved to get in. They came up close behind me.

"Doctor Harding," the same one continued, "if what we're hearing is true this town will be buzzing with hundreds more like us. This is huge news, wouldn't you agree? If there's a cure for Alzheimer's everybody is going to want to know."

"I have nothing more to say."

I drove around the block, came back and parked to watch the drive into our surgery car park. The reporters were still there. I took out my phone and called reception to warn them.

"They've already been in," our office manager told me. "I asked them to leave, Doctor Harding. I can see them outside. They're waiting to speak to patients as they leave."

That was only the beginning. The Mercury ran an article in the Friday edition and the editor's column featured an exposé suggesting that, in the interests of other sufferers, the patient's name should be revealed and criticising the authorities for not being more forthcoming with detailed information. Dalton brought a copy in the following Monday. We held a brief meeting with staff to discuss how to deal with any further enquiries and/or telephone calls. Dalton contacted Lauren Mills at the Firs and between us we thought we had the situation covered.

We were naïve. We had no previous experience of the way a sensational story runs like a tidal wave through a small community like ours. The nationals soon picked up the story and one of them ran the headline: *Pre-Christmas Miracle.* Compton was invaded before any of us had worked out the source of the leak.

31

Jenny Carter moved in with Wendy and Rob on the second of November. The chill in the air was nothing compared to the deathly cold Wendy felt at the thought of her mother's permanent presence in the house. She tried not to think about it. She told herself that if her mother had truly recovered from whatever had been causing her problems, she would eventually prefer a place of her own again. But when she and Rob had asked the doctors about Jenny's condition nobody had been able to give them a definite answer. Further tests were needed, they said. As soon as possible, they said. There would be an appointment sent through the post.

Wendy waited by the window, looking out for Rob's car bringing back her mother and the rest of Jenny's belongings. When she caught first sight of it pulling up outside her stomach sank and her feet felt like lead as she moved to open the door for them. Jenny swept into the house in a cloud of strong perfume, lunged into her bedroom and took possession. As soon as she'd put down her bags and, as she'd intended, she wanted to light a bonfire of clothes she refused to wear again. It was the very first thing she wanted to do. Not a cup of tea and a quiet talk. Not a gentle settling in around the table to give everyone a chance to take stock. Jenny hustled her daughter and son-in-law through the house and outside.

"Come on, you two. I can't wait," she said.

Rob found some cartons at the back of the garage and bits of wood he'd once bought to make shelves. He stacked them in a rough pyramid and Jenny hurried to her room and back outside again, her arms laden with skirts and tops.

Tucked under her arm was a pair of fluffy slippers. Rob opened a box of matches.

"No," Jenny shouted. "Don't light it. That's my job. I want to do it."

They stood at the bottom of the back garden and waited as the fire took hold. The clothes burned with fizzes and a spluttering noise. Acrid black smoke curled from melting man-made fabrics. Wendy watched the pyre. The bitter smell made her eyes water. Jenny had bought a bottle of pink champagne from the supermarket when they'd called in on the way home and insisted Wendy and Rob join her to toast the beginning of her new life. Wendy didn't feel like toasting anything. She recognised her mother's high spirits for what they were and knew only too well where it would lead. The pattern was familiar, locked away in her private thought box with the images and words she preferred to forget. The phone rang and Rob went indoors to answer. When he returned his brow was creased.

"That was somebody from the Mercury asking for you, Jenny," he said.

"The newspaper?" Wendy asked.

Jenny flicked her wrist. "Oh, that," she said. "We'll all have to get used to that. I'm going to be famous now. One of the tea ladies in that place said I'd soon be famous. Everybody will want to know about you, she said. So, what did you tell them, Rob?"

"How did they know you were here?" Wendy said.

Jenny ignored Wendy's question and linked her arm through Rob's. "What did they say, Rob? What did you tell them?"

"They wanted to speak to you and I told them you needed rest just now."

"Clever boy," Jenny said. She patted his arm. "Keep 'em waiting and wanting."

Wendy's heart sank. Who did her mother think she was? What was she playing at this time? The phone rang so many times that night they had to unplug it and in the morning a group of reporters was waiting at the front of the house.

"I told you I was going to be famous," Jenny said, peering round the curtain. Rob went out to ask them to move away. He opened the front door. In a rapid burst of sound cameras whirred; voices shouted; bodies pushed and scrambled to get closer to the house.

"Is she there?" one shouted loudest. "Is she coming out?"

"She needs to rest," Rob told them. "Please leave us alone. You're causing a disturbance."

"Is it the new injection? Have they used stem cells? Is Jenny Carter the first to receive the new treatment? Come on, Mr Carter. The world needs to know how it works."

More bodies pushed towards Rob. He stepped back and closed the door against them and their noise. He went into the living room where Wendy had pulled on the curtains for privacy. Jenny was smiling and checking her appearance in the hall mirror. Outside, the commotion continued. One of the neighbours came to the back door. He said he'd called the police because his dog wouldn't stop barking at the noisy crowd of strangers. He wished the Carters well and asked if there was anything he could do to help. When he left, Jenny said, "Do you think I should do something with my hair before I put in an appearance?"

The press moved away from the house and out of the avenue at the request of the police but they didn't leave Compton. Joan Spencer passed on the news that a core group had booked into the George Hotel and were hanging about the shopping centre during the day, questioning passers-by. Lauren Mills rang Wendy on her mobile to say that the newspaper people had turned up at the Firs looking for anybody who knew anything at all about Jenny. Lauren had refused to speak to them, she said, but couldn't vouch for everybody else.

Next day Jenny was in even higher spirits.

"Let's all go out together," she said.

Rob finished his work early and drove Jenny and his wife to an out of town shopping mall. He took the back roads out of Compton so they wouldn't be spotted. Wendy thought her mother was never going to stop spending. Jenny parted with cash like it was burning holes in her purse, hurrying into every designer outlet, collecting carrier bags and parcels as she went. They returned home under cover of darkness loaded to the gunnels. Jenny took down the blue curtains in her bedroom and replaced them with *personality* pink. She had Rob help her rearrange the furniture and filled the wardrobe with top of the range clothes and shoes. She stayed out of sight and unavailable for questioning. Jenny Carter played the game like a professional, biding her time and waiting for the optimum moment.

One week later she planned a press conference. She arranged it all herself. The house wasn't big enough, she said, to accommodate all the people who wanted to see her so she booked a meeting room at The George. Wendy wondered why her mother felt she needed to go through with all of it.

"Are you sure, Mum? Are you sure this is what you want to do? You've seen the newspaper reports. They've already had the story. What more is there to tell them?"

Jenny Carter drew herself up to her full importance and said, "They haven't heard it from *me*."

She searched through Yellow Pages and found a hair stylist who would come to the house.

" I want to look ten years younger," she told him.

She had streaks of caramel and honey put through a graduated bobbed cut. She ordered a professional standard straightening tong as well as conditioners and extra special serum. She wore McQ Black for the press conference with patent heels and white gold jewellery. Rob and Wendy went with her.

A large group was waiting in the drizzle in the car park at the side of The George Inn. They jostled for position as Rob parked. He got out first and opened the passenger door for Jenny. Cameras flashed as she got out of the car. There was a jumble of noises: the clicking and whirring of cameras; male and female voices shouting over the top of each other; the shuffling of feet and crunching of gravel. Wendy climbed out of the rear passenger seat. Rob took Jenny's arm and opened an umbrella for her.

"Mrs Carter, Mrs Carter. Over here Mrs Carter."

Jenny turned and smiled and the cameras flashed again. Rob held back the pack to protect Jenny but Wendy was swallowed up in the crush.

32

Joan

When Wendy said she was thinking of giving up her job at the supermarket I told her I thought it was unwise to do that.

"Wendy, my lovely," I said. "Don't you think you'd be better off out of the way? Wouldn't it be better for you to be out of the house?"

She said she couldn't face it much longer. She didn't have the energy for two jobs any more but she didn't want to let us down here at the charity shop. I could understand it, really. It can't have been easy putting up with all that palaver from the newspapers. They never left them alone for weeks. As soon as the story got out it was like a swarm of locusts in Compton. The dailies and the Sundays, they all came looking for more information about Wendy's mother.

Jenny lapped it up, so I'm told. Loved all the attention. From what I saw of her, she went about acting like some Hollywood film star. Posing for pictures. Going on the radio. She spent money like it was going out of fashion as well. Bought a flash new car, fancy clothes and handbags. I suppose it must have been the money from the house sale. I don't know the details. I didn't ask.

Wendy couldn't stand it. There were reporters waiting outside the house from morning till night. She told me it got so as she didn't dare open the door. They were followed everywhere they went. They tried coming in here once, the newspaper lot, but I saw them off.

"Get away with you," I shouted. "Have you no sense of decency?"

One of them, a nice-looking young lady, had a bit more about her than the rest and I listened to what she said. She had a calm voice, not shouting and screaming like the others so I let her in the shop. It's a narrow entrance. It was easy for me to hold the others back. I've got a bit of weight about me and I've still got strength in my arms. In any case, we're in the arcade, see. It was only a small group outside the shop. You can't get many bodies down here all at once.

"Thank you," she said. She told me her name and which paper she was working for.

"I'm Joan Spencer," I told her. "I'm the manageress."

"Mrs Spencer, I know it's a nuisance having all this noise and disturbance but, surely, you must see what hope this story brings to other sufferers and their families?"

Well, I could see that angle. That made sense to me. If the experts could get to the bottom of what had helped Jenny Carter get better it would be a good thing for all of us. So I let her go on.

"Mrs Spencer," she said, "is there anything else you know that we can tell our readers?" Her voice was buttery smooth and when she smiled she showed a lovely set of white teeth, but her eyes were like that crystal candlestick on that shelf over there. Fake. Mmm, I thought. You're going to have to be careful here, Joan.

"Such as?" I said.

"I'd say you know Mrs Carter's daughter very well."

"Yes," I said, not knowing where she was heading.

"It would be interesting for our readers to learn more about Mrs Carter from a different viewpoint.

"Which Mrs Carter do you mean?" I asked. "The mother or the daughter?"

"Ah, yes," she said. "I'd forgotten that Wendy is Mrs Carter too."

I started getting suspicious right then. You can't tell me that this woman had forgotten a fact like that. If she had, she was in the wrong job. I got myself ready to tell her where to get off.

"Do you think Mister Carter's suspension from work could have had any bearing . . ."

I didn't let her finish. I grabbed her notebook from her, opened the door and threw the thing out into the arcade.

"And you can follow it right now," I said. "Unless you want a kick up the arse."

She put on a false sort of smile and I could tell she was going to have a go at bringing me round. Fat chance. I grabbed hold of her shoulders and turned her around to face the door.

"That's the exit there," I said. "Use it." And I gave her a bit of a push. I slammed the door behind her and locked it. Coming down here with all her fancy talk! What do they think we are? Idiots? Think we're all Moonrakers, do they? Scraping the moon's reflection off the village pond thinking we're gathering cheese? How dare they come sneaking around looking to pick up dirty little titbits? What possible good could come out of me telling them what I knew about Rob Carter?

I didn't like the man. I know I've only ever had Wendy's side of things but I saw for myself what a pompous piece of work he was. Full of himself. Arrogant. Maybe he didn't deserve to have his name soiled like that but that didn't make me like him any more than I did. Still, there was no way I was going to go blabbing to the papers about all that business. They weren't going to find out anything about that from me. When Wendy came into work next time, after the newspaper lot had disappeared, I told her what had happened.

"What did they want to know about that for? How did they know in the first place?" she said.

I said, "I don't know, Wendy. Don't worry yourself about it. It's not worth it."

She went to hang up her jacket in our little cloakroom and when she came back she was blowing her nose. Her eyes looked a bit red.

"I'm sick of it," she said. "Why can't they leave us alone?"

She said nothing more for a while and then, very quietly, "He's never told me who it was."

I was thinking off on a different tack and at first I didn't know what she meant.

"The girl who accused Rob," she said. "He's never told me who it was."

I felt awkward. I don't often find myself in a position of not knowing what to do but at that moment I was right between a rock and a hard place. I knew who the girl was. My granddaughter had told me. She used to be best friends with her until she found out what the girl had done. She'd actually boasted about it to our Louise. Got her to swear secrecy and then laughed while she told what happened. She thought it served Rob Carter right because he'd refused to accept one of the girl's written assignments for being too late.

The college hushed it all up, you know. Oh, yes. They didn't want it getting out. The girl's mother went up there and sorted it. Pleaded with the principal not to expose her daughter. Begged them, she did. They had their own standing in the community to consider, apparently. Standing in the community? My left foot. It wouldn't be good for Compton the mother said. Well, the girl repeated all this to our Louise and thought it a big joke that her mother had had the embarrassment of going up before the headmaster, so to speak. What a little tyrant. I bet she's spoiled as a burnt rice pudding. Well, she's a good girl is our Louise and dropped the little madam straight off. The mother can't be better than she ought to be, either.

I decided not to tell Wendy what I knew. She had enough trouble to cope with. What good would it have done her to know? I kept my mouth zipped but in a small town like Compton secrets like that can't stay hidden. You probably know as well as I do that the last people to hear gossip are usually the ones it affects the most, but Sophie Harding, the doctor's daughter wouldn't get away with it forever.

33

The solid, old semi-detached bungalow was in complete darkness. Jenny had gone to her bed early before the end of the television news. In their own room Rob was already asleep, the Stephen King novel he'd been reading face down on his nightstand at the end of a chapter. Wendy, as usual, was listening, straining to catch that first shimmer of movement from the shadows. Six weeks she'd been waiting and listening in the dark. Six weeks since Rob had been falsely accused and the Sandman had abandoned his nightly trysts with her. Six weeks since her mother had defied all the odds and baffled the doctors with the miracle of her recovery. And in that time Wendy felt as though her life had gone from bad to worse.

The press conference had been a nightmare. Those people were so rude, Wendy thought. They shouted over each other. Louder and louder. They probed and pushed for answers to questions that nobody knew the answer to, not even the doctors. Rob had had to ask them to take turns; they were all shouting out at once. The meeting room at The George Inn had been packed full of people from regional and national newspapers. Rows of chairs went right to the back and they were all full. The atmosphere was warm and steamy. It had been raining and the room smelled of damp hair and wet clothes and shoes. A stack of wet umbrellas leaned by the entrance, dripping puddles on the parquet. There were laptop cases all over the floor and overnight bags and holdalls squashed underneath the chairs.

As soon as her mother sat down the questions began to fly. A chorus of voices made the room buzz.

"When did you first feel ill, Mrs Carter?"

"What was it like at the Firs?"

"When did you begin to feel better?"

"Did you have any unusual treatment?"

Jenny said, "It was all unusual to me."

The room buzzed again.

"Tell us about the treatments they gave you."

"I don't remember any treatments. I just got better."

"They must have given you something, Mrs Carter. What did they give you?"

"They didn't give me anything."

"You had tests?"

"Yes. I had tests."

"What tests did you have, Mrs Carter?"

"I don't remember."

"Are there any more tests planned? Mrs Carter? Mrs Carter?"

The buzzing faded to a hum.

"What would *you* say is the cause of your recovery, Mrs Carter?"

"I have no idea. But isn't it marvellous?"

The hum weakened but the questions went on and on. Jenny sat between Rob and Wendy at the middle of a white clothed table at the head of the room, facing the crowd, flashing her eyes and smiling. Questions from the floor slowed, diminished, petered away to a thin trickle. Wendy sensed the cooling of interest. It seemed her mother couldn't give them what they'd come for. They were dissatisfied with Jenny's responses to their questions.

Wendy heard the beginnings of mutterings and grumbling. One by one they put away their laptops and pushed back their chairs. They picked up their overnight bags and began to leave. Wendy thought perhaps they would be left alone now.

Afterwards, at home, Jenny had been high-spirited and wanted to relive what she believed had been a triumph.

"Don't forget to buy al the Sunday editions," she said to Rob. "Oh, isn't this all so exciting?"

Jenny had been unable to sleep that night. She'd stayed up watching television until the early hours and, when she finally went to her room, Wendy heard her mother moving things about. The screech of clothes hangers against the metal hanging rail in the wardrobe and the scrape of drawers being opened and closed sounded as though Jenny was trying on all her new clothes.

Though national interest in her diminished Jenny was still feted locally. They wanted her on the radio and the six thirty regional television news wanted to do a piece. Jenny tried on all her clothes again and had the hairdresser come back to refresh her style.

"What do you think about these shoes with this dress, Rob?"

"Silver or gold jewellery with this one, Rob?"

"I'm not sure about this colour with my hair. What do you think, Rob?"

It went on day after day.

If only they had waited, Wendy thought, before they'd sold her mother's house. If only things hadn't happened in so much of a rush. *If only* . . . such small words with the weight of the world behind them. Who could have imagined that a cash purchaser would immediately appear and the transaction complete so rapidly? In any other usual chain of buyers there would have been time to pull out of the agreement, time to delay the exchange of contracts and prevent the sale going through. Why couldn't it have been like that for them? Jenny would still have had a home of her own to go to and she wouldn't now be in the next room, settling in like the new lady of the house, taking away Wendy's position, acting as if it was her own house.

It would soon be Christmas. Wendy imagined the scene: mother fussing over the boys, stealing her family away from her with talk of all the famous people she'd met. There was even mention of a book. A publisher had called with the offer of a ghost-written account of Jenny's story. It was sickening the way her mother soaked up all the attention like a pathetic C-list celebrity. Embarrassing. Wendy dreaded another tiresome evening of sitting around the table while her mother recounted every last detail and Rob encouraging her with his annoying questions about cameras and studio people like some star-struck groupie.

Six weeks of agony. Six weeks of mounting frustration. Six weeks of lovelessness. And it was in the middle of these unsettling thoughts that Wendy sensed *his* presence. The air rippled. As she lay beside a sleeping Rob she felt the Sandman's approach coming to her in waves, undulating through the house. It was unmistakable, that shift in the atmosphere. With each wave she could feel the change of pressure in her ears. Her nose twitched; her eyes widened in readiness and a lump came to her throat. He was here! She felt her head swim as the darkness parted at his coming and her woman's fluids rushed to receive him.

He was coming nearer. The feeling was growing stronger. He was in the hall. A step nearer. She caught her breath in anticipation of his touch. She closed her eyes against the tension tightening her body. She bit down hard on her teeth to stop herself from crying out. He was at the door. The pressure drummed against her jaw. Surely, his mouth would find hers any second now. The air swelled with waves of expectation. The silence flickered.

Then a light, glowing orange-red through the tissues of her eyelids. She opened them. Light from the hallway seeped under the bedroom door. Footsteps padded across the carpet to the bathroom. More light. A cough. The flush of the toilet and the running of water from the bathroom sink. Her mother coughed again as she returned to her room and closed the door. The lights went out with a click. Then silence and return of the still, stagnant dark. Her mother had disturbed him and frightened him away.

34

Joan

They were planning a pre-Christmas pantomime up at the sixth form college and my granddaughter, Louise came round to mine with a couple of her friends to tell me she'd been given a part. She was thrilled to bits was our Louise and not the least bit bothered they'd cast her as the witch.

"I'm going to be perfectly horrible," she told me. "Do you want to hear my witch's cackle?"

She gave me a loud demonstration and finished up coughing and spluttering. I had to get her a glass of water.

"You'll ruin your voice if you go at it like that," I said.

"I'll just have to keep practising," she said. "I'll get used to it."

"Will you have a green face and a hooked nose?" I said.

"Oh, no," she said. "They don't want that kind of witch. I'm going to be glamorous. Still wicked, but glamorous. It goes better with the story. Trouble is, I've got to find my own costume. Can you sew something for me, Grandma?"

"I might not need to," I said. "We've got some lovely things in at the shop. Why don't you come in and have a look?"

She screwed up her nose at that suggestion.

"Here, don't you be so fussy," I said. "We get some beautiful things. You'll be surprised."

"Designer labels?"

"Sometimes."

Her eyebrows lifted at that and she had a little think.

"Okay then. I'll give it a go."

She came in on her own the following Tuesday afternoon after she'd finished college for the day. We'd just had a couple of boxes of toys brought in and Norma was sorting them out into piles of different qualities. We always get toys in the run up to Christmas. Children have so much these days and I expect people need to have a clear out to make space for the expected new things. But not everybody can afford brand new, can they? So we make up a display of boxed games and toys that don't look too bashed about. Not jigsaws, though. You never know if all the pieces are there.

Anyway, in comes our Louise. I looked out through the windows, down the arcade, expecting the rest to come in.

"Haven't you brought your friends with you?" I said.

She shook her head and I said, "I thought they might want to help you choose."

"Grandma," she said in that tone of voice that means you've just said completely the wrong thing to a teenager. "It's a charity shop."

"And?"

"Most of my friends wouldn't be seen dead coming in here."

"Time you got some new friends then," I said.

Wendy stepped forward and said, "I'd like to help. Tell me what you're looking for."

"Well," says our Louise, "I'm not sure exactly but I want it to be sophisticated. The most glamorous witch ever."

They went through the racks together and found a full-length, long-sleeved, black chiffon affair. It had a few crystals sewn on under the bust line. Louise looked at the label inside it and grinned.

"Can I try it on, Grandma? What do you think?"

When she was satisfied I offered to buy it for her. Norma said she looked lovely and asked who else was going to be in the pantomime.

Louise said, "The usual suspects."

"And who are they?" Norma said.

Louise rolled her eyes and let out a sigh.

"Sophie flaming Harding," she said.

"What?" Norma said. "After what she did?"

I thought, oh dear, the cat's coming out of the bag. I pulled a face at Norma, flashed my eyes at her to get her to stop but she didn't see me.

"Huh," she said. "She's the one who ought to be the witch, Louise, not you."

"Yes, but she can sing," Louise said. "And dance. They can't put on a production without Mademoiselle Harding. Doctor daddy's darling. Anyway, I'm not bothered. I don't have anything to do with her any more."

"Why? What happened?" Wendy said.

Norma puffed up her chest and said, "Well, you know, she's the one who caused all that trouble with . . ." She clapped her hand over her mouth and went very red.

"What's wrong?" Louise asked.

"Nothing, love," I said and passed her the dress in a plastic bag. "Here you are, Louise, my lovely. Don't forget to get me some tickets. Won't your friends be waiting for you now?"

"They're in the Internet Junction. See you later, Gran," she said and gave us all a little wave as she went out.

I turned round to see Norma with a flushed face looking down at the floor. Wendy's face was white.

"Are you going to tell me the rest of it, ladies? Or can I guess?"

"Norma, I think it's time for a cuppa, don't you?" I said.

When she'd disappeared into the back I took hold of Wendy's hand.

"I'm sorry it's had to come out this way, Wendy. Our Louise meant you no harm. But Norma should have known better, the old blabbermouth. Look, my lovely, the only reason we didn't tell you before was we thought you'd enough to be going on with."

Something happened inside Wendy's eyes. Her face was deathly pale but her eyes were burning. Fiery and fierce. She stood staring for a second and then the corners of her mouth turned up in a funny, crooked smile.

"That's all right," she said. "I know now. I can wait a bit longer."

35

The following Saturday morning after Wendy found out about Sophie Harding she came to the breakfast table late. Her mother was busy at the kitchen sink.

"Spitz-poff," Jenny said in a Mary Poppins voice, "or you'll be late for work."

The sourness that rose in Wendy's mouth threatened to escape in a snarl but she took the bowl of cereal her mother offered and said, "Thank you."

"I'm doing some grilled bacon for Rob," Jenny said. "I know you don't care for a cooked breakfast but that shouldn't mean Rob can't have one."

Wendy took a deep breath and let her mother get on with it. Wendy had other priorities. She had Sophie Harding on her mind and how she was going to deal with her. She was finishing her cornflakes when Rob appeared, freshly showered and shaved and took his place at the table.

"That's a nice shirt, Rob," Jenny said. "Doesn't he look nice, Wendy?"

Oh, please, Wendy thought. It was sickening but Rob seemed to enjoy the attention.

"Thank you, Jenny," he said. "And is that grilled bacon for breakfast? Jenny, you're spoiling me."

Isn't she just? Let me get out of here, Wendy thought but she smiled and said nothing.

Jenny flitted around the kitchen, removing Wendy's used dish, checking the grill pan, watching the eggs on the hob. She had on an apron that she had once given to Rob as a jokey Christmas present. Wendy thought it was tasteless: a female body in a bikini with huge breasts spilling over the top, printed larger than life-size. Jenny said it would make for a laugh at a summer barbecue. Rob had never worn it. When her mother leaned over Rob to put his plate in front of him the printed boobs were just centimetres away from his mouth. He pulled a stupid face and put his hands over his eyes and her mother laughed a girly, tinkly little laugh that set Wendy's teeth on edge. Jenny playfully shoved Rob's shoulder.

"Now then," she said. "Dear me. What a sight you must think me," and she hoisted the apron higher and shimmied her shoulders.

"I'll bet you were quite a handful when you were younger, Jenny," Rob said.

Jenny placed her hands beneath the printed breasts and winked at him.

"You could say that, Rob. You could say that."

They burst into laughter. Wendy couldn't watch any more.

"I'd better be going," she said.

"Dinner will be ready at seven tonight," Jenny said as Wendy reached for her coat from the hall stand. "Rob's taking me to the Causeway shopping mall this afternoon, aren't you dear? A bit of Christmas shopping." She winked again. "Secret things. Isn't that right, Rob?"

It ought not to matter to me, Wendy thought as she opened the front door and stepped out onto the drive. *So she's doing the flirting thing again. I've seen it all before. I know where it ends.*

It was part of the pattern and belonged with all the other dark memories Wendy chose to put on one side. Her mother's high-spirited flirting was not specifically directed at Rob, Wendy knew. It was simply a part of how her mother had always been. Some of the time she would be hyperactive, hyper-chatty, hyper-everything, as if she was on drugs. She would sweep everybody along with her, get enthusiastic about this and that and flit from one thing to another like a butterfly.

At other times she would turn nasty, just like when she fell ill with the dementia and afterwards at the care home. Say spiteful, hurtful things. Like when she said Wendy had only married Rob for the good pension he would get one day, or when she said her boys were the ugliest babies she'd ever seen. When Wendy was a schoolgirl her mother would laugh at her sometimes and say she was getting too fat for her school uniform. Then she would be sad and sleepy and Wendy would have to take care of her own washing and ironing, do the shopping and the cooking and all the other household jobs until her mother started feeling better again.

It had never occurred to Wendy to ask for help. She didn't know help was available. She wasn't aware she was in a situation requiring help. Her mother was just her mother and this was how things were. She grew up believing that you had to get on and do the best you could.

It ought not to matter now. Wendy was used to it. But still, there was a dull ache nagging its way into Wendy's head every day. It was there as soon as she woke in the morning and she took it to bed with her at night. Wendy's house didn't feel like *her* home any more. Her mother was taking it over, putting her influence on everything. And Rob was allowing it. More, he was enjoying it.

Well, one day he'll be sorry when he learns the truth. One day, he'll find out what my mother is really like. There's no point in me trying to make Rob see it. He wouldn't believe me. He'll have to experience it for himself.

For now they were like new best friends, Jenny and Rob getting on with their happy lives and ignoring Wendy's pain. She closed the door behind her without saying goodbye to them. They probably wouldn't have heard her anyway. She dismissed them from her thoughts as she drove to the supermarket. At least there was one little problem she could deal with. *Look out, Sophie Harding*, she thought. *I'm on my way to sort you out.*

She hung her coat in the staffroom and put on her work uniform. From the floor below Christmas muzak looped endlessly through hits of the sixties and seventies. There was no sign of Sophie Harding. Wendy checked the work rota but Sophie's name was missing. On the shop floor Wendy looked out for her and when she had to go into the stockroom for the fresh bread trolley she searched there, too. Wendy took her turn on the till and she leaned back to see as far down the line as she could. Still no Sophie. Just a long line of cashiers wearing silly Santa hats decorated with bits of tinsel. The muzak rolled around again and the announcement speakers hummed and crackled with news of the latest special offers.

"Have you seen anything of Sophie?" she shouted to the women on the checkouts either side. They shook their heads. When the supervisor came to empty her till Wendy asked again.

"Yes. She's been moved," the supervisor told her. "She's going to be Santa's helper in the grotto. The Christmas fairy. Did you want one of us to pass on a message?"

"No. No, thank you. It doesn't matter. I'll catch her later," Wendy said.

The Saturday queues grew longer and noisier and the hum of people and muzak and tills ringing and announcements and more muzak made Wendy feel hot and uncomfortable. She was grateful when it was her turn for a break. She rushed to the staffroom for her coat and scarf. Outside, in the car park where the marquee for Santa's grotto had been set up, daylight was fading and the fairy lights around the entrance tunnel swayed in the late afternoon breeze. Wendy fastened her top button against the cold and steeled herself for the confrontation. She wanted to stare into the girl's eyes and accuse her of what they both knew to be true. She would stand her ground in the full knowledge that she was the one who had been wronged. She wanted to expose the girl in front of other people and savour her downfall. Sophie Harding deserved it.

But the queue of joyous little people waiting for their surprise gifts stopped her in her tracks. She looked at their happy little faces, cheeks all red with waiting in the cold, tiny fingers gloved and mittened hanging onto mother's coat or dad's sleeve. How could she spoil *their* day? That would be unforgivable. She stood at the entrance to the grotto and saw, standing next to Father Christmas, a slim figure with shining dark hair pulled back into a sophisticated chignon. Sophie was exquisite in her fairy outfit with its spangly wings and glittering crown. She was pretty and pouting and *nice.* She had on pale pink ballet tights and her legs were long and shapely. She was helping the little ones reach into the gift barrel; her eyes were bright and sparkling; her teeth white and even as Christmas snow. She looked so different from when she wore the shop floor uniform. She'd done something special with her makeup too so that her whole face gleamed.

She's so pretty, Wendy thought. *I don't understand why she would lie like that.*

Wendy stood and stared. Why would such a pretty young thing want to cause trouble for Rob? It didn't make sense. Sophie Harding looked like butter wouldn't melt. And yet, and yet, what about last week and the week before when they'd worked together filling shelves? *She* had known. Sophie Harding had known all the time they were working on stock rotation in canned goods, emptying the shelves first onto trolleys, putting new stock to the back and then replacing the old at the front. Wendy could see the scene in her mind's eye: Sophie, chatting away like anything about the show at college. Nice as you like. Charming and friendly. And all the time, she *knew. She was lying and she was damned good at it.*

'Isn't the grotto beautiful?' a woman in the queue said. 'They've done even better this year.'

The woman's nose was turning red with cold and the little boy at her side was hopping up and down and pulling on her arm.

'Yes, you're right. It's lovely,' Wendy said.

'I'm going to see Father Christmas,' the little boy said to Wendy and hopped faster.

'Are you, sweetheart? That's nice.'

It's a shame you can't trust the Christmas Fairy, though, she thought. She crossed the car park and back into the building. She went back to her work, trying to empty her mind of all thoughts of Sophie Harding. *Let it go now,* she told herself. *There'll be another time.*

36

Sarah

Sophie was upstairs getting ready to go to college for the pantomime and I was ironing a shirt for Marcus while he went to collect his mother from Barleycroft. A foul fog had settled across our part of the county, cold and damp dripping from hedgerows and trees, deadening the night air. Sophie was in one of her matching moods.

"Have you borrowed my pearl lip gloss?" she shouted from the top of the stairs.

"No."

She shouted something else but I couldn't hear.

"Sophie," I yelled up at her, "if you've got something to say to me come downstairs and say it properly."

She thumped her way down and stood staring at me with her arms folded across her chest.

"Somebody's taken my lip gloss."

"Ask your father."

"Don't be stupid, Mum."

"Listen to yourself, Sophie. Who in this house would ever want to use your lip gloss?"

"Well it's not where it should be."

"And you're surprised?"

"What?"

"Sophie, you're always losing something and then trying to put the blame on someone else. But lip gloss? Come on. Go and have another look for it."

"I don't know where to look."

I hung Marcus's shirt on a hanger behind the door and folded up the ironing board. Sophie was still leaning against the wall being stubborn.

"Well aren't you going to help me look for it?" she said.

"Actually, Sophie, no I'm not. Your dad will be back any second with Grandma and I've still got things to do."

"Oh, and I haven't? I wish I'd never said I'd be in this stupid pantomime."

"Sophie, this can't be about a tube of lip gloss. You're nervous, darling. You'll feel better when you're in college with all the others putting on your costumes."

"Not without my lip gloss," she screamed and ran upstairs.

I heard the clunking of a car door close and Margaret came through from the hall.

"Did I hear shouting?" she said.

"First night nerves," I said. "Come and get warm. It's a nasty night."

I took her coat and she sat at the table.

"No Christmas tree yet?" she said. "Or is it in the sitting room?"

"Next weekend. We don't like to decorate too soon."

"Oh, we're already swamped at Barleycroft. Trees and baubles and fairy lights everywhere, even outside in the gardens. But I quite like it. It seems to give everybody a lift."

"Well, we could all do with something in this dreadful weather," I said.

"Sophie," Marcus shouted up the stairs. "Time to go."

She came thudding down with her hair tied up in a scarf to protect it from the damp air.

"Hi, Grandma," she said and gave Margaret a peck. "Sorry, got to dash. I said I'd be there at half past."

"Off you go then, sweetheart. We'll see you after the show. What do they say? Break a leg."

Marcus said, "Got everything?"

Sophie patted her Samsonite make up case. "It's all in here."

When they'd gone I poured Margaret a sherry and another for myself. We took them into the sitting room and sat by the log burner

"I'm really looking forward to tonight," she said.

"Good. Yes, so am I. How's everything else at Barleycroft aside from the Christmas decorations?"

"Wonderful, Sarah. It's one of the best decisions I ever made to move there."

"Have you heard from Anthony?"

"Yes I have and I have a favour to ask. Would you invite him to spend Christmas with you and Marcus? I don't like to think of him being alone. It's the worst time of year to be by oneself."

"I'm glad you brought it up, Margaret," I said. "Marcus and I were discussing it just the other night."

She settled back on the sofa and sighed with relief. "Good. That's settled then."

"What will you do? I saw the announcements on your notice board the other day. You're spoiled for choice."

"I know. Wonderful, isn't it? I shall be beautifully busy."

"Could you eat a little something? There are refreshments later but I don't know if . . ."

"No thank you," she said.

The phone rang and I took it in the hall. When I went back to the sitting room Margaret was leaning back in the corner of the sofa. She had kicked off her shoes and looked so relaxed and well. Her eyes were bright, her complexion fresh. She looked contented.

"That was Marcus on the phone," I said. "He isn't coming back for us. He's offered lifts home to some of the cast. He says visibility on the roads is atrocious and he didn't want any of the kids walking home. We'll go up in my car."

"Very sensible too."

I drove slowly with dipped headlights. Full beam bounced back off the fog and made visibility even worse. It was difficult to distinguish between the edge of the road and the soft verge and I had no taillights in front of me to follow. I crept along until we made the safety of the main road where street lighting helped. I thought I'd offer to do the same as Marcus and give lifts home to anyone without transport. There are no footpaths along some of our lovely country lanes. Any pedestrian wouldn't be seen until it was too late. It didn't bear thinking about.

The college was buzzing with parents and friends, aunts and grandmothers, milling in the corridor outside the drama studio and filtering through to take their seats. There were fewer men in the audience. Sophie gave a lovely performance as did many of the others. They have such talent, these young people and seem so polished for their years. I was especially impressed by the music and lighting, all produced and controlled by the students themselves. There were some very clever effects.

We helped ourselves to refreshments afterwards and stood in small groups around the studio. The college principal moved among us thanking everyone for their support. I had turned to speak to another parent and I didn't see who was approaching from the other side of the room. I heard his voice and knew immediately who he was. I heard Marcus say,

"Mother, I'd like to introduce you to Mr Carter, Sophie's English teacher."

"Hello," Margaret said, "I'm so pleased to meet you. Congratulations on a superb pantomime. I've enjoyed it tremendously."

"Good," he said. "Though not much of the credit is mine, I'm afraid. We have to thank our Miss Granger in Performing Arts. She's your granddaughter's tutor, Mrs Harding."

For a moment I didn't know what to do. I hardly dare turn around to face the man but I had no choice.

"Good evening, Mr Carter," I said, hoping to stay in control of my voice. Surely, I thought, he would see through me and my efforts to act normally. "Another excellent production."

"Thank you," he said. "We do pride ourselves in putting on a good show and we've had a fantastic turnout. It makes such a difference to the cast, you know, to have a good audience."

He was speaking from the heart. There was no undercurrent of bitterness in him. His eyes were smiling and his expression was open and honest. I looked from his face to my husband and then to Margaret and back to Rob Carter again. The fluttering of nerves in my stomach calmed and I felt a sense of relief.

"Would you like a drink?" Rob Carter said. "We have wine for our parents this evening."

I shook my head.

"No, thank you," Marcus said. "We're both driving. Mother?"

"Yes, I think so. Thank you, Mr Carter."

"Wait here," Rob Carter said. "I'll bring one for you. Red or white?"

Sophie arrived to join us. She'd removed her stage makeup and tied back her hair.

"I see you found the lip gloss," I said.

"No," she said. "This is a different one."

Behind her Rob Carter was coming back from the drinks table with a glass in his hand for

Margaret. My stomach fluttered again.

"Here we are," he said, handing it over. "Lovely performance, Sophie as always. We'll see you in the West End one day."

"I hope so, Mr Carter," she said. "And I'll send you and Mrs Carter two front row seats."

"Make sure you don't forget. I'll be depending on it." He looked at each of us in turn and excused himself. "Got to do the rounds. Drum up more support for next year. Thank you again for coming. Will I see you in February at parents' evening? Good."

"What a lovely man," Margaret said when he'd gone. "They didn't have teachers like him when I was a girl. I think I should have had a crush on one as handsome as him."

She laughed and I tried to laugh with her but it turned into a spluttering cough. Had I been blind? Was Sophie's explanation another of her inventions? I looked straight into her eyes but there was not a flicker of embarrassment. It seemed our daughter was born for a career in acting. I don't know which one of us she gets it from.

Marcus began to gather up the people he was taking home.

"Room for one more," he said. "How about you, young lady? As long as you promise not to put a spell on me on the way."

The girl stared first at Marcus and then at Sophie. I recognised the one who had played the witch.

"No, thank you," she said and turned her back.

Marcus said goodbye to us and left with Sophie and three others. Margaret took her gloves from her handbag and as she pulled them on we heard the girl say to her friends,

"Huh. I wouldn't get in a car with *her*. Stuck up little cow."

One of her friends said, "She's okay."

"No, she isn't. You don't know what she's really like."

"What do you mean? Come on, what do you mean?"

"I can't. I promised Mr Carter I wouldn't say anything. But trust me, she's poison. Dirt. You don't want to have anything to do with her. Honestly. I know what I'm talking about."

I saw Margaret's mouth open wide in surprise. I had to stop her from stepping in. I linked my arm in hers and, forgetting about anything else, I hurried her to the car park.

"Let's go home," I said. "Stoke up the fire. How about toasted crumpets? Marcus still adores them. I think it would be a good idea if you stayed over tonight, Margaret. One of us will run you back home in the morning. This weather is atrocious and . . ."

I almost bundled her into the car and kept on talking, saying the first things that came into my head, anything to cover up the fearful feeling I might have to explain about Sophie.

"What on earth was all that about?" she asked me on the way home.

I lied. I simply couldn't bring myself to tell her what Sophie had done.

"Teenage jealousies I expect, Margaret," I said. "Best not to get involved. You know what they're like. Enemies one day, best friends the next." I was glad of the car's dark interior so she couldn't see my face flush.

37

Jenny Carter was invited on regional television during the Christmas week, part of the follow up on the *Christmas Miracles* theme they were running. Jenny said she was too excited to drive and wasn't sure how to find Prospect Place in Swindon. She didn't want to make a mistake and wind up late. Wendy drove her to the studio. Rob was feeling under the weather and stayed home. Every five minutes, Jenny checked her appearance in the passenger mirror, pouting up her lips and flicking at her hair. Wendy pulled into a guest parking space and her mother took one last check on her appearance.

"You don't have to come in," Jenny said as Wendy pulled on the handbrake. "I know what to do."

She got out and brushed herself down.

You look ridiculous, Wendy thought. *Way over the top.*

Jenny's dress sense had fallen into a time warp. Her skirts had grown shorter and her heels so high she could barely walk in them. She couldn't lock back her knees and had a graceless, bent-legged gait, plonking down her feet in a flat-footed stomp. Wendy waited until her mother was out of sight. She got out of the car and approached reception.

"I'm with my mother," she told the receptionist. "Jenny Carter. She's going on the teatime news show."

The young woman quickly made a security card for her. She followed the receptionist's directions and took a seat in a room opposite one marked *Makeup.* Both doors were open. People were dashing about, in and out of the make up room, up and down the corridor. Wendy picked up a magazine and waited. The noise from across the corridor continued. More people came in and went again. She could hear rapid footsteps getting nearer and then fading away again. Then she heard her mother's voice. The sound grew fainter and Wendy guessed that Jenny had been taken to await her slot. Two voices began as soon as the corridor was silent.

"Jesus," one of the voices said. "She walked in done up like some forties or fifties glamour puss. Chrissie in makeup was having a fit."

"I know, Fiona. I heard. What did Chrissie say?"

"She said, '*We can't let her go on looking like that.*'"

"Christ, no."

"I agreed. We were supposed to be running a serious slot. Covering the medical background, treating the whole thing, well, like properly, you know? So she comes in like a World War Two pin-up. Pencil skirt. High heels. Arched eyebrows and bright red lips like some weirdo Picasso. Hair all platinum and fluffed out at the sides. Jesus, we didn't know where to look. She had a great figure for her age, I'll give her that, but nobody was ever going to take her seriously looking the way she did."

Wendy squirmed. *Stay where you are,* she thought. *Sit still. Don't make a noise. You don't want them to know you're here.* She pressed her magazine flat on her lap so it didn't rustle. She closed her eyes and tried not to listen.

"So, what did she do?"

"Chrissie made up some tale about studio lighting. Told her they'd need to make some small adjustments. We knew we'd have to do it quickly. Eddie and Joy usually make a point of having a quick word with guests beforehand, just to put people at their ease. Well, you know Eddie's got this giggle. He sounds like a right girl once he gets going. And then he can't stop and sets Joy off. We were heading for a disaster and all because this silly old bat fancied herself as Norma Desmond. You know, *Sunset Boulevard.*'"

"Elaine Paige?"

"That's the one. Chrissie rushed her away into make-up and I warned cameras. Head and shoulders only, I told them. For fuck's sake, I said, don't let the viewers see the rest. The producer would have my head on a plate. Anyway, so, Chrissie sorts the old dear out. Tones down the cosmetics, smooths out the hairstyle and that was the outward appearance fixed. But that was only the half of it. When I rushed down to see Chrissie ahead of Eddie and Joy, I only had to take one look at Chrissie's face to see there was even more to worry about."

"No. What?"

"Chrissie squared her mouth and crossed her eyes at me as I came through the door. Cruella was in full flow. '*My daughter blames me. I know she does,*' she said. '*But it's not my fault she's depressed. Actually I think everything is working out well. When I came out of that dreadful place I had nowhere else to go, did I?*' "

"Oh, God. No."

"Oh, God. Yes. She went on and on. '*I shudder to think what it must have been like in there,*' she said. '*I'm glad I don't remember any of it.*' I looked at Chrissie and rolled my eyes. She did the same. Cruella was still at it. '*Oh, you hear such tales about those places,*' she said. '*I suppose in days gone by people with dementia would have been locked away for good. They'd have said they were loonies, wouldn't they? They'd have sent them to the mad house. They don't call them that now,*' she said. '*They call them the Firs.*'

I thought, Oh, my God. This is *so* not what Eddie and Joy are expecting. I skimmed through my clipboard notes hoping to hell and back there were no questions about the daughter."

In the waiting room Wendy cringed. She prayed for them to stop.

" *'Well I can't have had dementia, can I?'* she was still rattling on. *'People don't recover from dementia unless it's been caused by something else they've recovered from. I'm proud of myself that I've been able to put it all behind me and get on with my life.'* "

"She didn't."

"She did. *'I like living with Rob,'* she said. *'He's a very appreciative young man. I don't know why Wendy complains so much. He works hard. He pays all the bills. If I was ten years younger . . .'* Oh, shit. The woman's a nightmare, I thought. She was pursing her lips and tossing her head. Chrissie had her eyes closed and looked as if she was going to faint."

"Oh, Fiona. Poor you."

The blood drained from Wendy's face. She couldn't bear to hear any more but if she got up to close the door they would know she'd been there all the time and must have heard what they'd been saying. She remained still, hardly daring to breathe, her knees pressed close together, her shoulders rigid. She wished it could all go away.

The voice continued. "Jenny Carter was supposed to be a little old lady at the centre of a human interest story. Instead, she was sitting there preening in front of the mirror like some ageing prima donna, batting her eyes and showing her yellow teeth. She was like a macabre circus act."

"Well they certainly won't invite her back. Will they, Fiona?"

"Look, I've got to go. See you later."

The corridor fell silent once more. Wendy waited until her breathing returned to normal. She found a tissue and blew her nose. Then she took a deep breath, put down the magazine and went outside to wait in the car.

38

Rafe

Christmas was disappointing to be honest. We'd had a good laugh on Christmas Eve with a group of friends over in Swindon at the Apocalypse. It finished around four in the morning and we all crashed in somebody's flat afterwards. I woke at about two on Christmas Day afternoon and woke Richie so we could get back to Compton in time for mum's dinner. We always have it late afternoon, sometime between three and four. It's kind of tradition in our family. We'd borrowed mum's car. The roads were dead quiet. We got back in plenty of time and walked straight into some kind of nightmare. It was hell in the house.

Mum was crying on the sofa and my dad and grandma had launched world war three in the kitchen. Richie and I got out of the way. We went to our room and listened through the open door. We'd had to share the spare room since Grandma had moved in.

"Jenny," Dad was saying, "you're being unreasonable."

"No, I'm not. It's her," Grandma argued. "Lying around all day crying. It's Christmas bloody day, Rob. Why does she want to go and spoil everything by bursting into tears every five minutes?"

Richie nudged me with his elbow and said, "Merry Christmas, brother."

We put on a computer game and played against each other for over an hour. We'd had no breakfast. My stomach was rumbling.

"I'm starving," I said. "Let's go and see what's happening."

"Boys, there you are," Grandma said. "I've made you a chocolate pudding for after the turkey. I know you don't like traditional Christmas pudding. There's custard too."

Dad had his eyes closed and was shaking his head. The table was set in the dining room but instead of the tablecloth

Mum usually puts out each year, the one with a holly and candle design, there was no cloth at all. Instead there was a narrow strip of flimsy fabric down the centre of the table in a kind of shimmery bronze colour. Mum's Christmas place mats had been swapped for matching bronze frilly things. The wreath that went round a fat candle was missing from the middle of the table too. There were two stemmed glasses, like giant goblets, with tea candles inside them.

"Doesn't it look lovely?" Grandma said as we took our places. Mum had gone to the bathroom and came out a few minutes later. She sat in silence with her head down. She didn't look at us. Dad carved and Grandma put out dishes of vegetables and brought warm plates from the oven. Still Mum said nothing. We pulled our crackers and made a stupid show of wearing the paper hats and reading out the jokes but Mum didn't join in with us.

"Take no notice of your mother, boys," Grandma said. "She's just in a bad mood."

I glanced over at Mum, expecting her to say something but she kept her head down and stayed completely silent. I didn't like the feeling I was getting but Richie and me were ravenous. We cleared our plates and helped ourselves to seconds. Grandma didn't have any roast potatoes, Dad passed on the sprouts but Mum ate hardly anything at all.

"Wendy, aren't you hungry? Can't you try just a little?" Dad said. "Jenny's worked all morning to put this meal together."

"Oh, leave her alone," Grandma cut in. "Don't pander to her. She's behaving like a child."

I nearly threw down my knife and fork.

"Will somebody tell me what's going on?" I said.

Grandma humphed. Dad sank back into his chair.

"Your mother feels put out because I cooked today," Grandma said. "She's sulking because I have dressed the table and she's mad that I have gone to the trouble of making you boys your favourite pudding instead of forcing you to eat stodge."

Richie looked across at Mum and said, "Aren't you going to say anything, Mum?"

She didn't answer. She tried to smile but her eyes were red and watery. I'd seen enough. I jumped up and pushed back my chair.

"Grandma," I said. "This is not your house. We like to do things *our* way."

I fully expected Dad to take control of the situation but he sat as quiet as Mum and turned his head away.

"It was time for a change," Grandma said.

"We didn't want to change," I said, still standing.

Richie's head was swivelling from side to side like watching tennis.

"Sit down Rafe," Grandma said. "You're making yourself look stupid. If you're not careful you'll turn out just like *her*."

"What's happened to you, Grandma?" I said. "You didn't use to be like this."

"Maybe I should have. Your mother's been too soft with you. Maybe I should have taken over sooner."

My face went hot. It must have been bright red. I could feel my jaw pulsing. I walked round the table to where Grandma was sitting and stood over her chair.

"I liked you better when you were ill," I said and left the room. I grabbed my coat and went out. I was so mad I didn't know where I was going. I was just walking. The streets were empty. I ended up in the pub. The bar was nearly empty too but the dining room was full of families enjoying their Christmas dinner and having a good time. There was a lot of noise. Christmas music and laughter, some little kids running around and blowing those curled up squeaky things with feathers on the end. I ordered a drink and took it to a table by the fireplace and sat, staring into the fire. Richie turned up about half an hour later. He sat beside me and put his arm round my shoulder.

"I thought I'd find you here," he said.

"There isn't anywhere else to go."

"You were great, Rafe," he said. "I've never seen you so fired up about anything before. I didn't know you had it in you."

"What happened after I left?" I asked.

"Grandma didn't even flinch at what you said to her. She started collecting the plates and asked who wanted pudding. I felt sorry for Mum. I was annoyed with Dad for not saying anything to support her so I decided to be obstinate. You know me, Rafe. I'm good at obstinate. I said I wanted traditional Christmas pud. They all stared at me. At last Mum spoke. She said there wasn't any. I could have eaten some of Grandma's chocolate pudding to be honest but I wanted to show solidarity with you. I knew you'd be here."

"Thanks, Richie," I said. "What do you think's going to happen now?"

He took a swig of his beer and shrugged. "Not our problem," he said. "We go back to uni."

"No, I mean before then. We've got the rest of Christmas to get through."

"We'll think of something."

"It's driving me crazy," I said. "It isn't like our home any more. I really don't want to be there."

"Mum'll be back at work tomorrow. You know. The sales. Mum and Grandma won't be able to wind one another up so much."

Richie was trying to make light of it but I couldn't remember ever having felt so unhappy at home before. Grandma was spoiling everything.

39

Sarah

Marcus phoned his father to invite him to stay with us over Christmas. He went upstairs to make the call from his office. I knew why he needed to do that, to be alone without the distraction of the radio or Sophie's music. He has to concentrate and focus hard on keeping his voice calm and controlled whenever he's speaking to his father. I heard him close the study door and was surprised when he came downstairs to find me shortly afterwards. I was sorting through a box of candles and baubles and, when he didn't say anything, I stopped what I was doing and looked up.

"What's the matter?" I said.

"He doesn't want to come."

Marcus slumped onto a sofa in the sitting room and began drumming his fingers on the arm. I waited for a moment. He looked troubled.

"Marcus?" I said. "Did you say the right things, darling? I mean, how exactly did you put it to him?"

"I invited him for Christmas, Sarah."

"No, darling, what I mean is did you be sure to let him know we wanted him to come?"

"Yes. It's him. He doesn't want to come here." He ran his hand through his hair and shook his head.

"Perhaps he felt a little awkward about it what with Margaret being so near. Maybe it's too soon for him. Maybe it's . . ."

"No. It isn't anything like that," he said. "Dad says he's made other arrangements."

"What other arrangements?"

Marcus shook his head again and said, "I can't believe it."

"What? Marcus?"

"He's going away for Christmas."

"Oh," I said. "Well that's probably a good idea. Where is he going?"

There was a long pause before Marcus said, "India."

"India? But he's never been out of England. He hates travelling."

"I know."

"Where in India?"

"Kerala. Right down in the south. It's all booked. He says it's supposed to be the best time of year to go there. To avoid the double monsoons they get, apparently."

"Oh." I didn't know what else to say. Marcus was still drumming his fingers and biting at the inside of his mouth. I said, "There's something else, isn't there?"

He stopped drumming and looked up at me, an expression of sheer disbelief creasing his face.

"What?" I said.

"He's going with a woman."

"What? Who?"

"Someone he met recently."

"Where?"

"It's incredible." I sat on the sofa arm beside him and waited for him to find his words. "You know Dad's been doing up the house? He says he gave himself a stiff neck after painting the ceilings. His shoulders were painful as well."

"Why doesn't he find a decorator to do it? He shouldn't be climbing ladders at his age."

"I agree but that's beside the point. Someone recommended him to a kind of alternative massage. He says it worked a treat. It's her who's going to India with him. The therapist."

"The masseuse?"

"Yes. Her name's Maya. She's younger than him. In her fifties, he said. How the devil could this woman persuade him to go to India? He moaned about visiting us here."

"Marcus, nobody ever persuades your father to do anything he doesn't want to do. Dear God. Has he told your mother?"

"I didn't think to ask. I was rather taken aback."

I slipped my arm around his shoulder but he was staring blankly at the fireplace as if he didn't know what to do next. We sat in silence for a few moments.

"Should we tell her, Sarah?"

"Maybe we can find out if she already knows. Leave it with me. I'll call her. She's expecting to hear from me anyway."

Margaret was full of news of Barleycroft activities when I phoned. She had joined the bridge club and was thinking of volunteering for a stint in the co-operative grocery shop. It was obvious how much she was enjoying herself in her new place. I hardly dare bring up the news about Anthony. I didn't want to spoil her mood. I needn't have worried. She laughed.

"The old fool," she said. "He was probably too embarrassed to tell me himself. I hope he has a good time. You've got to admit, Sarah, he needed some loosening up."

When I put down the phone Marcus was pacing the kitchen, waiting to hear how his mother had taken the news.

He said, "She laughed?"

"Yes, darling. She laughed."

"Wasn't she the slightest upset?"

"Not a bit."

Christmas passed quietly. Sophie was out with friends most of the time, Margaret was busy with Barleycroft party nights and bridge afternoons and Anthony was in India. The house looked forlorn with just the two of us in it as if it was overdressed for the occasion. We'd exchanged gifts on Christmas morning as usual. Three of us for Christmas lunch. Two for the Queen's Speech. After Sophie had gone out Marcus and I sat looking at each other across the quiet living room surrounded by festive garlands and twinkling lights in the window and on the tree in the corner. The perfect English Christmas cottage. He shrugged his shoulders.

"It feels like we're the old fogeys now," Marcus said.

"I know. Strange, isn't it?"

"There's my parents off doing their own thing, acting like teenagers. Yours are living it up at a ski lodge somewhere in the Troodos mountains and here we are with nothing more exciting to do than decide what to watch on television."

"Maybe we should go away somewhere next year, " I suggested.

He stared at the ceiling and said, "Maybe you're right."

40

Margaret

I soon grew to love my little house and become accustomed to the changes in my life. There's very little cleaning to do compared with the old place in Kent. I can keep on top of it quite easily. A quick wipe down on the kitchen surfaces and everything comes up sparkling. I have more time to do other things, take part in activities, go on trips.

There were so many small pleasures in the early days, things I hadn't before considered. I had electricity sockets in handy positions; kitchen wall cupboards at the right height for me; no steep stairs. No need for a cumbersome, heavy vacuum cleaner. Windows that tilted and turned so I could easily clean them. Even hanging up a brand new tea towel made me feel pleased. Small things, I know, but each tiny pleasure added up to a sense of contentment. I got rid a lot of things, too. I went through the packing cases Marcus brought for me and donated some pieces to our fund- raisers here at Barleycroft. Others went to charity. I felt de-cluttered and that simple act of de-cluttering made me feel well.

I've learned quite a lot about myself. One would think at my time of life there ought not to be much you don't already know about yourself. You've had years to get to know who you are, after all. But some things have surprised me. I never thought I was the type to enjoy group activities. I used to say disparaging things about what I called Darby and Joan clubs. I didn't understand why elderly people enjoyed being with other elderly people. I always thought it must be healthier to mix with all age groups. Elderly folk were dull, I thought. They talked too much about the past and their health problems. How wrong I was. What a little snob I must have been when I was younger.

Now it's me who is elderly. It takes quite some getting used to. You think you're going to stand by all your preconceived ideas about how you will behave in your own old age but then, one day, you find you've become subject to the same influences as all the other old people you used to criticise. Other people's music is too loud. Your sleeping patterns do change. Sometimes you can be wide awake at four in the morning and at others you find yourself nodding off in the afternoon. There are vague aches and pains which seem to come and go so that, at times, it can become quite a feat simply to pull on your tights. If you're lucky, that is. If you can manage to keep your health and a good pair of hips or legs; if you can still check your change from the newsagent; if you can remember to switch off the gas before you go out. And, for goodness sake, don't pay too much attention to what is happening in the mirror. The pale face with creased skin that looks back at you from underneath hair that has thinned so much you can see your own scalp will shock you. Bristle like hairs will appear, sprouting from your chin and you will need your reading glasses or a magnifying glass to pluck them out. Then, when you browse through your old photographs you will ask yourself if you can remember appreciating your life when you were thirty, forty, even fifty. All those years have flown by and now, here you are, feeling as if you are the same person you always were but the aching back and the face in the mirror tell you something different.

Sarah says it's been a very similar pattern for her parents in Cyprus. They have come to depend on the ex-pat group for all their social life just as I now join in here with the organised coach trips and tea dance afternoons. We are growing old. No. We are old.

Anthony wouldn't have been able to live this kind of life. He would have fought against it all the way. His obstinacy would have prevented him from making any friends here. He doesn't know what he's missing. There is Andrew, who plays piano beautifully and David who knows more about World War Two than anybody I have ever met. Admittedly, there are more women in our little community than there are men, but that doesn't seem to matter. We are all simply human beings in need of the company of other human beings.

I do think about Anthony a lot. You can't spend all those years with a person and then, in a flash, wipe them out of your life. One of the residents here told me it took her seven years before she experienced a day without thinking constantly about her late husband. Then she felt guilty, she said, for not thinking about him.

"But life goes on," I said. "You can't spend the rest of your life in the past, can you? You've still got some living to do."

She patted me on the hand and said, "Guilt is a sneaky emotion, Margaret. It can creep up on you in disguise."

I think Brenda and I will become exceptionally good friends. She seems so wise. They say that wisdom comes along hand in hand with old age, but sometimes, during conversations like that one with Brenda, I feel she has reached a stage of understanding that I have yet to learn.

"I worry that Anthony must feel very lonely," I told her.

Loneliness is a terrible thing, especially in one's old age. I worried that Anthony would be miserable, rattling around in that big house by himself. Would he be eating properly? Would he be taking proper care of himself? His laundry? Was he walking around in soiled underwear beneath his dirty shirt and trousers? Of course, this was before I found out about his new friend, Maya and their trip to India.

I was happy for him, then. I was glad he'd found a companion. Admittedly, it did seem strange that he'd taken to this alternative medicine scene. It all sounded very new age to me, something that went completely against Anthony's traditional views and love of rules and procedures. If I had suggested, what is it called, Reiki? If I had brought it up I know he would have called it poppycock and made fun of the idea. But Maya had helped him see things differently, I supposed. Whereas I had tolerated Anthony's stubborn ways for so many years Maya been able to change his set patterns in a matter of weeks. Whether that was due to Maya or her Reiki, I couldn't say. That did rankle a little I have to admit but it served no purpose to dwell on it. That sort of thing only makes one feel bitter. I mentioned it to Brenda.

We'd gone into Devizes to do our Christmas gift shopping and I suggested we take a break in the little tea shop where I'd been with Sarah in the autumn. We sat in the same place by the window looking onto the courtyard. The tubs outside had been cleared of flowers and were filled instead with illuminated topiary style trees.

"It makes me quite cross when I think about it, Brenda," I said. "How quickly he has changed to please someone else."

"Yes, I can understand how you must feel," she said. "You must be wondering whether you should have insisted on him making those changes for you. Whether you should have put your foot down."

"Yes, that's just what I mean. Should I have?"

"Margaret," she said. "We'll never know." She took a huge bite out of her toasted teacake and butter ran down her chin. She dabbed at it with a paper napkin and pulled a silly face. She made me laugh and, immediately, I stopped feeling sorry for myself. I brought out my shopping list and we discussed where we wanted to go next. I still hadn't chosen a gift for Sophie.

"What can you buy for a young lady who already has everything?" I said.

Brenda said, "More," and made me laugh again.

41

Rafe

We were all doing different things on New Year's Eve. Mum and Dad had been invited to a gathering at the college principal's house, Richie had gone up to London to stay with friends of his and Grandma had some sort of charity do to go to connected with the Compton Women's League. She was still riding high on a publicity wave that had carried her into her new and exciting world. She loved that people treated her like a celebrity. She liked to think she'd gone upmarket. She was a somebody now, she often said. She would put on a kind of telephone voice whenever she talked with anybody from this new world of hers. I heard it on the radio and when she was interviewed on the local television news. It might have been funny if it hadn't been so unbearable to see strangers making a fuss of her, calling her things like remarkable, redoubtable, telling her what a paragon she was. They didn't know what she was like at home.

I asked Mum about it when we were on our own watching an episode of Eastenders. The cast was acting out the usual Christmas soap drama and it prompted me to bring up our own situation. Our story was more unbelievable than what was on BBC.

"Has Grandma always been eccentric?" I asked Mum.

"Yes," she said. "As long as I've known her."

"How come I never noticed?"

"You wouldn't have seen it before. You were just a child."

"So how about when you were just a child? Was she weird then?"

"Yes."

"So you noticed it, Mum. Why didn't I? Why didn't Richie? Or Dad?"

She sighed and said, "Because she's always been good at hiding it, Rafe."

"So she can choose when not to be like it?"

Mum picked up the remote and turned down the volume. She came to sit beside me.

"Rafe," she said. "Grandma is just different. It doesn't mean she doesn't love you."

I said, "I never used to doubt that, Mum. When Richie and I were little she baked cakes for us, hugged us, was nice to us. She was a proper grandma. At least, that's what we saw in her. We had no doubt she loved us. Now, if she still feels the same way she has a funny way of showing it."

"I don't think you need to worry about it. Grandma isn't your problem. I'm sure things will work out."

I searched my mother's face and realised something that hadn't before occurred to me. She had lived with it all her life.

"When you were young, Mum, how did you cope? After your dad died you were by yourself with her. It must have been awful."

"Sometimes it was."

"Didn't she ever go to see someone about it? Didn't you?"

Mum shrugged her shoulders. "I suppose neither of us knew what to do," she said.

"I could look it up on the internet for you if you like," I offered. "There's all kinds of stuff on there. That's where I found out more about Alzheimer's."

"Yes, Rafe, I know. But I don't think it would do any good. It wouldn't change anything, would it? Grandma would still be as she is."

"But at least you'd have a name for it, Mum. You'd know what you were dealing with."

"I don't think we'll ever really know," she said. "The tests they did haven't shown anything and she won't go back."

"What do you mean?"

Mum paused and I thought she wasn't going to say any more. Then she cleared her throat and carried on.

"I found something in the bin," she said.

"What?"

"Two things, actually."

"Go on."

"A packet of pills." She reached down beside the sofa and picked up her handbag. She opened it and lifted out a small carton.

"What kind of pills are they?"

"I think they're painkillers," Mum said, sliding out the empty foil blister packs. She pushed them back into the box and stashed them in her bag.

"What was the other thing?"

"It was torn into pieces and at first I thought it was a bill that had got into the wrong pile. It was an appointment date for Grandma. For a scan. Last week. She didn't keep it."

I wondered whether I should mention I'd seen Grandma taking pills from a similar pack when I'd gone to see her at Easter but I didn't get the chance. Dad came in and said it was time Mum started getting ready to go out.

42

In the solid old semi-detached bungalow, on the sought after avenue, in the pretty market town, everybody was getting ready to go out. Wendy and Rob had been invited to the college principal's New Year celebration. Jenny was going out later.

The idea of the passing of the old year appealed to Wendy. She couldn't wait to see the back of it. Even the positive things that had happened had all turned into negatives. And the bad? It had grown even worse. The New Year brought with it the hope of putting all those worries behind her and the tantalising prospect of starting afresh. Maybe there would be something to look forward to after all. Maybe the Sandman would come back to her if she could only lift herself out of her persistent gloom.

"You're not wearing that are you, dear? I thought you said you were going to the Principal's house."

Wendy tried to ignore her mother's cutting remark.

"It's all I've got, Mum. Everything else is too big."

"I told you, you should have gone to the sales. Pritchards have some lovely things just now." She held up the jersey cocktail dress she was pressing on the ironing board. "This was over three hundred pounds originally. A bargain at one eighty-five. So I spent the savings on earrings. I love earrings."

"I know you do. They're very nice."

"When was the last time you treated yourself to something new?"

"I don't know."

"Go on, tell me."

"Really, I can't remember. It doesn't matter. It isn't important to me."

"Well, it should be. You can't expect a handsome man like Rob to stay interested if you let yourself go."

An image flashed through Wendy's mind of her mother wearing a shabby wrap around her shoulders and someone else's knee socks.

"I'm glad you look so nice, Mum," she said.

"I have to make the effort more than ever now," Jenny said. Wendy half expected her mother to continue with something like *my public expect it* but Jenny said, "You never know who you might meet." She treated Wendy to one of the flirtatious winks she'd perfected since she moved in with them.

The door opened and Rob came in. "Anybody for a gin and tonic before we go out. Get the party started?"

"What a lovely idea, Rob. How kind," Jenny said.

Wendy said, "Not for me just yet, thank you."

Jenny tinkled with fake laughter. "Party pooper," she said.

Rob made a big show of preparing the glasses, frosting them for a few minutes in the freezer, rubbing the rims with lime juice and tipping ice cubes into his mini ice bucket, part of the Ultimate Bar Accessory pack Jenny had given him for Christmas. He laid out the tongs in readiness and carefully measured a finger of export Gordon's when the glasses were ready. Jenny fizzed with anticipation. She bubbled more than the Schweppes.

Wendy wondered why Rob played along with Jenny's games. Why was it he seemed unable to see what a monster her mother could be? There they were, strutting like exotic prize birds around one another. It was nauseating and the horrible truth was that her mother had no intentions of ever leaving them to go to a place of her own. When Wendy had brought up the subject Jenny snapped out of her usual arrogance and put on her little girl voice.

"Oh, Wendy dear," she'd said. "I'd love to have a place of my own again. You know I would. But the doctors say I might have a relapse. I shouldn't feel safe at all on my own. Oh, no, dear. I'll have to stay here. If I was by myself and something happened, how would you feel? You'd never forgive yourself. I wouldn't want to put you through that. Not after all you've done for me."

And Wendy had been beaten again. She shook off the recollection of that conversation with her mother and tried to think positively.

Rob handed Jenny her drink. "With a slice of lime, Jenny. Not lemon. Just the way you like it."

Jenny took the glass and kissed him on the cheek. "You remembered," she said. "Isn't that sweet of him, Wendy?"

Wendy folded up the ironing board and put it in its place in the hall cupboard. From the kitchen behind her she could hear the clinking of glasses and the rattle of ice cubes. She thought it a hollow sound. It didn't mean anything close to companionship, a comforting sharing of a celebration night. It was the sound of people pretending that everything was normal.

Rafe came out of his room. "I'm going now, Mum," he said.

"Okay, sweetheart. Everything all right?"

"Fine. We're meeting at the pub."

"Come and have a drink with us, son, before you go out," Rob called from the kitchen.

"I can't, Dad. They'll be waiting."

Jenny came into the hall. She linked her arm through Rafe's and pulled him toward the kitchen.

"Don't be such a spoilsport, sweetie," she said. "It won't hurt to do something to please your father for once."

"Really, Grandma. I've got to go."

"No, you haven't."

Rafe looked at Wendy with pleading in his eyes but Jenny marched him away. Wendy followed.

"I've changed my mind, Rob," she said. "I think I'll join you."

Wendy thought she saw the briefest flash of anger flicker across Jenny's face and knew, in that instant, she would need to protect her son from her mother's manipulations. She took a deep breath and pushed the thought aside. Rafe accepted a beer. The four of them touched glasses. In the warmth of the kitchen with her mother, husband and son next to her, Wendy's heart was as cut as their crystal tumblers, cold as the ice inside them.

"Rob, we'll have to get a move on as well," she said.

He looked at his watch. "You're right." He took his jacket from the back of a chair and said, "I'll start the car. Get it nicely warmed up."

Rafe downed the last of his beer. "Right, everybody," he said. "I'm off. See you tomorrow, Happy New Year."

Wendy put the glasses by the sink but her mother picked hers up again and poured a refill of neat gin.

"I suppose you've left me some hot water," she said with a whine.

Wendy's breath caught in her throat. There was a hard lump deep inside her ready to explode.

"You know there's always hot water. Mum, why do you always have to say things in that way?"

Jenny shrugged. "I don't know what you're talking about." She walked down the hall, sipping from her glass. Wendy followed as far as the bathroom. "Rob's waiting. You'd better go."

Jenny switched on the power shower and took another drink. She moved the setting on the shower dial. "You never have it hot enough. Well, off you go then. You wouldn't want him to go without you, Wendy, would you? I mean, you never know who he might meet."

"What?"

"There must be plenty of women who'd like to swap places with you."

"Don't start, Mum."

"An attractive man like him? Even the young girls at school have got their eye on him. Who was that student he had a fling with?"

"Stop it, Mum."

"All men are self-centred, Wendy. You must remember that. They'll take whatever they can get."

"Stop it."

"Why? It's only the truth. They're all as bad."

"I'm glad I'm not like you."

"Oh, you think you're like your father, do you? He was the most selfish one of all."

"Please stop it now."

"You thought he just upped and died? Oh no, dear. Here's another piece of truth I've been saving for you. He killed himself. Yes. Took his own life. He hung himself in the garage where he knew I'd be the one to find him. That's how selfish he was."

Wendy was trembling. "You're lying," she said. "You're making it all up. I won't listen to you any more. Mother, you're poison." Wendy confronted her mother in the bathroom doorway. She brought her face close. "And I'm warning you right here and now. Keep your claws off Rafe."

Jenny laughed. "He'll turn out just as selfish as the rest."

"You know what?" Wendy said. "You're twisted. There's something really wrong with you. I don't think you know you're doing it. You can't really mean to be so cruel."

Jenny laughed again and crunched on an ice cube from her drink. In the bathroom steam billowed from the hot shower. She wiped it from the cabinet mirror and smiled at herself. She took another swallow of gin.

"I suppose you think your secret lover isn't selfish at all."

"What did you just say?"

"Did you think I'd forgotten about him? Your lover? The Sandman? He's gone now, hasn't he? Would you like me to tell you why?"

Wendy turned her back on her mother. "It's New Year's Eve, Mum. I have to go."

Jenny stepped forward and stood in the bathroom doorway. She shouted down the hall. "He was only ever on loan, you stupid, little mouse-girl. *I* sent the Sandman to you to cheer you up. But he was mine first. He's back at home now where he belongs. With me."

Wendy rushed back along the hall to challenge her mother. "What?"

"You heard me. I lent him to you. I was the one who sent him to you. The Sandman. I told him, go and give my daughter what she needs. Was he good, Wendy? Did you like it? I taught him well, didn't I? We're back together again now. Haven't you heard us at night in my room?"

Wendy screamed. She backed away from her tormentor with her eyes closed tight against the sight of her mother's leering face. She pushed out her arms in front of her to keep it from coming closer. She was still screaming as she ran to the front door. A door slammed shut behind her as Wendy ran outside into the drive.

43

Rafe

There wasn't a mini bus to be in time for. I made it up. I didn't want the rest of the family thinking I was a Billy-No-Mates. There was a special late night at the pub with a DJ and bar snacks and everything, so I thought I'd just stay there. It had to be better than sitting on my own watching television. I thought so, anyway. The atmosphere was lively and the place was all festive red and green with strings of fairy lights all over the walls.

There were a couple of lads in I recognised from schooldays. I joined them and we got to talking about what everybody was doing. One of them, Jamie, had a sister at sixth form college and she was coming up later with a couple of her friends.

"I left them getting ready," Jamie said. "Couldn't wait to get out of their way. They won't get here till about ten. They get through a bottle of vodka first before they come out. It's cheaper."

The group of girls turned up just as Jamie said. They were loud and boisterous. Most of them had on too much make up and clothes that wouldn't have looked out of place on a Greek island summer holiday. They must have been freezing. One of them looked different from the rest. She had her hair pulled back away from her face so you could actually see her features. Her eyes were amazing. I don't know what she'd done to them. I think it might have been her eyebrows. I couldn't stop looking at her. She wasn't falling about laughing like the others. I wanted to go over and talk to her but I waited too long. By the time they'd finished their drinks they made moves to leave again. A taxi driver came inside and called out one of their names and they all disappeared. I carried on talking to Jamie for a while but, somehow, everything had gone flat. I felt bored with the music. Bored with the company, actually, so I went home. Sod the New Year, I thought. I'll just go to bed. How sad is that?

When I got in I decided to make a drink. Dad had left the gin out so I had a go at making one of his specials with the lime and everything. As I crossed the hall to the living room I heard the shower running. I thought, that's funny. Who's in the shower? They've all gone out. Then I thought maybe Grandma had come back early or something, and I ignored it for a while. I got hungry and went to make a bacon sandwich. I ate it in the kitchen and finished my drink. Then, I needed the toilet.

The shower was still running. I looked at my watch. It had been on since I came in. More than twenty minutes. I knew something was wrong. Maybe whoever was last in the shower had forgotten to turn it off. I was getting desperate for the toilet and the sound of all that running water didn't help.

I shouted out, "Is anybody in there?"

No answer. I shouted again and banged on the door. I banged louder. Still the only sound was the water running. I tried the door. It opens outwards into the hall. Dad had somebody hang it the other way round to save space in the bathroom so we'd have room for a bath as well as a shower, but you can still lock it from the inside. I pulled it a bit. It wasn't locked. So, I thought, somebody had forgotten to switch it off. I wondered if it was Grandma starting to forget things again.

I pulled back the door and stepped inside. The room was completely full of steam. It was so thick it was like smoke. To begin with I couldn't see a thing. I thought I should open the window but first reached out to turn off the shower. I stepped on something soft and nearly lost my balance. I looked down and nudged whatever it was with the toe of my shoe.

Jesus! My bladder let go and I wet myself. I peed into my pants and it ran down my leg all over my shoes. At the same time I felt the gin and my bacon sandwich coming up and I leaned over and vomited into the sink. I hardly dare look up again.

Grandma was lying on her back on the floor with her head crushed up against the shower tray. Her eyes were wide open, staring blindly at the ceiling. There was a piece of jagged glass sticking out of her throat. More pieces of glass were scattered across the floor. I recognised it. It was the same pattern of cut glass as the tumblers we'd all used earlier. There were blood splatters everywhere except for around my feet where there was a pool of my own urine.

I forced myself to look at Grandma again. For a second I didn't know what to do. Should I touch her? Should I turn off the shower? Call 999, idiot, I told myself. I went to the phone on the kitchen wall. My hands were shaking as I dialled and I felt sick again. I asked for the ambulance service. They asked me to describe what I could see and took the address.

"Is she still breathing?" the voice asked.

"I don't think so," I said. There was a fucking great piece of glass sticking out of her neck, for fuck's sake.

"Are you sure she's not breathing?" the voice said. "Have you checked?" What's your name, son? Hello? What's your name?"

I thought, Please don't ask me to go back in there.

"Hello? Are you still there? What's your name, son?"

"Rafe."

"Listen to me now, Rafe. There's an ambulance on its way right now. How old are you, Rafe?"

"Eighteen."

"Okay, Rafe. Stay calm. Help is on its way." Stay calm? "Are you on your own? Rafe? Are you on your own?"

"Yes."

"Stay there."

The voice kept asking me if I could go back to check if Grandma was breathing. I didn't want to. I couldn't face going back in there. I wandered around in the kitchen with the phone to my ear answering yes and no, but not really concentrating. I was thinking about Mum.

"I've got to call my mother now," I said and hung up. I called Mum's mobile. I don't remember my exact words but I think I told her I thought Grandma was dead. Then I went to change out of my clothes. My jeans felt cold and wet against my legs and I didn't want people to know I'd actually peed myself. It didn't occur to me they'd see the pool of piss on the tiled floor anyway. I put the soiled clothes in the washing machine. I didn't go back to the bathroom. I left the shower running and everything just as I'd found it. I was afraid to touch anything. And I was afraid to look at Grandma's face again with its horrible staring eyes and purple-red, scalded-looking skin. One side of her face was blistered and her skin was peeling back, wet and sloppy. It looked like jelly and custard. My stomach heaved again. I tried to concentrate on something else. I thought about the girl in the pub. While I waited for the ambulance to arrive I thought of her pretty face, her lovely shiny hair and the way her eyebrows arched over those beautiful eyes.

Part Three

44

Sarah

On New Year's Eve we had an unexpected visitor. Actually, it was past midnight so in fact it was already January. High winds which had been gusting through the day and evening, whistling through the trees in the garden and screaming down the chimney dropped away quite suddenly to nothing and the temperature plummeted again. Everything went very still. When I heard the knock at the door my heart shook and I immediately panicked. Sophie was staying with friends and I imagined something awful had happened to her. Marcus answered the door and brought Seamus Dalton back with him.

"I hope I'm not keeping you from your beds," he said.

Marcus said, "Not at all, not at all. Come in. What can we do for you, Seamus?"

I took his coat and offered to bring us all a winter warmer. I went to the kitchen to heat some mulled wine. While I was bringing out glasses I could hear Marcus and his colleague talking in hushed tones. It all seemed very strange to say the least. Seamus Dalton wasn't in the habit of calling on us so I knew straight away that something unusual had happened. I waited until their conversation tailed off. I knew Seamus wouldn't discuss whatever it was in front of me especially if it was anything to do with their work. When I heard Marcus opening the burner to throw on another log I went in with a tray of drinks.

"Your decorations are beautiful, Sarah," Seamus said.

"Thank you. I like to make a special effort at Christmas."

He took a glass and tasted. "Wonderful. Most welcome." He refused my offer of a snack. "No, I won't keep you, my dear. I must get along home. My wife will be waiting for me. She worries I'm getting too old for this job. I do apologise for disturbing you but there was something I thought Marcus would like to know."

"That's perfectly all right. No trouble at all."

He drained his glass and thanked me again. Marcus saw him to the door. I waited. A blast of freezing air pierced the warmth of the house as the door opened. Marcus came back in and sat by the fire with his arms folded across his chest. For a split second he looked like his father. His face was set with the same tight mouth.

"Can you tell me?" I said.

"Seamus is worried."

"Yes, I gathered that. What is he worried about?"

"A patient of his died suddenly at home tonight."

"Oh, dear. The poor family. What a dreadful time of year. How awful. New Year will never be the same again for them."

"You're right. It won't."

"Who was it? Are you allowed to say?"

He lifted his shoulders on an intake of breath and brought them down again with a sigh. "It's Jenny Carter," he said. "Rob Carter's mother-in-law. The one who . . ."

"Was on television the other day. My God. That's terrible. It's tragic. How cruel. How can they bear it?" A lump tightened at the back of my throat. How could Fate be so cruel? Hadn't that family gone through enough? "How did she die?"

He shook his head and said, "That, I can't tell you. There'll have to be a post mortem. Apparently there are some suspicious circumstances."

45

Rafe

By the time Mum and Dad came home on New Year's Eve the house was crawling with people. The police had arrived shortly after the ambulance. There must have been a policeman and woman waiting outside to meet my parents as well because they all came into the kitchen together, through from the front door. We weren't allowed to use the back door for some reason. Mum was grey in the face.

I was sitting on one side of the kitchen table. Mum and Dad sat opposite. I've no idea what time it was. Mum was asking me questions but I couldn't concentrate on what she was saying. Inside my head felt blurred. There was this rolling emptiness in my mind something like white noise, cold and freaky. And stuck in the middle of it was this picture, an image of Grandma lying in all that blood and that jagged piece of glass sticking out of her neck, the skin of her face all puffed up and blistered, red and yellow and watery. My stomach was empty but I still felt sick. My heart was thumping and I was kind of short of breath.

"It must have been a terrible shock for him," I heard someone say. I tried furiously to think of something else. The girl in the pub with the pretty face and nice hair. She was lovely and she smiled at me but I hadn't had the balls to ask her name. I thought about her eyes, the way they looked big and sparkly, but they disappeared out of my head and all I could see was Grandma's dead ones, open and staring at nothing.

Somebody passed me a drink of water. I took a sip but my throat wasn't working properly and I couldn't swallow it. I made a dash for the kitchen sink and some sour stuff came up. I looked at the glass in my hand and saw that same crystal pattern, like snowflakes or stars and I tried not to think about shapes with sharp points. Doctor Dalton came in then looking solemn. I don't know who called him. A plain clothes person went up to him and they discussed something quietly. The uniforms were standing around everywhere and I couldn't understand why there were so many of them. Police inside the house. Police outside the house. Flashing lights and an ambulance waiting to take away Grandma's body. When the doctor had finished talking with the detective my mum asked him something.

"It's out of my hands. There'll have to be a post mortem," he said. "I'm sure you understand."

She nodded but didn't say anything.

Dad said, "I don't know what we should no next. A death in the house? Do we need to inform the registrar?"

"I'm afraid that will have to wait until after the post mortem," Doctor Dalton said. "And if there's need for an inquest into Mrs Carter's death we . . ."

"An inquest?" Dad said.

Doctor Dalton pulled a sad smile and said, "Under the circumstances."

"Can I see her now?" Mum said.

"No!" I shouted. "Don't do that, Mum. It's too horrible."

The detective interrupted. "The boy's right, Mrs Carter," he said. "Sorry. It's Rafe, isn't it? Rafe's right. We're waiting for CSI to finish in there."

Mum said, "CSI?"

"Crime Scene Investigator," he said. "Or Scene of Crime Officer if you prefer."

"Crime? What crime?" Mum said.

"Just procedure, Mrs Carter. That's all."

"You think someone came in the house and killed her?" Dad said.

"We don't think anything yet, Mr Carter," the detective said but I noticed he was looking at me when he said it.

I sat down at the table again with my back to him. I didn't want him staring at me. If it had been Richie instead of me who'd found Grandma he would have handled it better than me. He doesn't lose confidence like I do. I began to wish he'd stayed home or that I'd gone with him. I hadn't done anything wrong but the way that detective was watching me made me feel as though I had. Richie would have spoken up. He would have come across better than me. And he would have asked that girl's name. I folded my arms onto the table and put my head on them. I closed my eyes. I wanted it all to go away.

I must have dozed off for a while. I woke to movements in the hallway. I opened my eyes to find Mum weeping quietly and Dad holding her from behind as they watched the paramedics manoeuvre a stretcher through the door to an ambulance by the front gate. Some woman was calling out instructions to the men with the stretcher, telling them to be extra careful. I wondered why. Grandma was already dead. What did it matter how careful they were? Doctor Dalton was talking to my dad. He was telling him something about the family's right to attend the post mortem or to appoint a deputy. Then the detective asked us to accompany him to the station to help with their enquiry. I'd heard those words loads of times on the telly so it didn't bother me too much. As we moved along the hall I kept my eyes straight ahead. I didn't want to see the bathroom but I could tell there was a lot of activity going on in there. I guessed they were taking photos and stuff. We all still had our coats on so we stepped outside just in time to see the ambulance pulling away. Police cars were lined up all down the avenue. Mum got into one with a policewoman, Dad was taken into another and I had to ride alone in a third.

At the police station I didn't see where Mum and Dad went. I was taken into a small room. It was small and a bit dirty, not anything like you see on supercop TV shows where there's flash new equipment and decent furniture. This room can't have been used much. A layer of dust covered the chair they gave me and when they switched on the light it smelled rank once the bulb had heated up. I asked where my parents were and was told they were answering questions in another room. I wondered if that one was just as dusty. The grey-faced detective sat opposite me across a small table. I supposed he was pissed off because his night had been ruined. He needed a shave. His face was turning greyer with stubble.

"I'm Detective Inspector Peachey," he said. I had to stop myself from sniggering. *Peachey*? I could hardly look at him. I kept imagining a round furry fruit with his features stuck on the front of it like those Mr Potato Head toys we had when we were little. I hoped he hadn't noticed my reaction. "Where's your brother?" he asked me.

"In London."

"Where exactly?"

Peachey. I couldn't get it out of my head. "I don't know."

"You must have some idea."

"I don't. He's with friends."

"Which friends?"

"From university." *Peachey*. Why couldn't I stop? It wasn't that funny. None of it was funny. Why did I want to laugh?

"You don't know your brother's friends? I thought you were twins."

"We are. But we have different friends. I don't know where they live. They might be on his email contacts."

Peachey nodded at a uniform who left the room and returned almost immediately to whisper something in the peach's ear.

"Do you have the same contacts?"

Wasn't he listening to me? Why would I have Richie's email contacts? "No," I said. "Why do you keep asking me about my brother?"

Peachey didn't answer my question. "You'd been arguing at Christmas."

"Me and Richie? No. No way."

"You and your family. Arguing with your grandmother." I wondered how he knew that, then I guessed he'd already got it from my parents. "You were arguing on Christmas Day."

"Yes."

"What about?"

"Not much. Grandma wanted to do things differently. That's all."

"But you left the house?"

"Yes."

"So it was a heated argument?"

"I was angry, yes." I heard noises from the corridor and the door opened. A policewoman was with my parents.

"Sir?" the woman said.

"Okay. Bring them in."

"Rafe, are you all right?" Mum said.

Peachey said, "Please, no interruptions."

"I think that's a perfectly reasonable question to ask our son," Dad said.

The peach said, "Yes, indeed Mr Carter. But without interruptions we'll get through here a lot quicker. Please take a seat."

The policewoman showed my parents to some chairs at the back of the room. Mum wiped hers with her scarf. The peach looked at me again.

"Why were you angry with your grandmother?"

"Because she was bossing everybody about."

"Did she often do that?"

"Yes."

"And now she's dead."

I felt my face flush. "I was angry with my dad as well but he isn't dead. Am I being accused? Dad?" I swivelled around to look at my parents and Dad stood up.

"Sit down, Mr Carter. I must ask you to trust my line of questioning."

Peachey sounded bored. Maybe he was just tired.

"Look, all I did was find her," I said.

"No need to get upset, son," Peachey said. "We only want to get to the bottom of what happened."

"I don't know what happened. I was just the first one to come home."

The peach scratched behind his ear. *Fruit flies*, I thought. *Fruit flies on a peach that's gone bad. An old peach with grey mould sprouting out of it.*

"Were there any more arguments after the one on Christmas Day?"

"Not that I know of."

"But your grandmother was still being bossy?"

"Yes. She was a pain, if you must know. She always wants her own way."

"Tell me about when you were getting ready to go out earlier tonight."

"I don't know what you mean."

"You wanted to leave early. You had a minibus to catch. Which minibus was that, Rafe?"

I gulped and I felt my face flush again. Now I'd been caught in a lie. I thought, *Oh, shit. This isn't going to make me look any better.* "There wasn't a minibus. I made it up."

"Why would you do that?"

I puffed out my cheeks and knew I'd have to tell the truth. What a sad bastard they'd think me. "To make it sound as though I had somewhere to go," I said.

"Oh, Rafe," Mum said softly. "You could have come with us."

The door opened again and another police officer came in to whisper in the peach's ear. Detective Inspector Peachey stood up and nodded his head. He smiled at me and at Mum and Dad and said, "That's all for now. Thank you for helping with our enquiries."

I said, "We can go home?"

"An officer will accompany you," he said. "Unfortunately we've been unable to complete all our investigations at the house. Holidays, you know. People we can't get hold of. Is there anywhere you can stay for the rest of today? You'll be able to collect a change of clothes and other personal items. The bathroom is off limits, however."

I wouldn't want to go in there anyway, I thought.

We were driven back home and allowed to go to our rooms to collect clothes. I felt suddenly cold and I'd started shivering. I stuffed as much as I could into my backpack but I didn't have another pair of jeans. There was tape across the doorway into the bathroom. I didn't look at it. Dad made a call to a Roadside Inn, the only place he thought might still have someone on duty at this time on New Year's Day, and managed to book us two rooms. I left Richie a text and a message on his voicemail to get back to me urgently but he must have had his phone switched off.

46

Listen. Wendy was so relieved when the police allowed Rafe to leave Compton and go back to his studies she collapsed onto a chair and cried. They had no further need to ask him questions and they told her they'd also sent officers from a force local to the university to check that Richie's whereabouts on New Year's Eve could be reliably accounted for.

But the house was still in turmoil. A special laboratory team returned to take even more photographs in the bathroom. They had some sophisticated-looking equipment with them and they measured everything including the exact size of the door handle and its height from the floor. They recorded the distance between the door handle and the hand basin. They recorded the height of the hand basin, the height of the toilet. They ran the shower very hot to see how quickly the room filled with steam with the window closed and tested the floor tiles. They left the bathroom door ajar, opened the kitchen door and opened and closed the front door. Then they repeated the exercise with the kitchen door closed and again with the bedroom doors opened and closed.

"Why is all this detail important?" Wendy asked from where she stood watching in the hall.

"It could be very important in determining exactly what happened," one of the team replied but would say no more. Rob and Wendy had to use a neighbour's toilet for the day. Rob hated having to do that.

"It's embarrassing," he said. "I feel like the whole neighbourhood is watching."

"It's only natural to be curious," Wendy said but Rob stayed in a filthy mood throughout the day.

The boys were clear from suspicion and that was all that mattered to Wendy. In her heart she knew neither had contributed in any way to their grandmother's death. That was unthinkable. The police detective who'd pursued that line of questioning had got it completely wrong. All the same it was one less thing to worry about.

Doctor Seamus Dalton attended the post mortem examination acting as the Carter's deputy. Wendy didn't really want to hear anything about it. She simply wanted it all to be over and done with as soon as possible. The very words post mortem made her feel sick. Her life had gone from bad to worse and just when she'd thought things couldn't possibly get any worse, they had. She couldn't eat and, for the most part, she couldn't sleep either. She was afraid to sleep. She hadn't witnessed the horror of Jenny's body like poor Rafe had, and she had no intentions of viewing her mother when the time came for the funeral, but her thoughts were full of wild imaginings and when she closed her eyes there were pale grey ghosts coming at her from frightening corners of dark, evil-smelling forests. There were no gentle whisperings from her handsome Sandman. It seemed he had deserted her forever. From the deepest corners of her thoughts there was only the sound of loud and cruel laughter.

Dalton came to the house during the evening after the post mortem concluded.

"Come in. Come in," Rob greeted him at the door.

"Will this winter ever end?" Dalton said, stepping inside and wiping his feet. His face was white but the skin on his nose was turning purple like his hair.

Wendy came into the hall. "A hot drink, Doctor?" she said.

"Well now," he said. "If you have some I wouldn't say no to some hot chocolate."

They took their drinks into the sitting room and talked of the weather and the state of the roads and how residents of small market towns like Compton missed out on public expenditure to care for such things when there was a large metropolitan district on their doorstep. When Dalton had finished his drink he leaned back in his chair and looked directly at Wendy.

"Thank you," he said. "That was exactly what the doctor ordered."

Wendy managed a weak smile and said, "I'm ready."

Dalton laid his hands flat on his knees and leaned towards her. His eyes were soft and kind and for a moment she could imagine her father might have looked at her like that.

"It would have been over very quickly, my dear."

Wendy brought a hand to her chest and her eyes filled with tears.

"Even though there was so much blood?" Rob asked.

Wendy glowered at him. "Rob. Must you?"

"I can't discuss details of how it happened, Mr Carter," Dalton said. "That's for the inquest to decide."

Wendy looked puzzled. "So what was the post mortem for?"

"To establish, if possible, the cause of death."

Rob said, "And that has been possible?"

"It would appear so."

"And?"

Dalton cleared his throat. "Mrs Carter, it would seem that your mother died from a cerebral embolism."

"I don't understand what that is."

"To put it plainly, Mrs Carter, an embolism is a bubble or bubbles of air which restrict the flow of blood. In this case the flow of blood in the venous system. In the veins. Death would have been almost instantaneous, say within two minutes of the original trauma."

"You mean the cut from the piece of glass," Rob said.

Wendy closed her eyes against his crassness but opened them again for fear of images of blood and the cold stare of her mother's cruel eyes. Dalton stood and made to take his leave.

"I understand we'll be able to go ahead with the inquest formalities quite quickly," he said, "which is a blessing. Sometimes the wait can go on for months, even years in some cases. There are some benefits from living in a quiet, rural spot like ours, it would seem. Well, Mrs Carter, we can now release the death certificate and the funeral can take place. Families always say they can't have closure until all of that is out of the way."

He stepped toward the door then turned back. "You do realise that both yourselves and your son will be requested to attend the final hearing?"

"Yes," Rob said. "We've been given some literature on what to expect. An outline of procedures."

"Good. Well, that's it then. Once again may I say how vey sorry I am for your tragic loss, Mrs Carter."

Rob saw him to the door. Wendy could hear what they were saying. "Your wife is under a great deal of strain, Mr Carter. It seems to me she has lost weight since last I saw her. Don't hesitate to make an appointment if there's anything I can do."

"Be careful of the step at the gate," Rob called after him. "It's probably frozen over again."

Rob came back into the living room to face Wendy's tight expression.

"What have I done wrong now?" he said.

"If you don't know there's not much point in me telling you," she said. "You wouldn't understand. There's a novelty, eh, Rob? *You* not understanding *me*."

47

Joan

Norma and me went to the funeral service over at the Crematorium. As a mark of respect for Wendy we closed the shop for the day. Norma was wearing her full length navy blue.

"Do you think this'll be all right?" she asked me. "I haven't got a black coat."

"Neither have I," I said. "We'll have to do, Norma." I buttoned up my own brown coat and tucked a black scarf at the neck. "It's more important to keep warm today."

I've never liked that Crematorium place. It doesn't look right to me. There's no effort been put into making it formal, serious enough for the occasion. It could be a branch library or a doctor's surgery. It's too modern. You go into a porch and it's like stepping into reception at a primary school. Then, through these glass doors into a room full of plain wooden benches just as if you'd turned up for a school assembly. No. It's not solemn enough for me. It's not that I think everybody should be weeping and wailing but I do feel there ought to be something grand, something larger than life about a funeral. I think people need to sense a kind of majesty to make them remember this is where we'll all end up one day. Not on a trolley in a school hall. It doesn't hit the right note.

Oh, it was cold. Bitter. Everybody had on scarves and hats and gloves. We went to the back, Norma and me and watched people as they came in. There was a group from that Compton Women's League and I recognised the coat one of them was wearing. I bet her fancy friends didn't know where she'd got it from.

I had a good look at Wendy's sons when they came in. It was the first time I'd seen them up close. Good looking boys, both of them, but the fair one wears some strange clothes. He looked like a Romany. They walked behind the coffin, each holding a single rose. I thought that was a nice touch but to tell the truth neither of them looked upset. So that was it. Not a big crowd. A bit sad, really.

I thought there might have been somebody from the newspapers. You know, after all that fuss and palaver you'd have thought they'd want to write the end of the story, so to speak. That's what newspapers do though, isn't it? They build people up so they can knock them back down again. I suppose they must have thought Wendy's mother's story was disappointing. They'd never got the story they wanted out of her, the one that gave the world the answers to her cure. Maybe it was an embarrassment that they'd built up a false miracle. Either that, or they thought Jenny Carter wasn't worth the trouble. Well, she did a good job of that herself, if you ask me. Posing and prancing around like she was a somebody. If she'd been a nicer person maybe they would have had more sympathy.

I can't say I ever knew her well. She wasn't from Compton originally so I never knew her family but I think she was a Farmer or Falmer before she married Gordon Carter. Now Gordon, there was a lovely man. Born and bred in Compton, he was, and the nicest man you could ever wish to meet. When Wendy first told me she'd lost her father when she was a girl I didn't realise she was Gordon's daughter. Then, once I fitted it all together, I could see the likeness.

Oh, all the girls used to have a soft spot for Gordon Carter. There were a few broken hearts when he turned up with Jenny on his arm. He met her at the cinema somewhere, you know. Yes. Ice cream girl, that's all she was. Stood at the front of the cinema with a tray strapped round her neck and they used to put spotlights on her during the interval between films. You got two films in those days and you could sit there all day if you wanted to and watch them round again. I never saw her at her work but I can imagine what she looked like. I bet she just loved it when they turned the lights on her. She wore her hair done up like Diana Dors, you know what I mean? Bleached to high heaven, backcombed on top and curled under onto her shoulders. She must have thought she was a somebody even then.

She didn't want to mix. I remember coming across them a time or two just after they were married and you couldn't have a proper conversation with her. You'd just get a yes or a no out of her. She'd hang onto his arm as if she couldn't stand up by herself and drape herself all over him. She'd have this bored face on her and never quite looked at you properly. Her eyes would be going here, there and everywhere, looking round to see who else was about. She always gave the impression they had somewhere more important to be, other more important people to be with. Then she'd pull on his arm some more and lead him away. I don't know why Gordon let her boss him about like that. He was just too nice.

I think Wendy inherited his quiet nature. You know, the shyness, the lack of confidence. In the shop she liked to hear me talk about her father in his younger days.

Go on Joan, she'd say. Tell me about when Dad used to give all the little kids a ride on the back of his motorbike.

"He was just a teenager, my lovely," I'd say, "and he used to run errands for the old folk round the new estate. Fetch a paper or go to the post office, that sort of thing. Then, as soon as he got his first paid job he saved up for the bike. He said he'd be able to get about faster."

"And fit in more errands," Wendy would add just like a child who's familiar with a bedtime story.

"That's right, my lovely. He was a very special young man. We got used to seeing him riding up and down. There goes Gordon, we'd say. Then all the little kids started lining up and asking for a ride. 'Course it wouldn't be allowed now not without crash helmets and all but it was different then. Your dad was so careful. He only took them up to the park and back, nice and slow. Everybody loved your dad, Wendy."

She loved to hear me talk like that. Her face would go all dreamy and, to be honest, it gave me pleasure to see her looking happy. 'Course, things changed after her mother died. After the funeral she told me she was thinking of looking for a new job. I said it would do her good.

"A change is as good as a rest, Wendy," I said. "There's a lot of truth in those old sayings." She didn't tell me where she was applying.

"I'll tell you when and if," she said. "I don't want to tempt fate." There, another old saying. You can't get away from them. Sometimes nothing else will do. They just fit the bill. I think it's a good thing to hang onto some of the old ways. Not all change is for the good, if you ask me. The trick is in knowing which is which. We all have to decide for ourselves.

Wendy had a lot of deciding to do in the weeks after Jenny's death. She didn't look well, but oh, the expression on her face when I told her about the old days. You'd think she'd been touched by an angel. She fairly glowed. She never asked any questions about her mother, though. I supposed it was still a touchy subject. It takes a long time to get over bereavement, especially one like that.

48

Rafe

I read through all the stuff about what happens at an inquest. Most of it's online, anyway, so I knew that in March I'd most likely be called to say what I knew. I learned that coroners don't have to be medical experts. A lot of them have degrees in law or criminology. They act independently. They're not part of the police or the government. They're paid for by the local authority. It's not the same as giving evidence in a criminal court because an inquest is not a trial. That was one of the first things the coroner said at the opening of the hearing. After all the scraping of chairs and sounds of people shuffling into their places, she looked around at everybody and began.

"We're not here to apportion blame," she said, "but merely to establish the facts. If it becomes apparent that there is, indeed, any element of blameful negligence or deliberate misdemeanour, it will become a matter for the police. At this stage, I remind you, nobody is on trial. I have witness statements taken at the time of the death and I may call upon those witnesses for further questioning."

I looked over at Mum who was sitting on the other side of Dad. Her face was pale as the moon and there were dark circles under her eyes. I looked away quickly. I didn't like to see her looking so ill. I glanced around and saw Peachey. He was freshly shaved. There was no grey fuzz on his face like the last time I'd seen him. He didn't acknowledge me. I saw Dr Dalton and he nodded and smiled. Behind us was a kind of a public gallery. It was nearly full. A lot of the people there looked like students. I guessed medical students. The room was tidy, like a school classroom after the cleaners have been in and before the kids mess it up again. I could smell the same kind of furniture polish Mum uses at home, a sort of honey smell.

The coroner shuffled some papers and then asked for the author of the report she was looking at. There was a witness stand like the ones you see at a trial and even though the coroner had only just explained about the purpose of an inquest, it still felt very formal to me. I felt my anxiety level shoot up a few notches as the coroner began by asking the first witness to verify her identity.

"You are the pathologist who carried out the post mortem?"

"Yes, Madam."

I recognised the woman. She was the one who'd wanted the stretcher bearers to be extra careful on the night Grandma died.

"Tell me, Doctor Owen, is it usual procedure to first X-Ray a cadaver before any other examination takes place?"

"No, Madam. It isn't."

"Why did you feel it necessary in this case?"

Doctor Owen launched into a detailed explanation and I couldn't keep track of most of the technical stuff. Mum and Dad both looked mystified, too. It was something to do with how fast Grandma had died. It wasn't pleasant listening to the gory details and I saw Mum put down her head as if she was looking at her knees. Grandma had fallen backwards into the shower with one side of her face under the hot water. The water was hot enough to blister her skin, therefore the pathologist made an early assumption that Grandma was already dead when she fell, otherwise she would have attempted to move away from the near scalding water. I didn't know skin could blister if you were already dead.

The coroner said, "You suspected a particular cause of death?"

Doctor Owen said, "I did, Ma'am."

"An air embolism?"

"That's correct. We X-Rayed with the piece of glass intact to prevent release."

"And your suspicions were confirmed?"

"Yes, Ma'am. Cerebral embolism."

"You were able to ascertain the exact location?"

'Yes. Once air enters the central venous circulation the lower specific weight of air bubbles as compared to blood will cause bubbles to rise to cranial in a patient positioned upright, provided the air bubbles move at a velocity greater than that of the opposing blood flow in the vein. The deceased was in an upright position when the injury occurred."

"Thank you. We will return to the subject of the deceased's position. How did air enter the venous circulation?"

"The piece of glass was lodged in the throat and had cut into the internal jugular vein. Gas will travel retrograde via the internal jugular vein to the cerebral circulation."

"Am I correct in thinking that an injury to the jugular vein such as in this case in itself would have resulted in death if not attended?"

"Most likely, Ma'am."

"But in this case death occurred before loss of blood became the reason?"

"That's correct."

The coroner shuffled more papers. The room was eerily quiet. I noticed some students up in the gallery taking handwritten notes. The coroner began again.

"I have here the report concerning forensic evidence gathered from fragments of glass recovered from the scene. Three sets of fingerprints have been identified. Elucidate, please."

"As you know, Ma'am, I did not personally conduct all the forensic examinations at the scene nor of items recovered from there, such as the fragments of glass. These examinations were, however, conducted at our laboratory which I represent."

"Indeed."

"The three sets of fingerprints are identified as those belonging to the deceased, Mrs Jenny Carter, her daughter, Mrs Wendy Carter and her son-in-law, Mr Robert Carter."

"Thank you. Would you take a seat? I have further questions for you later, Doctor, but at the moment I'd like to speak to Mr Robert Carter." Dad stood up. His face and neck were flushed. "Will you come to the witness stand, Mr Carter?"

I watched my dad walk to the front, step up to the witness stand and turn to face us all. I felt nervous for him but I don't know why. Yes, I do. It was the way he walked. He usually has a long stride and he often holds his hands behind his back as if he's at work, pacing up and down a classroom. In the courtroom his hands hung limp at his sides and he took small, unsteady steps like an old man.

"Robert Carter?" the coroner said.

"Yes, your honour."

I cringed for him. He hadn't remembered how to address her.

"You may call me Ma'am," she said. "Tell me, Mr Carter, how your fingerprints came to be on the glass your mother-in-law was using."

Dad began to speak but his voice cracked and he had to cough. My stomach flipped. He must have been feeling really uncomfortable. He was used to speaking all day at college but up there in front of everybody in the courtroom his nerves had got the better of him. I don't ever remember seeing my father nervous before.

"I can't be sure, Ma'am," he said, "but I think it might be because I was the one who made Jenny's drink and gave it to her."

The coroner reached to her side and picked up a cut glass whisky tumbler similar to the ones we have at home. A court aide moved it closer to Dad on the witness stand.

"Would you pick up this glass, Mr Carter, and hand it out to me in your usual way."

Dad did as she asked. He picked it up then he held it out towards the coroner as if he was offering her a drink. I took a quick look around the room. Everybody was staring at my father. What exactly were they looking at? He was only holding a glass. What could be so interesting?

"Thank you, Mr Carter," the coroner said. She looked at the pathologist and said, "A clear indication, I would suggest, of the clear imprints found around the base of the glass. Mr Carter has demonstrated his way of cupping a glass like this in the palm of his hand, his fingers coming up around the base leaving clear imprints at the lowest part of the sides where the crystal is cut into a pattern." She turned again to my father. "After you had given your mother-in-law her drink you did not touch the glass again?"

"No, Ma'am. I went outside to start the car."

The coroner lifted her head from her papers and looked straight at him. 'Tell me about the bad feeling in the house."

"Ma'am?"

"Your mother-in-law was causing arguments."

I thought, *Peachey made a big deal out of this as well*.

"Yes," Dad said. "There were frequent arguments. I'm not sure who caused them."

"What did you argue about with her?"

"Not much, really. Most of the bad feeling as you call it was between my mother-in-law and my wife. Jenny could be a touch on the arrogant side and liked to be in control. She insisted on taking over at Christmas. That upset my wife. Wendy was looking forward to cooking for the boys."

"Yes. I see. Thank you, Mr Carter. That will be all."

She waited until Dad had regained his place before she spoke again.

"Rafe Carter? There you are, young man. Come to the stand, please."

I gulped. My courage sank somewhere below my knees so when I stood up my legs felt unsteady. I wobbled my way to the witness stand. The coroner looked at me over the top of her reading glasses.

"Families do sometimes fall out at Christmas, Rafe," she said and completely surprised me. I was expecting a Peachey style interrogation but her tone of voice was warm and friendly. It threw me. Her whole demeanour was full of understanding. "It must have been a terrible shock to come home and discover what you found. You did all the right things, Rafe. You didn't touch anything and you called for help."

I felt like a little kid. I just nodded.

She said, "I have only one question for you."

"Yes, Ma'am?"

"Will you return to your studies, try to forget about the horror of these past months and get a good degree?"

"I hope so, Ma'am."

"We hope so too. Thank you. You may get down."

I went back to my seat feeling puzzled. What had she got me up for in the first place? She called out my mother next. Mum was so pale she looked as if she might faint. The coroner established Mum's identity the same way she'd done with me and Dad then began with the questioning.

"Mrs Carter," she said, "you accompanied your mother to see your family doctor in February of last year. Is that correct?"

"I think it was February, yes," Mum said.

"What were your concerns at that time?"

"She seemed to be forgetting things. And losing things. She got confused."

"So much so that it was decided she needed residential care."

"Yes."

"Were you surprised when she recovered enough to return home?"

"Kind of. That's a bit of a yes and no answer."

"In what way?"

"Well, on the one hand we'd been told she had dementia and I didn't think people ever recovered from that."

"And on the other?"

"She'd always had her ups and downs, Madam. I think she got depressed sometimes and then when it passed she'd be well and happy again."

"Did she ever seek medical help for her depression?"

"No. She wouldn't go see anybody about it."

"Why was that?"

"She didn't want anyone to think she was, you know, not right in the head."

The coroner did a lot of writing then and the whole courtroom waited. It was so quiet I was scared everybody would hear my stomach rumbling. It always does that when I'm nervous. In the public gallery people were still taking notes too.

"Mrs Carter, you told Detective Inspector Peachey that you had argued with your mother on New Year's Eve before you went out."

"That's right," Mum answered. "I wish I hadn't argued with her. I should have ignored her the way I'm used to but she went on and on. I shouted at her and went out and that was the last time I spoke to her."

"Where did this argument take place?"

"In the hall."

"You were both standing in the hall?"

"No. I was in the hall but my mother was standing in the bathroom doorway."

The coroner put down her pen and smiled at Mum. Her eyes were kind like they'd been when she was talking to me.

"You mustn't blame yourself, Mrs Carter," she said. "The argument with your mother had no bearing on her death."

"Thank you," Mum said. She looked grateful and relieved.

"Tell me," the coroner continued, "how it is that your own fingerprints were found on your mother's glass?"

"It must be because I picked it up with the others and put them by the sink for washing up later."

"But your mother took hers back again."

"Yes. She poured herself another drink."

"A large gin?"

"Yes."

The coroner made a note and pulled out a report from her pile. It looked as if she was checking what Mum had said with something written on the paper. I saw her nod her head and look across at Doctor Owen. The doctor nodded too.

"One more question, Mrs Carter. Why was the shower so hot?"

"Oh, that," Mum said. "That was typical of mother. She complained we never had the shower set hot enough. She always turned the dial right up. She'd let it run until the bathroom was really steamy. I suppose she'd turn it down again just before she got in. She didn't seem to care it was a waste."

No, I thought. *Grandma didn't really care about a lot of things except herself.*

The coroner said, "The bathroom would become full of steam?"

"That's right. You couldn't see your face in the mirror. It made the floor a bit slippery as well. I bought some non-slip mats to put down."

"Your mother understood the reason for using the bathroom mats?"

"Yes, but I kept reminding her. You know, just in case she forgot."

"Thank you, Mrs Carter. You may return to your seat."

I didn't understand why the coroner wanted to go into all these details. It seemed to me as if the whole thing was going nowhere. I was trying to keep up with the different aspects of investigation but I couldn't put them together in any way that made sense.

49

Margaret

We had a wonderful time at Barleycroft over the festive season. I can honestly say it was one of the best Christmases I've ever had. Hard overnight frosts turned the gardens and surrounding countryside into picture postcards in the mornings. Trees looked like a set for Swan Lake. The hedgerows were like tunnels of ice. I loved the peace and tranquility of my early morning walks. I'd wrap up warm and put on a pair of walking boots I've had for years and go for a wander. I'm lucky to be still reasonably sturdy. Many of my new friends here wouldn't dare to go walking alone in winter conditions for fear of falling. One hears such dreadful stories of an elderly person taking a fall and that's the last time they leave the house. Worse than that, sometimes complications set in and that's the end of them. I don't want to miss one moment of good health at my age. I want to make the most of it, pack as much into my life as I can, while I can. I supposed that's how Anthony was feeling, too.

I didn't bother with decorations in my own small house. There seemed little point when there were so many beautiful decorations in the communal rooms and across the square in the row of shops. A group of us helped take them down and box them after the New Year celebrations were over and I popped in some things of my own for next year's display.

"Are you sure you won't want these?'" Brenda said, holding up a string of fairy lights.

"Quite sure. If I decide to trim the house next year I'll treat myself to some new ones."

"Good idea," she said and wrapped them in old newspaper. I often invited Brenda to join me on my early morning walks but she always declined.

"Motion is lotion," I'd say to her. "We've got to keep the old joints oiled, you know."

"It's not the walking, Margaret," she'd say. "It's the freezing temperatures I object to. Wait till spring and I'll come with you then."

One morning after my walk I called in to our little coffee shop across the square. It's a cosy wee place with just enough space for a few tables and chairs. The woman who runs it, Janice, is so pleasant. I know it might not make sense going out to pay for a coffee when you could just as easily make one at home yourself but I like to support our on-site amenities. Besides, it's an opportunity to meet up with others and get to know people better. I had a frothy hot chocolate and decided to order a cooked breakfast. I was the only customer and ate alone until Brenda appeared.

"I could smell that bacon from my place," she said as she came in. "Put some on for me will you, Janice?"

Brenda sat to join me and when she took off her gloves her fingers were blue.

"Too cold for me this morning, Margaret," she said. "How about you?"

"I've already been out," I said. "You'll be coming with me soon, I think. I'm sure we've seen the worst of winter now. I can feel spring in the air."

"Now that's good news. I've had enough of this."

"I always think spring is such a joyful time of year, don't you? Makes you want to do things. Go places."

Brenda said, "Where do you want to go?"

"I don't know yet. I haven't thought about it." I couldn't, however, stop a fleeting thought about India and whether Anthony had finally enjoyed travelling to see foreign sights. I'd hoped we would have been able to maintain contact with one another. I found it difficult that he didn't seem to feel the same need. Whereas I spent hours thinking about how he was getting on, he hadn't shown similar interest in me. I hadn't heard anything from him since his trip and didn't like to put Marcus and Sarah in a spot by asking them about him.

Janice arrived with Brenda's breakfast. "I'm off soon," she said. "Tenerife. We've got a timeshare. Can't wait."

Brenda swallowed a quick mouthful of her bacon sandwich and said, "Does that mean the coffee shop will close?"

"No," Janice said. "I'm bringing somebody in to take over while I'm gone. If it works out there may be a permanent job for her. Part-time to begin with. You know how busy we can get through the summer, Brenda."

More people came in and Janice went off to serve them.

"Do you fancy riding into town this afternoon on the minibus, Margaret?" Brenda said. "Now you've mentioned spring I'd like to buy a few packets of seeds for my window boxes."

"Yes," I said. "I'd like that."

The weeks passed and still I heard nothing from Anthony. Whenever I telephoned he had the answer machine switched on and never returned the messages I left. I wrote to him. I kept my letter friendly and enquired about his health and how much he'd enjoyed India. Still, he didn't answer. Neither of us ever got interested in computers and emails so there was nothing more I could do. I called Sarah.

"I don't like putting you in a difficult position, Sarah," I said, "but have you heard from Anthony? I'm wondering if he's well. I haven't spoken to him in such a long time."

"No. We haven't heard from him, either," she said.

"I'm worried about him. He might be ill. He might have come back from India with some dreadful tropical disease."

"I'm sure it's nothing like that," she said. "Would you like me to drive you over there?"

"No, no. Thank you, my dear. I don't want to do that. I could call one of my former neighbours. Yes, that's what I'll do. I don't know why I didn't think of it before. Don't give it another thought, Sarah. I'll let you know how it goes. How is Sophie? Doesn't she have her driving test soon?"

"Next Friday afternoon. Not a good time. The roads are always busy then. I think she's a bit nervous."

"Tell her I expect a visit from her. Once she has her own car she has no excuse."

I called one of my former neighbours. Not much ever escaped Mrs Livesey when we lived along the same avenue. She was the best choice. I didn't like letting her know my business but I was never going to see her again so it didn't matter if she went round gossiping. I was stunned by her answer. Anthony seemed to be very busy, she told me. She'd seen his car out and about much more than usual. He always looked very smart. And there'd been a lot of workmen at the house. Plumbers, she thought, judging by the name on the big white van parked outside.

"Maybe he discovered a leak somewhere," I said.

"Oh, no, dear. I don't think so.," she said. "They've been fitting new units in the kitchen. I saw all the old ones in a skip outside in the drive."

"Well, thank you, Mrs Livesey. Just as long as everything's all right. That's all I needed to know."

"No, it isn't," she argued. "I think you should know he's had a woman there as well. I've seen her driving the car, too."

I swallowed hard before I managed to respond. "Ah, that will be Maya. That's okay then. Thank you again. Goodbye."

I spent an unpleasant evening alone and had no appetite at all. I went to bed early and attempted to read a chapter of my book but my mind kept wandering and I realised I'd read the same sentence three times. I got up again and warmed some milk. That usually did the trick. I picked up the book and tried again.

Come along, Margaret, I ordered myself. *This won't do. You made your bed . . .*

I was glad of my turn in the grocery store next morning. The co-operative is a wonderful idea and should be more popular everywhere, especially during these times of financial difficulty. By managing and running the store ourselves as volunteers, we're able to keep prices down. So, on a limited range of products we can compete with some supermarket prices. For those last minute emergencies or if you don't need a full stock-up at home, you can fill the gaps on your shelves very conveniently. There's another system in place for when residents are ill. It works exceptionally well: we all help each other. What could be better? We're putting together a Barleycroft cookery file too. I know this will sound sexist but I'm from a generation where the man of the house very rarely learned how to cook for himself. A few of us wrote out some simple dishes and one of the caretakers printed them out on postcards and laminated them. We keep a stack on the counter and everybody is welcome to borrow them.

My predictions of an early spring proved optimistic. When I stepped outside to walk to my work I wished I hadn't forgotten gloves. Perhaps I'd only imagined the end of winter, conjured up what I wanted to see, as if my new life had to be perfect in every sense. I turned up the heaters in the shop and when I pulled up the blinds I could see dust rising and swirling above the heater grille where I'd disturbed it. Harsh winter rays highlighted dust and grime everywhere. Like looking in an illuminated mirror, all the blemishes were in sharp relief. I rolled up my sleeves and got stuck in.

Keeping busy is like medicine to me. If your hands are occupied you don't have too much time to worry about things. I believe you can worry yourself into an early grave. I swept and mopped the floor and then set about the window at the front. Then when that was finished I gave the toilet a thorough bleaching, and the sink. Gradually, in between serving customers and cleaning, I wore myself out and by closing time I was looking forward to a good hot shower and putting my feet up. So it was a complete shock to open the large brown envelope that had been delivered while I was out and read its contents.

Anthony wanted a divorce.

50

Rafe

After the coroner had spoken to me and Mum and Dad she called Dr Dalton next and repeated the ritual of the business of taking the witness stand.

"Am I correct in establishing that there is nothing in Mrs Jenny Carter's medical records which would support the notion that she suffered from some condition which may have contributed to her death?"

"Yes, Ma'am. You are correct," Doctor Dalton said.

"And yet she had been receiving treatment for symptoms of dementia. I have here the file from the Firs residential care home. Her behaviour was erratic, would you say?"

"Yes, Ma'am. I would."

"But she was prescribed no medication other than that administered while she was in care?"

"That is correct, Ma'am."

No, it's not, I thought. *What about the pills I saw her take? And the empty packet Mum found?* I wondered if I should stand up and shout it out but I didn't have the nerve.

"How would you account for the remarkable improvement in her health, Doctor Dalton? Such that she could return home to live normally even so far as speaking lucidly on broadcasted interviews?"

Dalton shook his head and said, "I have to admit to you, Ma'am, it is a puzzle. We are accustomed to seeing bouts of lucidity so that one might think the patient was in a period of remission, so to speak. But never to this extent."

"You are aware that as part of the post mortem a section of the deceased's brain was examined?"

"Yes. I was there."

"You are also aware that in a cross section of the brain of a person suffering from Alzheimer's disease there are unmistakable signs?"

"I am."

"How do you account for the fact that the deceased's brain showed no such indicators?"

I heard a gasp like a sharp breath and when I looked around I realised it had come from Mum. She had her hand over her mouth and her eyes were wide with surprise.

"It can only mean that Mrs Jenny Carter did not have Alzheimer's. It is possible, Ma'am, that she may have been suffering from some other neurological condition which was never diagnosed."

You could have heard the proverbial pin drop. It seemed the whole courtroom was stunned into silence.

"How could that be so, Doctor Dalton? One might be tempted to think there had been some negligence in this case?"

"Certainly not, Ma'am. If a patient neither presents with symptoms nor seeks medical advice how would anyone know?"

"Quite so," the coroner said. "Just as the deceased's daughter has already explained."

She stopped writing, addressed the court again and announced a break. My stomach was rumbling louder and I was glad to get up.

Mum and Dad and I left the building to get some fresh air and find somewhere to eat. We left the car behind the courthouse on Castle Street and set off on foot. We'd no idea which way to head as we didn't know Salisbury well. I switched on my phone as we walked and saw there was a message from Richie.

Howzit going, bro? he wrote.

Lunchtime, I answered. *let u know l8ter.*

We found a McDonald's not far from the courthouse. Dad and I had a full meal but Mum took only a hot drink.

"Please don't make a fuss," she said when Dad queried it. "I'll get something later at home when all this is behind us."

We had to be back by two pm and I began to feel nervous again as we approached the courthouse building. I wondered what else there could be for the coroner to consider. It seemed to me that all her questions so far didn't add up like a jigsaw with too many missing pieces.

All the lights were on when we went back inside. They were too bright and gave the place a sickly atmosphere. Everything looked faded. Some of the people who'd been in the gallery didn't come back. I could see spaces where before there'd been faces.

There was something different about the way the coroner looked when she came in. She was quicker in her stride like teachers when they're in a rush, eyes straight ahead, chin up. She carried fewer papers to her desk than she'd had with her at the morning session. It made me think we wouldn't be kept much longer. We took our places and the coroner recalled Dr Owen to the stand.

"I have considered your laboratory's report on the layout of the bathroom, Doctor Owen. Please explain how important it is to this case."

"Certainly, Ma'am." She went on to describe our bathroom. It was embarrassing listening to her outline how small it is. Mum used to say you couldn't swing a cat in it and then when I asked her to explain a dumb saying like that, she said that's how Grandma had described it when she first went to visit. "The door originally opened into the room as you would expect but at some point it was made to open the other way into the hall to create more space for bathroom fixtures."

"And this has relevance, Doctor Owen?"

"I believe so."

"Yes. Go on, please."

"We investigated several factors, Ma'am. Before Mrs Wendy Carter left the house the deceased was standing in the bathroom doorway. It was exceptionally windy during the early evening of December thirty-first. We have ascertained that the opening and closing of the house front door causes a draught through the house along the hall, especially when other doors and windows are open and the bathroom window is closed. In conditions like those on that date the strength of the gust blowing through the hall would have been enough to force the bathroom door to close."

"To close with some force?"

"Not necessarily with great force, Ma'am, but the door would have closed against a person standing there."

"Go on, please."

"The bathroom floor was very slippery. It's my belief that the floor tiles were not suitable for use in a bathroom. The glaze is the wrong kind for wet rooms. Fragments of glass had chipped into it and thus provided us with samples for testing. As we heard from the deceased's daughter earlier, there were suitable mats available but as you can see from photographic evidence, Ma'am, these were not in place."

The coroner assimilated this and thought for a while. I watched her pursing her lips. You could tell she was piecing things together.

"So, we have Mrs Jenny Carter standing on a slippery floor with a glass in her hand when the door moves into her."

"Correct."

"She lost her balance?"

"I believe so. Leaning backwards to avoid colliding with the door."

"Tell me about your findings with regard to the position of the door handle."

"Yes, Ma'am. You will see from our report the correlation between the height of the deceased and the height from the bathroom floor of the door handle."

The coroner looked at her papers and said, "The glass in her hand was broken by the handle swinging backwards against her."

"Yes. We can't be certain whether the glass was broken before she slipped or at the same time."

"She then stumbled further backwards into the room."

"Indeed, Ma'am. Against the hand basin. We found fragments of glass there."

They must have been covered in my vomit, I thought.

Doctor Owen continued. "With a shattered glass in her hand Mrs Jenny Carter stumbled backwards and caught her right elbow on the hand basin. This would have knocked her arm in an upwards direction toward her face, specifically towards her neck."

"So that she was still in an upright position when the glass penetrated?"

"Yes, Ma'am."

"The scenario begs the question why she did not attempt to remove it."

"Shock, perhaps. Breathing would have become an immediate problem. And, as a result of the amount of strong spirit she had consumed, as detailed in the autopsy report, Ma'am, her reactions would have been impaired."

Ten minutes later we were out of the courtroom. Dad drove us straight home. Nobody spoke in the car and when we got in I scooted past the door to the bathroom. I hated going in there. The first time I'd had to use the toilet it made me feel sick just to be in the place where I'd stood on Grandma's body. Even though there was no sign of what had happened, the memories of what I'd seen were too fresh. Dad had given the room a coat of paint to make it look different but it didn't help much. After everything we'd just heard in the courtroom the memories came back as clear as ever.

One more night in this house, I thought, *and then I'm out of here.* I had to get back to my studies. I wanted to. My extra winter holiday had been no fun at all. I couldn't wait to get back to university. I sat in the kitchen. My phone beeped.

Howzit goin bro?
Finished. Accidental death
How's Mum?
Okay, I think
See you tomorrow
Yeh

I put my elbow on the table and my chin in my hand and sat, staring out of the kitchen window. In the dim light outside the garden looked grey and gloomy. The house felt quiet and still like it was waiting for ordinary life to begin again. Mum came in and put the kettle on and the three of us had yet another cup of tea. We spent a lot of time glued to those kitchen chairs during the time after Grandma died. It was as if none of us could relax enough to sit in comfort. Hard facts seemed to call for hard seats and those interminable discussions were as endless as the cups of tea and snatched snack meals.

The inquest result ought to have been the end. It was a clear case of accidental death, the coroner said, but Mum seemed to think she was partly to blame.

"I'll never forgive myself, Rob," she said. "I shouldn't have argued with her."

"What were you arguing about?" Dad said.

"Rob, we've just been over all of this at the inquest. Going over it again won't change anything and it doesn't make me feel any better. It's not so long since there was something *you* didn't want raking over. You told me to stop asking questions about it. Remember?"

I didn't understand what Mum meant by that but I noticed Dad looked away from me when I caught his eye. He looked like a kid caught with his hand in the cookie jar.

"Nobody died," Dad said. "You can hardly compare. . ."

Mum jumped to her feet and started shouting.

"It's *my mother* who died. You're making it sound as though I don't care."

"All I'm saying is I find it difficult to understand that you can't remember what you were arguing about."

Mum threw her mug across the room and it smashed against the wall. Cold tea ran in streaks down the paintwork like rain on a car windscreen.

"And I find it difficult to understand a lot of things about you, Rob Carter," Mum screamed at him. She ran down the hall to their room. Dad started to go after her but I stopped him.

"Please don't, Dad. I think she needs to be by herself. Leave her alone for a while."

I fetched the dustpan to clear up the broken cup. Dad sat back down again and put his head in his hands. I tipped the smashed pieces in the bin and wiped at the wall with a cloth but I made it look worse. It looked streakier than before. Dad was still slumped over the table.

"Are you and Mum all right, Dad?" I said.

He puffed out through closed lips. "Not really, Rafe," he said. "We haven't been all right for years."

I sat down across from him. He looked really tired.

"Grandma was difficult right through Christmas. Wouldn't you say so?" I wanted him to agree, to pass some comment that he'd realised how she'd messed up Mum's life and how hard it must now be for Mum. I'd hate it if the last thing I ever did with my mother was argue with her.

Dad said, "Difficult?"

"Don't you think she grew very bossy?"

"I suppose so."

There was a long pause.

"Dad, if Grandma never had that disease what was the matter with her?"

He shook his head when he said, "We'll never know now, Rafe"

"Mum said she refused to go for the scan they booked for her. You know, after she came here to live. If she'd had that . . ."

"It's too late now, son."

"But something must have caused it. You know, the odd behaviour. Don't you want to know? Doesn't Mum?"

"Not now. Not after what's happened."

"Why didn't she buy a place of her own when she got better?" I said.

"I think she liked it here."

"Mum didn't like it."

"They would have got used to it. Got used to sharing," he said. "They would have been company for one another so I wouldn't have to feel . . ."

"Wouldn't have to feel what, Dad?"

He raised his chin and slapped his hands down on the table.

"Rafe, I've said enough. It's not for you to worry about."

"You can't leave it like that."

"I can and I must. Rafe, I'm going to have a word with your mother now. Would you be offended if I asked you to clear the decks? Give us a bit of privacy?"

I was glad to get out of the house. It was already growing dark and the temperature was dropping fast. I double-wrapped my scarf around my neck against the freeze and pulled on a beanie. The snow crunched under my shoes. Winter was lasting forever. I put my head down and speeded up. As I drew closer to town the roads were clear but the pavements sparkled with a new layer of frost. By the time I wandered into the pub on the high street my fingers were stiff with cold.

Happy hour was in full swing. *At least some people have got something to be happy about,* I thought. It was only five o' clock but there was a group playing pool and another lot fooling around by the dartboard. I walked to the long bar and ordered a beer.

"Would you get one for me as well?" a female voice whispered behind me. "No, don't look round yet. I'll pay for it. I'll wait round the corner by the cigarette machine."

Whoever she was she left her perfume behind her, a powdery smell, something like vanilla. It was a lot nicer than the polish in the courtroom. I bought another bottle of beer and went to find the owner of the voice. She was waiting by the cigarettes machine as she'd said. I did a double take. I couldn't believe it. It was *her*, the girl from New Year's Eve, the one with the amazing eyes. The one whose face had saved me from going crazy that night.

"Thank you," she said. "How much do I owe you?"

Her voice was soft and low-pitched. Some girls' voices make me shudder. They talk too loud in Bacardi-fuelled screeches. Hers was like cream.

"My treat," I said.

"No, really."

"Yes, really."

We took a table away from the bar. She slid along the bench seat under a window. She looked cute in a short skirt, thick tights and some kind of fluffy jacket with a hood. Her eyes were doing the sparkly thing that makes my insides tingle.

" I don't usually do this," she said.

"Do what?"

"Come into a bar by myself. In fact it's the first time ever I've done it but nobody's home yet and I forgot my key."

"And you were freezing."

"Right. And another thing is, they wouldn't serve me in here anyway. They know I'm not eighteen yet. That's why I slinked off out of the way of the barman."

"And got me to commit an offence for you."

"Yes. Sorry about that. But I could hardly sit here without a drink in front of me, could I?"

She looked even cuter when she smiled. Her eyes tilted upwards like a cat's.

"You could have ordered a coke," I said and did my best teasing grin.

"Can't stand the stuff." She treated me to another of those smiles and said, "I suppose we should introduce ourselves."

"My name's Rafe."

"Hello, Rafe. I'm Sophie."

51

Sarah

I answered the phone and knew immediately there was something wrong. Margaret's voice was flat. She sounded exhausted. She wasn't the same person as the enthusiastic woman who'd been delighted with her new life. There was no bounce in the way she spoke. I thought she might be ill.

"Have you had your flu injection this winter, Margaret?" I said. "Marcus can arrange it for you."

"No, I'm fine."

"You don't sound fine. Margaret, if you don't mind me saying, you sound tired." I tried to soften my message with a light-hearted quip. "Have you been partying too much?"

"No, no," she said. "I'd like to see you."

"I'll come straight away."

"No, dear. I mean I'd like to see you both."

"Would you like me to come and collect you?"

"No, thank you. I think it would be better if you both came here."

I knew something must be very wrong. My heart was in my mouth.

"Margaret, you're making me feel very worried. What's going on? What's happened?"

She wouldn't say. I decided to take matters into my own hands. "I'm coming for you. Don't try to put me off. I'll be there in twenty minutes."

I practically flew down the lane and over the hills. I dropped down into Barleycroft and took the first parking space available, ignoring the allocated house numbers. I hurried across the central courtyard to Margaret's bungalow. I knocked briefly and went straight in. Margaret was waiting indoors. She already had on her coat and was ready to go. She greeted me with a kiss and said,

"I'm glad you talked me into coming with you."

"Well, aren't you going to tell me?"

"I was going to wait until Marcus was with us but I suppose it wouldn't hurt . . ."

She took off her coat. "We'll have some tea," she said. "Would you like something to eat with it?"

I put down my car keys and took off my own coat.

"There's an envelope on the dining table, Sarah," she called from the kitchen. "It's in there."

I slid out a solicitor's letter. I gasped. My hand shook.

"I can't believe it," I said. "Oh, Margaret, what is he playing at?" I stared at the words. My hand continued to shake. Margaret came in with a tea tray and set it down.

"I think he's playing at house, or cowboys and Indians. Something like that."

"He can't be serious."

"I'm afraid he is. Once he assumed I'd received this letter he started answering his phone."

"So you've talked to him about it?"

"Yes."

"Why? I mean, why does he feel he needs to do this?"

"Have some tea," she said.

"Margaret! What's going on?"

"He wants to get married."

I dropped the letter on the table and leaned against the back of Margaret's sofa.

"Oh, Margaret. You must be devastated."

"Not really, my dear. I've had time to think about it. I'll admit it was a shock at first." She handed me a cup and helped herself to a digestive. I picked up the letter and looked again at the date.

"Margaret, you've known about this for weeks."

"Yes," she said. "I've been thinking what to do about it."

I said, "I knew it must be something serious. You sounded not quite yourself on the phone."

"I'm a little under the weather, dear. That's all."

"I'm not surprised after news like that."

"There are worse things that could happen at my age. Listen, Sarah. I'm concerned about Marcus. Niall will take it all in his stride. He wouldn't even flinch. I'm sure he'll come to visit just as soon as he can get away, but Marcus? Well, you know he's always been the more sensitive one."

"His first concern will be for you," I said.

"It shouldn't be."

"I don't know what you mean."

She put down her cup and thought for a moment. "I'm not going to say any more just now, Sarah. I want Marcus to hear the rest of my concerns."

We finished our tea and I carried the tray to the kitchen. I washed and dried everything while Margaret gathered her handbag and coat again. She got into the car and looked straight ahead. I don't remember if she said anything as I drove home. I think I was too stunned. When we arrived at the cottage Sophie was already home from college. She came to meet us in the hall and kissed her grandmother.

"Hello, sweetheart," Margaret said. "You're home early."

"My English teacher is absent this afternoon," Sophie explained. "He's taken a few days off. There was a court hearing he had to attend."

"Oh, yes. I heard about that poor woman. Dreadful business."

"Sophie, will you take Grandma's coat, please?" I said.

We made ourselves comfortable by the fire in the living room. Sophie managed to be polite and stay with us for about ten minutes and then made an excuse about homework. I thought it more likely she would spend the unexpected time off chatting with friends on Facebook. I made no comment. I wanted to talk to Margaret about what was bothering her.

"Marcus may be late this evening," I said. "Wouldn't you like to tell me what's on your mind?"

"No, dear," she said. "I'd rather wait."

I couldn't persuade her. Conversation became difficult. I ran out of things to say. In the end, I switched on the television and we watched a little trash TV until Marcus arrived. I went to meet him at the door and took him into the kitchen.

"Marcus, your mother is here."

"Good," he said. "Is she staying for dinner?"

"I don't know. Maybe. Probably. I don't know."

"What's going on, Sarah?"

There was no point in beating about the bush. "It's your father, darling. He wants a divorce."

Marcus said, "Idiot."

"That's not all. He wants to marry Maya, the woman who . . ."

"Oh, for goodness sake," Marcus said. He slumped onto a chair. "Is mother very upset?"

"You'd better see for yourself. There's something else she's been waiting to tell you. She wouldn't tell me what it is."

Marcus got up and we joined Margaret in the living room. I switched off the television. Marcus sat next to his mother and took hold of her hand.

"Mother," he said, "Sarah has told me. You don't have to do what he wants any more."

"Oh, I know, dear. He has no grounds on which to divorce me. Well, other than the fact that I was the one to leave if he wants to make a case out of that. And he would have to wait how long? Two years for desertion? I know I can make him wait should I choose. I'm not the one committing adultery."

I saw Marcus flinch at the mention of adultery. Margaret saw him too.

"Marcus," she said, "Maya is only in her fifties. You don't suppose she'll be content to lead a sexless life. Although I don't know how your father is going to be able to . . ."

"Yes, well," Marcus interrupted. "I don't think we need go into that."

I touched her shoulder and said, "You know we're always here for you. Whatever you decide."

"Thank, you, Sarah," she said.

"So what is it you were thinking about?"

She took a moment then said, "It all boils down to money."

Marcus shook his head. "I'm not with you," he said.

Margaret shifted in her seat and turned to face him. She looked straight into his eyes.

"Darling Marcus," she said, "if I agree to this divorce it will be quicker and cheaper. That's something I think both your father and I would agree on."

"Mmm, yes. I still don't see . . ."

"It seems Anthony has good reason to want the divorce to go through quickly."

"I wouldn't call it good reason, Mother."

"He wants to marry his Maya. Now, there are two ways of looking at this. If I disagree that our marriage is irreconcilable I can make him wait for years before he can marry again. Agreed?"

"Agreed."

"That may turn out to be an expensive option both in the court and in terms of annoying him such that he wouldn't want to listen to reason."

"What reason?"

"Wait a minute, Marcus. Let me finish. If, on the other hand, I agree immediately I should be in a stronger position to make some conditions."

Marcus said, "Now you've really lost me, Mother. What conditions are you talking about?"

Margaret placed both hands on her lap and smoothed her skirt. She wore a determined expression.

"It's really quite simple," she said. "I want to make sure that you and Niall don't lose your inheritance."

"Mother, that's the last thing I'm worried about."

"Well, it shouldn't be. It should be the first. This woman, excuse me, this Maya is much younger than Anthony. When he dies she will inherit."

"Mother!"

"Under the law, dear, unless he wills the house and everything to you and your brother, to put it bluntly she will get the lot."

"Bluntly? You're not kidding. What on earth has made you think this way?"

"Because that's the way the law works, isn't it? And I know your father."

Marcus got up and began to pace about. I took the opportunity to add my thoughts.

"Are you saying you'll offer Anthony a quick divorce in return for sight of his will?"

"Exactly, my dear. But with further provisos. I want to make it impossible for Anthony to write his sons out of his will. What do you think of my plan?"

I hoped if ever I was faced with such things I could be half as magnificent as Margaret.

52

I continued to feel Wendy's pain. I knew she was close to collapse. She didn't realise I was still with her but I'm never far away from any of you.

Rafe went back to university and the house felt like a tomb. The clocks went forward and spring arrived again but Wendy could find no joy in it. Apart from the days she called in to see Joan and Norma in the charity shop the weeks dragged endlessly in dull routines of household chores. Day after day, mindless cooking and cleaning. And for what? So she could do it all again the next day? But it kept her occupied, kept her from thinking. There were too many vague ideas she couldn't allow to take shape: Sophie Harding, for one. Wendy hadn't had the energy to face the confrontation she'd planned. Since New Year she'd had little energy for anything that required organisation. She'd requested a different rota at the supermarket so she wouldn't have to work alongside the little witch. She'd asked if she could avoid working Saturdays but she didn't give the reason. Instead, she said she was finding it difficult to cope with the busiest times since her mother's death. Human resources had been sympathetic but adamant in their refusal. And Wendy had lost the will to fight. She gave in her notice and left. Sophie had won. She'd got away with it. Wendy tried to keep thoughts of nasty little Sophie at bay. She stuffed them into the forbidden thought box, now crammed to overflowing.

She laundered and ironed things that didn't need it and kept the house scrubbed. The door to Jenny's bedroom remained closed, the room untouched, but the rest of the house including the bathroom gleamed like a television advert. But who was going to notice? Nobody came. Who would want to after what had happened there? Even the boys didn't want to come home for Easter this year. Richie had made excuses but Rafe had come right out with it.

"I don't want to, Mum," he'd said. "You understand, don't you? It gives me the creeps."

She felt as though she'd lost him and that even in death her mother had beaten her again, was still controlling her and manipulating her family. Jenny had had the last word. Wendy could almost hear her mother's laughter echoing along the hall and in the boys' empty room.

And what makes you so special? Look, even your sons don't want to be with you.

She opened the door to the bedroom her mother had used and stood in the doorway. Nothing had been moved. Everything was just as it had been the night Jenny died: p*ersonality* pink curtains drawn against the window as if the room were still in mourning, her mother's vast collection of cosmetics and hair products on the dressing table, an obscene, expensive outlay. Selfish. She could still smell the perfume her mother wore, a violent purple concoction like a witch's brew. It irritated the back of her throat and made her want to sneeze. There it was on the dressing table still, the biggest bottle Jenny could find, sitting beside the GHDs and the smoothing lotions and the finishing serum and the age-defying creams and day creams and night creams and hand creams and eye creams.

She hurried to the kitchen and got a black dustbin liner. With one sweep of her arm she cleared jars and pots and tubes in a clatter of plastic and glass. Some thudded to the floor and rolled across the carpet. She left them there, treading over them and on them as she flung open the wardrobe door. She would need more bags. She ran for them. She fetched the whole roll and began to fill them with her mother's clothes, shoes, handbags, scarves. She pulled down the pink curtains and stuffed them in.

I don't care how much they're worth, she thought. *I want rid of them.*

She was still packing things away when Rob came home.

"I'm in here," she called out when she heard him.

He came and stood behind her. He had his hands on his hips and looked as if he was going to start criticising. She caught his questioning expression and said, "Don't you dare say anything, Rob Carter. This is long overdue."

"I was only going to say I'm glad you feel well enough to do that," he said and backed away.

She sat on the edge of her mother's bed and stared at the clutter she had created: piles of clothes and accessories, heaps of shoes and high-heeled boots. *Ridiculous.* Her head was spinning. Her life was a mangled mess just like the piles of trash around her.

The final insult had come in her mother's will. As Jenny's executor Rob had explained it to Wendy. All of Jenny's possessions, including the new car and all the money from the sale of her house had to be accounted for, Rob said. Expensive items of jewellery must also be taken into account so that he could come to a valuation of Jenny's estate. And when taxes were paid, the residue was to be put in trust for Rafe and Richie until they were thirty. *Thirty.* Jenny had left nothing to her daughter.

Nothing for all the years of putting up with her moods. Nothing for taking care of her when she was too depressed to get out of bed. Nothing to help out the boys when they need it most. Right now.

Wendy felt poisoned. The burst of energy she'd expended had exhausted her. Her shoulders slumped and she realised she couldn't finish what she'd started. She had lost everything: both of her parents, her marriage and now her sons. She'd lost her Sandman, too. He'd been the only thing that had kept her going. And it was obvious he was never going to come back.

Look at me, she thought. *Who would want to come back to this?*

The face in the dressing table mirror was so pale and thin it made the eyes sink deep into their sockets. The hair was lank and flat and the nose looked too big for the face. She was tired. So tired. She wanted to sleep so badly. It would be wonderful to fall asleep and not have to think about anything.

She got up and made her way to the kitchen closing the door on Jenny's room.

"You look worn out, Wendy," Rob said. "Look, I've made you an omelette. Try to eat some of it , will you?"

She sat and did as he asked but could manage no more than a couple of mouths full.

"Why don't you see Doctor Dalton? Would you like me to make an appointment for you?"

She nodded. Agreement used less energy. Rob touched her shoulder and she shrugged him away.

"I don't want to be touched," she said. "Please don't do that."

"You can't go on like this. You need to sleep."

"I can't sleep."

"Dalton will be able to give you something."

His words were like a spell. The dark clouds in her head dissolved. There was the simple answer. It was so easy. Sleep. An end to all her pain. It would be wonderful to sleep. Maybe forever. So, of course Wendy was nervous when she went to the surgery in April to ask for sleeping pills. Nobody knew what she was planning. A secret like that would make anybody feel nervous.

But Dalton wasn't there. She nearly ran away when she entered the doctor's office. She knew whose father she was looking at, asking him for help. And he sat there as if he knew nothing about what his treacherous daughter had done, the damage she'd caused. He looked over his glasses at her with that innocent look asking how she'd been coping, nodding his head and pulling his fake sad face.

My darlings, are we not all guilty of making the same kind of assumptions? How often do we see what we think we see and, certain of our facts, make judgements about other people? Haven't I already shown you how easy it is to build a wrong impression even when people are telling you their truth? Wendy didn't know that Marcus Harding was making similar judgements about her. All she could see was another tormentor.

How could he pretend to care whether she was ill or not? How could he sit there nodding and commiserating, making his face look as if he was really paying attention to her troubles? What a family, she thought. They must all be alike. Every single one of them. Not to be trusted. Cheats and liars, the lot of them.

Doctor Harding's deceit fired Wendy's determination. A sudden burst of hot energy banished thoughts of sleeping. Indignation spurred her. On her way out, with the prescription in her hand, a new idea presented itself.

53

Joan

Wendy popped in to see us one Saturday afternoon. She brought in an extra big box of assorted cream cakes. I can't tell you how pleased I was that Wendy had picked herself up and was getting on with her life again. It was so lovely to see her on the mend compared with the way she'd looked at the funeral. She had a nice new haircut. She had on a lovely suit, a skirt and a matching jacket. In my day, we used to call them costumes. A suit was something a man wore. Well, anyway, it was very smart. I bet it cost a bob or two. I expect Wendy had come into a bit of an inheritance from her mother. And I wouldn't begrudge her one penny of it. Nobody deserved a little bit of good luck more than Wendy, I can tell you that for nothing.

"How are you getting on, my lovely?" I asked her.

"Really well, Joan," she said. "I got that job I applied for."

"Have you? Good for you," I said.

She said, "You were right, Joan. Giving up working wasn't the right thing to do. Not for me. It's no good having all that time to yourself to mull over everything that's happened. You need to be busy."

I didn't like to say I told you so, so I just congratulated her instead. I was about to ask Wendy to tell me more about her new job when Norma came in. She'd been up the bakery. We can't resist. We just can't resist. Norma put down her bag of vanilla slices next to Wendy's box. The counter was covered in cake.

"Oh, Wendy," Norma said. "It's lovely to see you. Oh, we do miss you."

"Are you sure it's me you miss or is it just the cream cakes? Is there one for me in that bag?"

We did laugh. We shared them out but we didn't get the chance to eat them right then because a woman came in.

Norma went in the back with the cakes to put them in our little fridge and put the kettle on. Wendy stood to one side while I turned my attention to the woman. She was about my age, I'd say, maybe a bit older. Very smart. Very smart indeed. I knew as soon as I saw her that she hadn't come in to buy. She put her fancy shopping bag on the counter and brought out a package wrapped in old newspaper and a bit of bubble wrap.

"Excuse me," she said. She had a nice voice. Quiet, like. Softly spoken. I could tell she wasn't from around these parts. A west country accent is always a west country accent. You never lose it. Well, it seemed to me she didn't have any sort of accent.

"I wonder if you'd like this for the shop? I don't want it any more," she said.

I waited until she'd finished unwrapping it and then I picked it up to look underneath. That's the first thing you do, you see.

"That's Sylvac, that is," I told her. Are you sure you want to get rid? It's collectable. Might be worth a bit."

"Yes, I'm sure," she said. "I haven't got space for it now and, to tell you the truth, its tearful face makes me feel quite miserable even if it is only an onion."

I thanked her very much. "I'm sure we'll be able to sell that straight away."

"By the way," she said. "Brenda asked me to say hello for her."

"Brenda? Brenda Wilson? You know Brenda?"

"Yes. I live at Barleycroft."

"Oh, lucky you," I said. "I wouldn't mind a place there myself."

Wendy's ears pricked up.

"I thought I'd seen you somewhere before," she said to the woman. "That's where I work. In the coffee shop."

The woman smiled and said, "I might have some more bits and pieces for you. I'll bring them in, shall I?"

I thanked her again. Norma came in with the tea and cakes. After the woman had gone I congratulated Wendy again.

"She's got a new job, Norma," I said. "At Barleycroft."

"Oh, well done you," Norma said.

"In the coffee shop," Wendy told her. "Well, it's more of a café really. It gets very busy when we do Sunday roasts. Not everybody wants to cook for one and eat alone. That lady who's just been in. She's a resident there. I've seen her a few times."

"Her?" Norma said. "Her that's just gone out? Lives at Barleycroft? Well, you know who that is, don't you?"

"No," I said. "Am I supposed to?"

"That's Margaret Harding. The doctor's mother. Who'd have thought it? The doctor's mother in sheltered accommodation. Well I never."

I saw Wendy's eyebrows lift in surprise but her mouth turned downwards. She didn't eat her cake.

54

Rafe

I couldn't believe my luck when Sophie messaged me when I got back to university after the inquest.

You coming home for Easter? she wanted to know.

No, I messaged back, *not this year.*

Shame. Thought we might meet up. What you doing instead?

Nothing.

So come home. I've got a surprise for you.

What?

If I told you it wouldn't be a surprise.

I've already told my mother I'm not coming.

So, ring her up and say you've changed your mind.

I'll think about it.

What's the problem?

I'll call you on your mobile. It's complicated.

Explaining my feelings about the house wouldn't feel right in a Facebook chat. It was too personal. I thought it would be better to hear someone's voice, a person who would understand. I assumed Sophie would get it. Her father was a doctor. She must have heard all kinds of conversations at home about people's illnesses and stuff. Her voice sounded warm when she answered. I guess I must have needed someone to talk to because I just let it all out. Everything. The arguments. Grandma's queer behaviour. New Year's Eve when I found her body in our bathroom. The inquest. And why I didn't like going back to the house.

"Why haven't you talked to your brother about how you feel?" she asked me.

"How did you know I have a brother?" I didn't remember telling her.

"You mentioned him before."

"Did I?"

"Anyway," she said, "I've seen you with him. You both came into college one afternoon to see your old tutors. You went home with your dad. I saw you again in the car park."

"So when you blagged that drink out of me you already knew who I am?"

"Sort of, yes."

"Why didn't you say?"

"I didn't think it was important. It was nice meeting the way we did, wasn't it?"

I agreed with her. I often thought about that night.

"If you don't come home, Rafe," she said, "you won't shake off that feeling you have about the house. It'll last longer. You might never be able to get rid of it. You have to face up to it."

"I know."

"Get your brother to come with you. It might make it easier."

"I don't know about that, Sophie."

"Ask him. You've got nothing to lose. Tell him you need him there with you."

She was making sense. The easy calmness in her voice persuaded me and I said, "Okay."

"Email me," she said. "Let me know when and I'll meet you at the bus station with my surprise."

We travelled on Good Friday. I felt reasonably okay to begin with but as we approached home that old nervousness started up again. My stomach churned as we passed villages and pubs I recognised. The closer we got to home the more nervous I felt. I tried to concentrate on other things. I thought about when Richie and I were little, family outings and happier times. Holidays, birthdays and Christmases.

No, I said to myself. Don't think about Christmas. Think about something else.

Instead, I pictured Sophie's beautiful face.

As soon as we pulled into the coach station in Swindon I knew what her surprise was. A blue Vauxhall Astra.

"Nice one," Richie said as I made the introductions. "Not a bad chauffeur either."

Sophie said, "Shouldn't that be chauffeuse? Come on, guys. Get in. Anywhere you want to go first?"

Mum was over the moon to see us. Sophie dropped us at the house but said she had to get straight off. I was going to invite her in for a coffee. Mum came rushing up the path and kissed us both like she hadn't seen us for years.

"Rafe! Richie!" she said in a fuss. "Come in. Oh, come in. I was waiting for your call."

"We got a lift, Mum," I said.

"Yeh," Rafe said. "He's got a secret girlfriend."

We waved Sophie off and I went indoors. I slunk past the bathroom like a scared kid. Richie saw me do it and slapped me on the back.

"Get over it, brother," he said. "It can't hurt you now."

"I've put you in your old room, Richie," Mum said. "It's all been painted, sweetheart. There's nothing to worry about."

"I'm not the one who's worried," Richie said and went straight in to put down his backpack. I followed him in and saw Mum's efforts to put things back as they'd been before. She'd painted Grandma's wardrobe white and replaced the dressing table with a set of Scandinavian style drawers from Ikea. The smell had gone, too. Grandma's smell: strong perfume and powdery stuff. The windows were open and the room felt fresh. I crossed the hall to my own room, put down my bag and sat on the bed.

Sophie was right, I thought. It's better to deal with it sooner rather than later.

"Fancy a curry tonight?" Mum called from the kitchen

I shouted back, "You bet."

When I went to the kitchen for a drink Mum was still in a fussing mood, talking about nothing in particular. She was chopping vegetables and there were pots of red and orange-coloured spices everywhere. The sink was full of stuff waiting for washing up. But she looked so much better than the last time we'd been together. At the inquest she'd been so pale, like a ghostly version of herself. In just a matter of weeks she was smiling again and her eyes were brighter.

"Bother and blast," she said. "I've run out of apples."

"Apples in a curry?"

"It's my new secret ingredient," she said. "Only it's not so secret now, is it? I picked it up at my new job. Janice always adds apple puree to curry to give it body."

"Sorry, Mum. I forgot to ask you about your new job," I said. "How is it going?"

Mum's face lit up as she said, "I love it. Absolutely love it. The people are so nice and friendly." She pulled off her apron and went into the hall for a jacket. "Rafe, I'm going to have to pop out. You and Richie help yourselves to drinks. I won't be long. Now, where's my handbag?"

"Is this it?" I said reaching behind some storage jars on the worktop. Mum went for it at the same time and we got in one another's way. We tipped the bag onto the floor. The flap opened and some things fell out. A bottle of pills skidded across the tiles. Mum rushed to pick it up. I knelt down to help but she stashed everything away quickly and closed her bag.

"Right then," she said. "I'll be off."

Richie came into the kitchen and we made a brew.

"Where's Dad?" he said.

"Don't know. Mum didn't say."

"So. Sophie, huh? Tidy. Yeh. Nice piece of tidy. Where'd you meet her?"

"Don't talk like that, Richie. It makes you sound stupid. I met her in a pub if you must know. She's in one of Dad's classes at college."

"No way. That's weird."

"No it isn't. What's weird about it? It's just the way your mind works."

The back door opened and Dad came in wearing an old sweater, a North Face gilet and dirt-caked boots.

"Hi, guys," he said, unlacing the boots. "Does your mother know you're here?"

"Yes. She's gone to the shop.," Richie said. "What have you been doing?"

"Walking."

"Walking?"

"That's what I said. Walking."

"Dad," Richie said. "You don't do walking."

"I do now." He pulled off his boots and checked the water level in the kettle.

"It's just boiled, Dad," I offered. "Do you want me to make you one?"

"Thank you, yes. I'll just get out of these clothes."

When he'd gone Richie pulled a face and popped his eyebrows. He said, "What's going on with him?"

"No idea. Nothing much, probably."

I put a mug of coffee on the table for Dad when he came back. He sat with us and said, "Your mother is so pleased you decided to come home after all. She needs to spend some time with both of you. I hope you'll make sure that happens."

I said, "She seemed much better to me, Dad."

"She has her good days. What did she want from the shop? She brought a mountain of food home yesterday."

"Some special ingredient for curry," I said.

"Another one of Janice's ideas, I expect."

Richie said, "Who's Janice?"

"Her new boss. It's Janice says this and Janice says that. Nobody ever cooked a meal before Janice according to your mother."

Richie laughed but I didn't like the tone of Dad's voice. He wasn't meaning it to be a joke. He didn't have a joking face. He meant it. People who are jealous of somebody or something use that tone of voice. I wondered why Dad felt like that. How could he object to Mum's new job when it was obvious it was making her so happy?

55

Margaret

Brenda and I went on a theatre trip up to Bristol just after Easter. It was a production of the same show Sophie had visited during her time in New York. I understand her love of live theatre. There's nothing like that moment when the lights dim and the overture begins. It gives me a tingle and makes me want to cry. Then the curtains pull back and you are whisked away to another world. The show was very good but, I have to say, I prefer the old Rodgers and Hammerstein musicals where the sets are traditional and one can understand the development of the story. That is to say, where Brenda can understand the plot.

She kept interrupting with questions. For all her worldly wisdom on all manner of life's challenges she wasn't able to set free her imagination and just go with the flow.

Why is she doing that? she'd ask. Or, *What did he tell her that for?* And, *It wasn't like that in the old film.*

On the coach journey home she said, "And you can't hum any of the tunes afterwards, Margaret. I always used to like it when you came out singing your favourite song."

"We have to have new ideas, Brenda," I said, "otherwise everything would stay the same. Wouldn't that be boring?"

"I suppose so."

"Well, I expect there has to be change in the theatre too. New ideas. New ways of doing things."

She pondered on that for a while and I saw her eyelids drooping. By the time we arrived at Barleycroft it was way past midnight. I invited Brenda in for a nightcap.

"Thank you, but I'm away to my bed," she said. "Another time maybe."

I was glad she hadn't accepted my offer although, of course, I didn't say so. My back ached from sitting so long in the theatre and on the coach. My throat felt tight and sore.

I hoped I wasn't starting with something. I filled a hot water bottle and went straight to bed.

I wasn't feeling well enough to bother with shopping next morning. I stayed in my bed and dozed a little longer than usual. I couldn't eat breakfast and passed on lunch. By mid-afternoon I was feeling rather sickly. I made a hot drink and took it back to bed. My throat felt as raw as if I'd been chewing razor blades. I woke several times through that night feeling hot and I began coughing. I knew then that I was in for it.

Next morning I felt stiff and sore everywhere. I could hardly get out of bed. I struggled to the bathroom and then to the living room. I flopped onto the sofa and felt utterly exhausted. I could have telephoned Sarah. I know she would have come. Then she would have told Marcus and then he would start worrying about me and I don't want them to feel they have to come running each time I feel under the weather. I pulled the emergency cord. A few moments later I heard a knock at my door.

"Come in," I squeaked.

I recognised the young woman who came in. She wasn't one of the usual carers. She stood in the doorway and looked nervous.

"Oh, hello," she said. "It's Mrs Harding, isn't it?"

She had her handbag clasped tightly in front of her and was hanging back in the doorway.

"Yes, dear," I said. "Don't be nervous. Come in, dear. Come in."

She stepped into the room still clinging to her bag. I said, "Where do I know you from?"

"Don't be alarmed, Mrs Harding," she said. "I usually work in the coffee shop but Janice offered my services to help out with care-taking. We've got two off with the flu, Mrs Harding. No need to ask you how you're feeling. I can see for myself."

Her words had come out in a tumbled rush that made me feel dizzy as I listened.

"Call me Margaret," I said. I was burning hot. The back of my neck felt damp and sticky. I felt extremely nauseous too although I'd had little to eat for more than thirty six hours. I tried to get up from the sofa but I was light-headed and my legs were too weak.

"Let me help you back into bed Mrs . . . Margaret. And then I'll call the doctor. Should I call Doctor Harding?"

"No, dear. Don't do that. Just whoever is on call. Thank you so much."

She put down her bag. She helped me up from the sofa and, holding onto her arm, I shuffled back to my room. I parked my backside on the edge of my bed and said, "I don't know your name."

"It's Wendy," she said. "Now if you're sure you're all right for a minute I'll call for the doctor."

I tried to swing my legs around into bed but they ached so. They felt too heavy to move. Gingerly I lifted them one at a time with my hands. Dear God, I thought. Is this what getting old is all about? I don't like it. I let my head drop back onto my pillow exhausted from the effort of moving my legs. I could hardly breathe. Come on, Margaret, I told myself. It's the flu. That's all. You'll be fine. Young Wendy is here to help.

56

Marcus

My mother didn't tell me she was ill. I had some time free one afternoon and, as my last home visit had been in the vicinity, I decided to call in at Barleycroft. To my surprise Wendy Carter was sitting reading a magazine in mother's living room. She leapt to her feet when I entered and grabbed her handbag.

"Mrs Carter," I said. "Where's my mother?"

"She's asleep, Doctor. She hasn't been well. I've been sitting with her."

I noticed she was wearing a Barleycroft cover all with an embroidered logo on the breast pocket. I said, "I didn't know you worked here."

"Yes," she said. "I'm helping out on the caring side." She tucked her hair behind her ears and looked nervous. She still gripped her bag in her other hand. "We're so short-staffed at the moment. It's the least I can do."

"Wendy, is that you?" my mother called from her room. "I'd love a cup of tea."

"I'll go," I said.

"Yes, yes. of course," Wendy Carter said. "I'll wait here."

I tapped on my mother's bedroom door. "It's Marcus, Mother. Surprise visit," I said and went in carrying my home visit bag.

"Marcus!" she said. "How lovely to see you. Who sent for you?"

"Nobody sent for me, Mother. I simply decided to call in. Now then, let's have a look at you."

I examined her and noted the medication she'd been prescribed. I said, "You'll be up and about soon."

"Good," she said, rearranging her bed cover. "I need to get my hair done. I'll ask Wendy to make an appointment for me. She's been such a help. I don't know what I would have done without her."

"You could have called me. And Sarah."

"I didn't want to make a fuss, Marcus. Don't you make one now, please."

"I'll go and see about that cup of tea."

I backed out of mother's room feeling admonished. I closed the door. Wendy Carter was waiting in the living room. "How is Mrs Harding?" she said.

"She's over the worst, thank you."

"I expect she's hungry. She hasn't had anything, you know. I thought I'd stay a little longer and make something for her before I go."

"That's very kind of you," I said. "I'm sure she'll appreciate that."

Wendy Carter went into my mother's kitchen. I followed her. I watched. She put down her handbag on the worktop.

"Would you like a cup of tea, Doctor?"

I didn't particularly need a drink but I agreed. I wanted to observe. With some sense of shock I realised that Wendy Carter knew where my mother keeps everything. She reached into mother's cupboards and brought out cups. She knew in which drawer she'd find teaspoons. She knew which storage jar held tea and which one was for sugar. I watched as she got out a clean tea towel, opened the washing machine and threw the used towel in the drum. Every now and then her eyes flicked to the worktop where she'd put her bag, as if she were afraid someone was going to snatch it.

"Here we are," she said, setting down the tea tray and putting out biscuits.

"Why didn't someone let me know that my mother was ill?" I asked.

"She didn't want us to, Doctor Harding."

"What if she'd become more seriously ill?" I was aware of the hard edge in my voice. I knew I sounded affronted.

"I have to report all my visits to our residents' homes to the manager, Doctor. I would have told her if I thought . . ."

"If you'd thought?"

"No. I mean, if the other doctor had said . . ."

I took a deep breath and pulled myself in. I took control of my responses. I had to tell myself that Wendy Carter wasn't the one making decisions about my mother's health. Of course my mother was in good hands. I was overreacting. I knew it was unreasonable of me but I couldn't shake the thought that Wendy Carter was up to no good. She looked as shifty as she had on the day I'd seen her at the surgery. She wasn't as thin and unkempt but her face was just as pale and her gaze flitted around as if she was avoiding eye contact with me. She was on edge, uncomfortable in my presence. She kept her head down. Her hands shook as she put out teaspoons and they clattered against mother's china. Wendy Carter didn't want to meet my eyes. What was she hiding?

57

Margaret

I enjoyed the time I spent with Wendy and was sorry to see her go. The house felt quite empty without her little body about the place. Too quiet, too. I'd got used to having regular conversations instead of listening to the radio. Wendy asked me all about my paintings and photographs. She wanted to know where I found inexpensive frames. I found it such a delight to talk to someone who really wanted to listen about things that interest me. I offered to show her how to make a simple mount for a collection of family photographs.

We discussed some of Janice's recipes. Wendy told me which ones she was trying out at home. I'd tried some too and we compared our results. We even tried some together, working alongside one another in my small kitchen when I felt well enough to stand. It was quite a novelty for me to cook spicy, exotic foods. Anthony would never touch anything that didn't look like meat and two veg.

"I can't imagine what he ate when he was in India," I told her.

"He must have had to learn to try something different, mustn't he?" she said.

Wendy reminded me when it was time for my medication and laid it out for me.

"You can't be too careful, Margaret," she said. "Not with tablets. You have to take them at the right time in the right way. Who knows what might happen if you got them mixed up?"

I enjoyed the caring way she supervised me. She collected my newspaper and favourite mints from the shop. Nothing was too much trouble. She was like a breath of fresh air. After she left I didn't like the stillness. Of course, she hadn't left Barleycroft. She'd gone back to work with Janice in the coffee shop. As soon as I was well enough and the weather had improved I went to see her. Her face lit up as I went in.

"Margaret!" she said. "Oh, it's lovely to see you. Come and sit down. What can I get for you?"

I ordered a drink and a toasted teacake. When she brought them to my table I asked her to sit with me for a minute.

"You're looking so much better," she said.

"Thank you. Yes, I'm definitely better than I was."

"I was worried about you."

"Were you , my dear?"

"I've already lost both my own parents," she said. "I don't want to lose anybody else."

When I was ill and Wendy came in to look after me we'd discussed the dreadful events that had taken her mother and what a terrible trauma that must have been for her and her family. She was such a sweet little thing. My heart went out to her.

I said, "I know this is rather an old-fashioned idea but I'd like to invite you to come to tea, Wendy."

She looked embarrassed and said, "You don't have to do that."

"I know I don't have to. I want to. Are you free on Sunday?" She nodded. "Well, that's settled then."

I was so pleased she'd accepted my invitation. I watched the weather forecast wondering whether it might be nice enough to sit outside on the terrace for a time. My pots were coming into flower and I'd hung plaques and pictures on the outer walls so that the whole looked like an outdoor room. I was looking forward to spoiling her a little, not simply because I wanted to thank her for all she'd done for me, but because I felt she needed a little pampering.

Next day I felt well enough to take the minibus into one of the supermarkets in town. Brenda came with me. We sat, like schoolgirls on an outing, discussing our shopping trip.

"What are we like?" she said with that comical look she's so good at.

I said, "Two old ladies."

"No," she said. "I mean, coming down with the flu at the same time. Can't I have anything without you wanting it as well? I'll tell you something. Don't ask me to come to the theatre ever again. Breathing in everybody else's germs. And as for being two old ladies? Age is just a number, Margaret. That's all."

Brenda's company always reminds me how we must make the most of time with our friends at our age. A lively companion is such a boost to one's own well-being. She helped me decide on my special tea menu for Wendy's visit and, of course, I invited Brenda along too.

She came to help set the table on Sunday and make everything look nice and welcoming. I brought out a fresh tablecloth and my new best china in a bright geometric design. Very Art Deco. I've grown jaded with floral patterns along with magnolia walls. Fresh new designs seemed appropriate for my fresh, new life.

The day was fine but too cold for outdoors. Wendy arrived on time and admired my new outdoor tile paintings. I introduced her to Brenda.

"Yes. We've met several times in the coffee shop," Wendy said. "Crispy bacon and toasted teacakes with lots of butter. Isn't that right, Mrs Wilson?"

"Come in, come in," I said. "Let me take your coat." I offered her the chair by the fire. "Are you warm enough? You look a little pale. I can turn up the gas."

"No, no, thank you. I'm fine. Just a little tired, that's all."

Brenda and I waited until she was settled. She seemed to take a long time. She shuffled about in the chair arranging her skirt, getting up to rearrange it, smooth it and sit down again. She put her handbag on the floor beside her and then she picked it up again and clasped it on her knee. Eventually she spoke.

"You know Joan Spencer," she said to Brenda.

"I certainly do," Brenda said. "Joan and I go back years. I can't tell you how many. I haven't seen her lately. How is she?"

"Very well. She's still at the charity shop."

"She'll work till she drops, that one. You used to work there yourself?"

"That's right. I loved working with Joan. And Norma."

I said, "I bet you miss them."

She cleared her throat. "Yes I do."

"Bit of an old lady magnet aren't you, my lovely?" Brenda said.

"Brenda, where on earth do you get those sayings from?" I said with a laugh. Brenda laughed too. I thought we'd broken through Wendy's discomfort because she began to laugh as well. She rocked in her seat, wiping her eyes and shaking. The handbag fell from her lap and I could see then that she wasn't shaking with laughter. She was sobbing. The poor girl was sobbing her heart out. We waited.

"I'm so sorry," she said after a moment.

"You don't have to apologise to us, Wendy," I said. "We know you've been through a difficult time."

"I've spoiled your afternoon tea."

"No you haven't," Brenda said. "We haven't had it yet."

Always the comedienne, Brenda's joke did the trick. Wendy wiped her eyes and perked up.

"Is there anything I can do to help?" I asked. "Is there . . ."

"Yes," Brenda interrupted. "Give the girl something to eat. She looks famished."

I invited Wendy to the table and Brenda helped bring in sandwiches and cakes from the kitchen. Brenda tucked in and so did I, but I noticed Wendy was eating very little. She nibbled at a sandwich like a mouse but much more slowly. She still had her handbag on her lap, tucked under the table.

"Are you sure you're quite well, Wendy?" I said. "Do you think you might have picked up that dreadful virus from me?"

"No. It can't be that," she said. "It would have come out before now."

Brenda said, "There is something though, isn't there?'

Wendy sighed and took a moment as if she wasn't sure whether to speak. "I think there might be." She hung her head and looked embarrassed.

"Would you like to talk to Margaret in private?" Brenda suggested. "I'll disappear if you like."

"Oh, no. Please don't go on my account. It's nothing, really."

"Well, you can tell that to the Marines, my lovely," Brenda said, "but it won't get past me and Margaret. We can see there's something troubling you."

"Well . . ." she began.

I heard a car pull up outside the front window. I stood up to have a look. It was a blue car. I didn't recognise it so I turned my attention back to Wendy.

"Sorry, Wendy," I said. "I thought that was someone coming here."

There was a sharp rap and the door opened.

"Hello, Grandma, it's only me. I've come to show you my new car. I want to show off. Oh, you have visitors already."

"Sophie! What a lovely surprise."

Wendy leapt to her feet. She gripped that handbag as if her life depended on it. What little colour she had drained away completely. I saw how unsteady she was and I knew she was going to faint. Her eyes rolled and her knees buckled. Her bag dropped from her grasp.

"Quick, Sophie," I shouted. "She's going to fall. Grab her."

We hurried her to the sofa and laid her down. I put a cushion under her head and Sophie lifted up her feet. Wendy was holding her stomach and groaning.

"We should call someone," I said. "We can't let her drive home by herself."

Sophie went for Wendy's handbag. "She'll have her phone. I could get her contact numbers."

"Good idea, Sophie," I said.

She found the phone in a pouch inside Wendy's bag and handed it to me.

"You do it, Sophie," I said. "You're more familiar with these things."

She slid open the case and her thumb flicked across the keys. "Here," she said. "Mr Carter's number."

"Call him, sweetheart, please. I'll talk to him."

She held the phone to her ear waiting for him to pick up. Then she handed it back to me.

"Mr Carter? It's Margaret Harding here," I said. "Sophie's grandmother. Yes, I'm using Wendy's phone. She's with me at my house. She isn't well, Mr Carter. I was wondering if you might be able to come."

He said he couldn't come immediately. He was out with his walking group and they were miles from where he'd left his car. I told him not to worry, that I would deal with the situation and get back to him.

"Sophie, is your father at home? Call him. Use my house phone."

Sophie handed over Wendy's mobile phone. Brenda took it and slipped it back into its pouch. From inside Wendy's handbag she pulled out a bottle of pills.

"Look," she said. "Maybe she's on medication and needs one of these."

"No, Brenda," I said. "I think we should wait until Marcus gets here."

58

Marcus

When Dalton told me the coroner had brought in an outcome of accidental death for Jenny Carter I went home to my study and took out the Carter file. I read everything from the beginning: surgery files, the reports from the Firs, newspaper accounts. *What was I missing?* There had to be something.

A month later when Wendy came to the surgery and I prescribed two weeks supply of sleeping pills I brought out the file again. I started at the beginning once more, trying to read between the lines, looking for a clue. Still I came up with nothing. It wasn't until my mother called me about Wendy's collapse that I began to look at Jenny's case in conjunction with her daughter.

I arrived at Barleycroft to find Wendy Carter, pale and sweating on mother's sofa. She'd been sick, my mother said, although she'd hardly eaten anything. Mother's friend was clearing away their tea things.

"It can't be anything to do with the food, Doctor," the woman said, "or we'd all be feeling the effects."

"She had these in her handbag," my mother said and held out a bottle of pills. I recognised them immediately. "She's been holding her stomach, Marcus. And wincing. I think she must be in pain."

I gave Wendy a brief examination. We called for an ambulance. Sophie wanted to wait with us but I asked her to go home. I called Rob Carter on the number mother had noted and told him what was happening. When the paramedics arrived I explained my suspicions. Mother went with Wendy in the ambulance and I followed in my car. I checked in with admissions and met my mother at the ward entrance. I took the seat beside her. At the nurses' station at the head of the bays staff had their heads down with paperwork. One was in conversation with the porter who'd brought Wendy in.

Mother said, "I'm going to wait here until her husband arrives."

I had the bottle of sleeping pills I'd prescribed for Wendy in my hand. I held it out.

"It's never been opened," I said.

"She never took any. She told me that."

"Did she tell you why?"

"Yes. Now, Marcus. She told me in confidence. I don't want to repeat what she said. You'll have to ask her yourself."

"But she always kept them with her? No, you don't have to answer. I know she did. They were in her handbag. She carried them about with her all the time."

"That's right."

"Why? What was she waiting for?"

"Marcus, I don't want to betray her confidence. Suffice it to say that she felt she no longer needed them."

"You're fond of her, aren't you?" I said.

My mother smiled at me and patted my hand. "Yes, I am. I'm very fond of her. She's such a kind little soul. She wouldn't hurt the proverbial fly. She's generous with her time and such good company. You know, when I look at Wendy, I often wonder how Claudia would have turned out."

Mother was playing with her fingernails but her gaze was distant. "Your sister had the same hair colour, Marcus. Do you remember? Almost the same style, too." She stopped fidgeting with her hands and raised her chin. "Look, Marcus," she said, "I realise I've known Wendy for the shortest time but it's been wonderful, like having a daughter again. We've discussed the same things one would chat about to a grown up daughter with children of her own. And, I suppose, for Wendy our friendship might have been like having a mother. She had a difficult relationship with her own mother, Marcus. I don't think anybody will ever quite understand how hard it's been for her."

"But you can't tell me anything about that either, I suppose."

"No, dear. Not yet. It wouldn't be the right thing to do."

I had to say what was on my mind. "I'm not sure about her, Mother. There's something making me feel things are not quite right."

"What do you mean?"

"Maybe I'm being over cautious but when I saw how at ease she was in your home, I didn't like it. I wondered what she was getting up to."

"Good heavens, Marcus. How could you possibly think like that?" At my mother's raised voice one of the nurses looked over at us. Mum shuffled in her seat and looked uncomfortable. "I'm sorry for shouting," she said, "but Wendy has been nothing but extremely kind to me."

"She seemed too familiar with your things. You hear about unscrupulous carers worming their way into people's affections just so they can get their hands on their belongings."

"Wendy isn't like that."

"Something simply doesn't add up, Mother. That's all I'm saying. I want you to be careful."

"You're being quite ridiculous." She folded her arms and shook her head at me.

I knew I was defeated. "Call me when you're ready to go home, Mum. I'll come for you," I said and slipped the bottle of sleeping pills into my pocket.

On the drive home I pictured Wendy's way of looking sideways at me and the way she had to keep sight of that handbag. Why would anyone who felt they didn't need sleeping pills keep a full bottle with them wherever they went? At home I was still distracted.

"You're lost in thought," Sophie said after dinner.

"Sorry. Yes. What were you saying?"

" I was asking about Mrs Carter. Is she going to be okay? She looked awful this afternoon."

"I don't know, Sophie. To tell you the truth there's a lot I don't know about the Carter women."

"Would it be wrong of me to let her son know she's in hospital? I chat to Rafe sometimes online."

"I'm sure his father will have told him by now."

"He might appreciate someone to talk to."

Sophie went to her room. I went to my study and picked up the Carter file again. Sarah came up with coffee and watched me flipping backwards and forwards through letters and reports.

She said, "You might never get to the bottom of it. Don't you think it's time to let it go?"

"I can't let it go, Sarah. The answer's in here somewhere."

"There might be more than one answer."

"What did you say?"

"It might not be just one thing. It could be a combination. Downstairs just now you referred to the Carter *women* as if the same thing affected them both."

Her words were like a bullet in my stomach. A thought began to form itself but, just out of my reach, I couldn't untangle it.

"You could have something there," I said and turned back to my papers.

Sarah moved toward the door. "Marcus," she said. "There's something on television tonight I'd like to watch. I'll leave you to get on. Don't stay up too late."

I finished the coffee Sarah had brought for me thinking *What's the matter with the Carter women?* I searched through my files. *Why did they seem so secretive? What were they both hiding?*

I got up from my desk and moved about the room. I went back to the file and flicked through the reports. What could trigger severe dementia symptoms in an otherwise healthy woman? It had to be something present during the period of Jenny's decline so that its absence, during the time Jenny was in residential care resulted in her so-called recovery.

But we had already assumed she wasn't otherwise healthy. Now add that to the equation. What did we have?

I heard the phone ring and Sarah's answer. She called up to me.

"That was your mother, Marcus. She got a lift home, darling. You don't have to go out again tonight."

"Right. Thanks," I said and got up to stretch my legs. Then I sat in the easy chair by the window watching night fall. The white horse faded into the hill until the hill faded into the sky. I pushed back the chair and paced around again. I went downstairs and looked at the kitchen clock. The house was quiet. Sarah and Sophie had gone to bed. I made a hot drink and paced about some more. Both Seamus and I felt that Jenny Carter had long been avoiding coming to terms with a long-standing health issue. He told me the subject was broached during the inquest but quickly skimmed over.

It would be. It was irrelevant to the investigation. It didn't contribute to the manner of her death.

What could you add to an undiagnosed condition to bring about symptoms of dementia?

Wait a minute.

I pulled up my chair closer to the desk and flipped back the file to Jenny Carter's strained muscle after her fall. I made a note of the painkillers Dalton had prescribed and clicked the search button on my practising physicians' medical website. I already knew what I would find there.

'*Side effects from painkillers (opiates) can include sedation, euphoria, dizziness, fatigue, depression, tremors, sleeplessness, anxiousness, flu-like symptoms, upset stomach, dry mouth, pupil constriction, itching, hallucination, delirium, sweating, muscle and bone pain, confusion, extreme irritability and muscle spasms. Severe side effects can include severe respiratory depression, confusion or stupor, coma, clammy skin.*'

The painkiller Dalton had prescribed was opiate-based. I searched further. I read another report stating that nearly one in four respondents of a survey conducted by one of the giants in pharmaceuticals said they did not know the difference between paracetamol, ibuprofen and codeine. It also found that forty-four per cent of respondents would use the same type of painkiller regardless of what type of pain they had. Plus nearly half admitted to mixing medicines without seeking the advice of a doctor or pharmacist.

I clicked on another site and read on to confirm my suspicions.

'*Painkillers containing opiates can cause **mental side effects** in some users. Difficulty sleeping, **hallucinations, confusion and nightmares** are sometimes reported.*'

But it was the following paragraph that made the hairs stand on my neck.

'*Many individuals who suffer from personality disorders and drug addiction experience more intense changes in their moods and become reckless in their behaviour, with social interactions and financially. Physical complications, too, are a concern as are suicidal tendencies and a general disregard for self- safety and the safety of others.*'

I had to tell Dalton.

59

Margaret

Rob Carter gave me a lift home on the day Wendy was admitted to hospital. I invited him in. I could see he was in complete shock. He hardly knew what to say. I made him some tea and pressed a plate of sandwiches into his hands. We took them into the sitting room and I put a side table next to where he sat.

I said, "Try not to worry. I know that's easier said than done but I'm sure Wendy will be all right. She's in good hands."

"Why won't she say anything?" he said. "Why won't she speak to me?"

"It's probably the trauma of everything that's happened," I offered. "These things sometimes take a long time to come to the surface. I'm sure she'll get better in time."

"I don't know what I'm going to tell our sons."

"There's nothing better than the truth, Mr Carter."

He nodded and took a bite of his sandwich. "Thank you for this," he said.

"Really, it's no trouble."

I took a sip of my tea and let him eat in peace. After a moment he said,

"Wendy likes working here at Barleycroft. Maybe she's worried about having to give up her job."

"Well, we'll soon be able to sort that out, won't we?" I said as if I would have any say in the matter.

He took a drink and said, "It makes her very happy being here. I can see that. She talks about Janice all the time, you know. Janice and cooking. Actually, I felt envious."

"Of her work?"

"No. That's not what I mean. She comes alive whenever she's talking about working in the coffee shop with Janice. She never looks that way talking to me. I felt envious I wasn't the one bringing her that happiness."

"I don't think you should blame yourself, Mr Carter. Wendy has had some difficult times," I said. I wasn't sure whether I should try to draw him into a deeper conversation. He looked like a man with a lot to get off his chest. In fact he looked like a grown man who needed his mother. I attempted an opening.

"She had an unhappy childhood, didn't she?"

He nodded and it took him a moment to say, "We both did. It was one of the things that drew us together in the beginning."

I knew he wanted to unburden himself. I recognised the signs. It wasn't going to take much encouragement from me.

I said, "I'm a good listener, Mr Carter."

His eyes wandered to the ceiling and back to me.

"I know. Wendy has told me about you and how much you've helped her. I believe she cares very much about you."

"And I care about her too. You might think it an odd friendship between an old woman like me and . . ."

"No. I don't think it's odd at all. I think you represent the ideal mother figure for her. The one Wendy never had." He shook his head and added, "The one I never had either."

"As I said, I'm a good listener."

He watched me finish my drink. He didn't begin to speak again until I got up to take away the plates.

"I'm not special," he said to my back. "I have a love of English literature and a gift for helping to get the best out of students. And that's all there is. I'm useless at all the things men are expected to be able to do around the house. Pathetic at DIY. In fact, I'm useless at anything you have to do with your hands."

I put the used cups and plates in the kitchen and stood in the doorway.

"We all have different gifts. My son is not particularly gifted in the DIY department either," I said remembering Marcus's efforts at fixing Sarah's rotary washing post.

"I live in a world of books and study and the analysis of virtual people in virtual worlds," he continued. "It's a salutary fact that while I have spent hours reflecting on fictional characters and the way they interact, I've been unable to recognise certain of my own characteristics let alone change anything about myself. I've planned my students' assignments around innumerable aspects of the human emotions we've encountered together in our examination studies. We've studied despair. We have inspected the colours of madness. We've stratified expressions of love. Yet I don't know how one is supposed to love a woman. Sometimes my students surprise me with their insights into human feelings. They are far in advance of where I was at their age."

I sat across from him and nodded just to assure him I was still listening.

"I never learned much about love," he admitted. "Throughout my own school education I simply regurgitated all the required responses to examination questions on the human condition expressed in the poetry and prose of Lawrence, Thackeray, Shakespeare. Even through university I relied on my copious notes and memory to achieve my grades. So you can see I'm not much of an academic, either. I can plan and I can organise. But don't ask me about love. Ask my students."

"I think you should be less hard on yourself," I said. He didn't respond to that.

"My parents must have loved each other at some point," he said, "but I never saw any evidence of it. Ours was a house without hugs. I thought that was how everybody lived. We scraped by from day to day on a meagre diet of work and duty. Responsibility was my father's catchword. Everything that happened in our household was reduced to an inescapable rota of who was responsible for what. You can't have any rights in my house unless you fulfil your responsibilities, my father would say if one of us begged to differ."

"You have siblings?"

"Yes. One sister. Susan is seven years older than me. She lives in Florida with her husband. She was the only one who would put her arm around me or allow me to be a little boy."

I looked closely at him and saw that little boy staring out from his eyes. In his troubled expression I could see Niall and Marcus on the days when they'd argued and needed me to put things right for them. Little boys are gentle souls. It's a frightening transition for them into manhood. They pretend that it isn't with a great show of bluster and bravado. Mothers must understand how much love little boys need.

I said, "Go on. I'm listening."

"I think my mother had become so accustomed to doing everything Dad's way that, after time, she forgot how to be a mother, how to be a woman. She was dad's accomplice and if my father was wearing a frown you didn't need to look at her face to know that she was, too.

I remember one occasion when we'd been watching Dr Who. I was six years old, I think, so that must have been about 1964. I was terrified. I cried and my father was embarrassed at what he saw as weakness in me. He ordered my sister to take me away so he didn't have to look at me. My mother did nothing. She wore an expression that said you know your father is always right, Rob, so I went upstairs in disgrace. Susan gave me a drink and read me a story to take my mind off the things that had frightened me. I told her I was afraid to go to sleep and she came into my room that night to sit with me until I nodded off. Whenever I hear that signature music I recall the shame of being a frightened little boy."

I wanted to ask if he had been abused physically but he wanted to keep going. He continued as if he'd been reading my thoughts.

"There was never any violence. My father was too controlled to lash out. But he kept us in fear of being made to look stupid. I grew up fearful of authority. I was frightened of criticism," he said, "and, although I didn't realise it for many years, desperate for love. But Wendy forgave me all of my faults. She'd look at me with adoration in her eyes. I would catch her staring at me as if I were a god, as if she couldn't quite believe that I had chosen her for my wife."

I could read the pain in his eyes as he stared beyond the wall behind me, beyond the room, as if her were watching his own past life. He carried on talking as though I wasn't there.

"At first it was exceedingly powerful, this sheer love, this adulation. Wendy was in awe of me and it made me feel bigger and better than I had ever felt before. She gave me a sense of pride in myself. At last, I was loved for being me. I could do no wrong in her eyes.

But I had never learned how to handle that amount of love. Like an over-sweet dessert it began to cloy. Wendy compensated for the paucity of my demonstrations of feelings for her by loving me all the more, telling me it didn't matter if I was sometimes cold and distant, that she could love enough for both of us. The more she loved me the more inadequate I felt. It began to eat at me that I couldn't return Wendy's devotion. She'd try to coax me out of a mood, try to please me in her simple child-like ways and her entreaties only served to make me despise myself more intensely and bred in me a need to put a safe distance between us, to keep her at arm's length.

When the boys were born I was grateful there was now some other focus for her attentions. For a very brief time, when they were babies, life became easier for me. I had some space to myself free from Wendy's ministrations and I told myself that we could recover, that I could recover. I resolved to be a better father than mine had been to me and learn how to give of myself.

But as the twins moved on from infancy Wendy carried on in the same way as before. She saw herself as a wife above everything else. That was the most important role of her life. She loved the boys because they were my children not because they were hers. She supported me unconditionally in all family decisions. It was like watching my mother all over again. As they grew older Wendy always took my side over the smallest of disagreements. I could almost hear my mother saying you know your father's always right. I wanted Wendy to take a stand against me. I needed her to stop raising me up to a level where I couldn't breathe. I wanted her to put right everything my mother had done wrong."

He looked at me then and read my face.

"I know it's not fair, Mrs Harding," he said. "But it's life. It happened that way and I don't tell you these things now to look for your sympathy or to find excuses for some of the things that have happened since. We did the best we could with the skills we possessed. Neither of us knew how to unlearn what we had brought into our marriage."

He cleared his throat and looked embarrassed. "When I started to reject her in the bedroom, instead of getting upset she'd simply accept and wait. I think she's spent years of her life waiting for me to love her properly. It seemed we would live out our lives not as lovers but as friends. Eventually, there was nothing left to withhold from her. She has taken years of my neglect without question. She deserved a better man than me."

"Mr Carter," I said. "Now you have your chance, wouldn't you say? You must tell Wendy what you've just told me."

"I think it's too late."

"There's a new life ahead for both of you now."

"She wouldn't listen to me."

"How can you be sure of that if you don't try?"

60
Rafe

When I came home to see Mum, Sophie drove me to the hospital in Swindon.

"I won't come in with you, Rafe," she said. "This is a family thing. I'll wait here." She went into the snack bar.

I didn't stay with Mum long. She was tired and still looked very pale, almost as white as the sheets on the bed. I said Dad was coming in after work and told her about Richie being tied up on his placement. He'd come as soon as he could. She didn't say anything. Her eyes had that empty look I'd seen before but she did manage to smile at me.

"I don't want you to worry any more," I told her. "Everything will work out. I'll help. I can take time out to help you."

She raised herself in bed and reached out to touch my hand. She shook her head.

"I want to help," I said. "You don't have to do this on your own. You can show me what to do. I can learn."

She shook her head again. Her eyes looked fierce and her brows knotted but her mouth stayed closed like she had her teeth clamped tight. I told her I loved her. I left her some flowers and a magazine and came away.

Sophie was waiting in the café area. She'd ordered a juice for me. I drank it in one go.

"How is she?"

"Not good. She won't speak. I don't know what's going to happen."

"I don't know what to say."

"You don't have to say anything."

Sophie reached out across the table and touched my hand.

"There *is* something I want to tell you," she said.

"What?"

"Not here. Let's go."

I followed her to her car and she drove out of Swindon and took the M4 east towards Marlborough. She took the first exit and followed the road out into the country. We passed Silbury hill and the turn-off for Avebury. Everything looked very green after the pale interior of the hospital. Sophie swung off the main road into the car park below the white horse hill where ramblers usually start their trek. There was one other car but no people in sight. She switched off the radio and turned to face me. I thought she was going to start snogging me but she put her head down and clasped her fingers.

I said, "What's wrong?"

"There's something I have to tell you."

She took her time putting her words together.

"I got your dad in trouble at college last year," she said. "But I didn't mean to. It all came out wrong and everything got blown out of proportion and my mum got involved and I felt stupid and . . ."

"Sophie," I said. "Calm down and start again."

She took a deep breath. "I got your dad in trouble."

"Why? What did you do?"

"I was so stupid, Rafe. I was showing off. Boasting."

"I don't know what you're talking about. You're going to have to spell it out for me."

"All the girls at college think your dad is brilliant," she said.

"Do they?"

"Yes. He's a great teacher. And he's good-looking. For his age."

I covered up how weird that made me feel. "Go on," I said.

"I told a friend I thought he fancied me. It was a stupid thing to say. I know that now. I made it all up. I made out he'd been smiling and winking at me and how when I handed in my assignments he brushed my hand with his fingers."

My insides lurched. *Too weird.* She looked away from me and blushed.

"How did that get him in trouble?"

"My friend reported him to the Principal. I begged her not to but she wouldn't listen. She isn't my friend any more."

"What? And the Principal believed her?"

"At first, yes. Your dad was suspended."

I went cold but I didn't want to admit I knew nothing about it so I said, "So it was you."

"Yes. It was all my fault. I'm so sorry, Rafe. My mum went up to college to sort it out and then your dad came back to work. Nobody talks about it now but at the time it was awful. I lost a lot of friends over it. People said I'd deliberately tried to harm his career. I'm not even sure whether my mum believes me." Her eyes were wide and tearful.

I looked away from her and said, "Now it's me who doesn't know what to say."

I got out of the car and walked across the gravel parking area. I sat on a bench next to a waste bin. The grass rippled in the breeze and I could smell spring in the earth at my feet. Sophie came to join me.

"Can you forgive me?" she said. I put my arm around her and pulled her closer. She let her head fall on my shoulder. She smelled of clean skin. Her hair felt silky and smooth. "I was so stupid," she said in a whisper.

"What did my dad say to you about it?"

"He was fantastic, Rafe. Just great. He never said a thing. I had some time off college and when I went back in, it was as if nothing had happened. I got on with my work and he was just the same as always. You're so lucky to have such a great dad. But it's why I've never come into your house. I wanted to tell you first."

I thought about what she'd said long after she dropped me off. Dad came home from work, we had a hurried meal and then he went to the hospital to visit Mum. All the time he was out I mulled over everything Sophie had told me. Pieces began to fall into place. I remembered the argument Mum and Dad had after the inquest and how Mum had said something about a subject he didn't want to rake over. She must have been referring to the incident at college.

I was watching television when he came back at about nine-thirty almost bouncing into the house. He was grinning like a teenager, prancing like a pony. He's a terrible actor. I knew he was putting on a *everything's fine* show for my benefit.

"It's all going to be all right, son," he said. "I've had a word with your mother's doctor."

"Has Mum said anything yet?"

"No, but they say it's only a matter of time. It's been a bit of a shock. For all of us really, hasn't it? But I don't want you to worry. Everything's going to be fine."

"I told her I'd take some time off studies to be at home to help her."

He sat on the sofa beside me. "No, Rafe. She wouldn't want you to do that. *I* don't want you to do that. I'll make sure she isn't left on her own when I'm at work. I'll manage it somehow."

"Good. I'm glad," I said. "Maybe now we can get some things cleared up."

"I need a drink first." He went for the gin and tonic. He offered me a glass.

"I don't feel like celebrating anything just yet, Dad," I said.

"Why? What's the matter?"

"You are. You and Mum. I want you to tell me what's been going on."

"I should have thought that was obvious," he said and I swear his cheeks flushed.

"That's not what I mean. It's not so long since you told me things had been bad between you and Mum for a long time. Why don't you ever tell me and Richie anything?"

"Like what, for instance?"

"Like about being suspended from work."

He put down his glass and stared at me. "How did you know? Your mother and I wanted to keep that from you boys. It was all nonsense."

"Sophie told me."

"It was all a silly mistake. You know Sophie Harding?"

"Yes. I know her. And what about Grandma?"

"What about her? Rafe, put that out of your mind now. You have to get on with your life."

"I am. And I've been doing a lot of thinking. Sophie was brave enough to tell me today that she made a foolish mistake. I have to be as brave. I've been keeping something to myself. Did you know that Grandma had been taking pills the doctor didn't know about?" Dad shook his head. "She was. I saw her taking some once when I went to visit at her house. Then when she came to live with us here she had the same kind. At the inquest Doctor Dalton said she wasn't on any medication. Dad, did you order drugs for Grandma online?"

"What?"

"Pills. Painkillers. Listen, Dad, I'm the one who showed her how to use the internet. I know she shopped online. You got rid of the old computer I gave her so we can't check which websites she visited. When she came to live here did she use yours or did you order things for her?"

Dad rubbed at his chin and said, "I showed her how to use my laptop."

"Right," I said. "Let's have a look."

We went to the dining room table and he stood beside me looking over my shoulder as I brought up Grandma's history. A quick check through her email account brought up confirmation of an order she'd placed for the same painkillers during the time she lived with us.

"Those are the ones I saw her taking," I said. "It's the same packet Mum found in the bin."

Dad said, "They're just painkillers. It's probably cheaper to buy them online than it is to get them over the counter."

"You can't get them over the counter, Dad. That's the point. They're addictive. You're only supposed to have them on prescription."

His jaw dropped. "You mean . . .?"

"Yes. That's exactly what I mean. It's possible Grandma was addicted to them. Why else would she keep using them?"

Dad was still rubbing at his chin and shaking his head. He looked as if he didn't know what to say next.

I said, "Will you make an appointment to see Doctor Dalton? I think we should make him aware. Don't you?"

He sucked at his bottom lip and said, "Hang on a minute, son. Let's think about that. If Jenny had taken those things on a regular basis wouldn't it have shown up in the post-mortem?"

I hadn't thought of that. I googled another question. Dad pulled up a chair beside me. Together we read through a British Medical Journal editorial.

Forensic medicine experts warn problems can arise because, unlike in cases involving living patients, toxicology tests after death can virtually never be informed by information about how drugs were administered and number of doses taken.

In addition, if a person has been a chronic drug user, and has developed a 'tolerance', it can be factored into toxicology measurements for living patients but cannot be measured in dead bodies.

"That doesn't help us," Dad said. "What else can you find, Rafe?"

Dad was as excited as me, if that's the right word. I found a report where overdose of the same

drug Grandma had used caused four deaths in the southwest during 2011.

"Jesus," Dad said. This stuff's lethal."

"So is alcohol if you don't use it properly and you can buy that over the counter."

He pulled his chair closer. "See what you can find out about blood tests. Post-mortem blood testing. Surely if Jenny had taken this regularly there would have been traces of it in her blood."

We looked at several sites. We learned how and which samples are taken during an autopsy and where they're taken from. A toxicology report would show how chemicals are released and distributed throughout the body after death. I was fascinated. Then I found a forum where people were asking exactly the same questions as us. *How long does it stay in your system?*

We had our answer. The painkiller Grandma used lasted, at most, six hours. Recommended dosage allowed for four-hourly repeats. Warnings included *not to be taken with alcohol.*

I leaned back in my chair and said, "Grandma was drinking on New Year's Eve, Dad."

He got up and went for the bottle of gin. He poured some for me too. I switched off the laptop and we went back into the living room. I turned down the volume on the television and we sat quietly, just looking at one another, drinking from the same snowflake-patterned crystal glasses that had killed Grandma.

Dad said, "It wouldn't change anything. Jenny's death was still an accident."

"I know."

"I won't say anything to your mother until after . . ."

"Right. Okay. Dad?"

"Yes, son."

"Why did you say things had been bad between you and Mum?"

He grunted and said, "Ah, Rafe. It's a long story and it's none of your business."

"Yes it is my business. You and Mum are the most important people in my life. I want to understand. Mum told me about when she was little and how Grandma treated her. Why can't you do the same and open up?"

I knew by the look on his face he wasn't going to tell me anything I didn't already know.

"You'll have enough problems of your own one day, son. Why would you want to hear about mine?"

"Because you're my Dad and I love you."

"There's nothing special about me, Rafe."

"Yes there is. Everybody says so. You're a special teacher. You're a special father. You were a special man to Mum."

"Once, maybe."

"That's what I mean, Dad. That's what I'm talking about. All right, so you won't tell me what I'm asking. It's all down to you then. It's up to you now to make everything all right from now on."

61

Marcus

I never told Seamus Dalton about my suspicions. The following Monday morning he called a staff meeting and announced his immediate retirement.

He grinned and slapped me on the back. "Don't tell me it's long overdue, Marcus. I know it is."

"How does Mrs Dalton feel about it?"

"Delighted. Absolutely delighted. She went to the travel agents on Saturday and brought back cruise brochures." He wore a smile as wide as the Irish Sea and his eyes sparkled with enthusiasm. "The Caribbean. Maybe New Zealand or Hawaii. She hasn't decided yet." He rubbed his hands for sheer joy. I put aside the Carter questions.

Two days later after his last evening surgery we had a hurried champagne treat in the outer office before Seamus took his annual leave pending his retirement. Before he left he came into my room and closed the door.

"Have you a minute, Marcus?" he said. "I'd like to have a private word before I go."

"Of course. Come in."

He sat where my patients usually sit and crossed one leg over the other. He sniffed.

"I don't like to leave you with all those unanswered questions," he said.

"What unanswered questions?"

"Carter questions."

"Oh, *that*."

"What do *you* think, Marcus? What do you think I missed?"

I answered quickly. Seamus Dalton might have been more than ready for his retirement but he was still astute enough to recognise that any hesitation on my part would signify there was something I didn't want to divulge.

"I don't think you missed anything, Seamus," I lied. "Jenny Carter's death was an accident."

He uncrossed his leg and leaned forward.

"Yes," he said. "Her death was an accident but that's not what I'm referring to."

He got up, left my room and walked into his vacant consultation room. I followed him. The desk was clear of his usual piles of notes. The walls were bare where he'd removed his posters. He looked as if he was saying his final goodbye to his workspace. He ran his hands along empty bookshelves that had held his *Gray's Anatomy* tomes and other medical volumes including a copy of *The Coming Plague: Newly Emerging Diseases in a World Out of Balance* by Laurie Garrett. It had been a gift from Sarah and me.

"I always tried to keep abreast of new thought," he said.

"As do we all, Seamus."

He turned and stared into my face. "Be honest, Marcus. Was I negligent?"

"Not in the least," I answered quickly. "Nobody could have done more with what we knew at the time."

He drew his lips into a thin line and said, "I hope so."

"Seamus," I said. "Go and have your well-earned holiday. Enjoy your retirement. Come back and tell me all about it and make me envious."

Next day the locum arrived with a box of personal belongings, rearranged the bookcase in Seamus's room, turned the desk at an angle and hung modern prints on the walls. Pat asked to have a word with me the same afternoon.

"It's about Doctor McCloud," she said. "She wants us to set aside five minute only appointments so we can quickly intersperse them with other patients if anybody's late."

"I see."

"Well it won't work, will it, Doctor Harding? What if a five minute patient is late? And how am I supposed to know which is which when they ring in?"

"Let's give it a try, Pat, shall we? Doctor McCloud is finding her feet. I'll keep my eye on it."

"Thank you, Doctor, but I don't like all these sudden changes."

I took some paperwork and headed toward my consultation room. On the way I popped my head around McCloud's door.

"Settling in?" I said.

"Nearly, thanks." She was unpacking cartons of her own medical books. In one corner of the room she'd placed a child-sized table and chairs and boxes of plastic building bricks. "I'll feel more at home when I've met more of my patients."

"Tomorrow then," I said and went to my room. I closed the door and sat at my desk. Steady drizzle pattered at the window. I had an image of Seamus Dalton in a Hawaiian shirt patterned with lilac flowers to match his hair. *Should I have told him what I suspected?* I thought. No. The thought didn't last long. I decided I'd made the right decision.

The role of a GP has had to change. In my parents' day the family doctor came to know his patients almost as closely as his own family. Then, your GP may not have had expertise in a special area as we do today as GPwSIs, (General Practitioners with Special Interest) but he was an expert in *you*. Most likely he was an expert in your whole family, your children, everybody. He had supervised your wife's pregnancy, your mother's ulcers. He knew that you were allergic to penicillin without having to ask. He prescribed creams for your eldest son's acne and lanced the boils under your arm right there in his office. The patient came to the surgery in ignorance of the condition most likely to be the cause of his symptoms and trusted his doctor's deeper knowledge.

Today they come armed with information gathered from the internet. They say things like, *I think I may have Celiac disease, doctor*, and then they go on to tell you the full range of symptoms they are experiencing. They already know what medication you are likely to prescribe and can discuss alternative treatments. I am in favour of patients taking responsibility for their own well being so far as a healthy lifestyle and healthy diet and the rest of it. But we must be careful.

One woman, at the Norfolk surgery where I worked as a locum before moving to Wiltshire, fought for years on behalf of her son. She *knew* there was something different about him but his school said he was a difficult child who simply didn't like physical education. Nobody believed the boy or his mother when they said it *hurt* him to run about. His doctors could find nothing wrong with the child. That boy was in his thirties and had developed problems with his eyes, aortic aneurysms and his torso and limbs were covered in stretch mark striations where the connective tissue of his skin had collapsed before his Marfan Syndrome was finally diagnosed. And all because his mother never gave up the fight and the fact that the World Wide Web had brought information into her home. His condition is rare, it's true, but the mother was the one who had put the time and effort into researching her son's symptoms. She had pursued and pestered her local 'experts' until they conducted the correct tests.

Yet I maintain that we have to be careful. For, if many patients are able to recognise that their symptoms may point to a specific illness so they can bring it forward to their GP, isn't it possible that many others could use that same information to *hide* what they have discovered? It doesn't matter what their reasoning may be. Denial perhaps, or fear of the outcome, life insurance disqualification, shame or embarrassment. But a little knowledge can indeed be a very dangerous thing. We know people self diagnose and buy medication online. It's an extremely precarious situation and I don't have the answers for what we need to do about it. Now, at least, I will be able to make McCloud aware of Wendy Carter's possible genetic inheritance.

62

Margaret

I visit Wendy as often as I can. She's improving slowly. Sometimes when I go she's out of bed and sitting in the chair alongside. The cotton nightgown she had was so old-fashioned. I remember I mentioned it to Marcus one day and he pulled the strangest face and asked me to describe it to him.
"It's a long, white cotton thing," I said, "with a bit of lace round the neck."
"Just like in Peter Pan," he said. "You know, Mother, Wendy in Peter Pan. Not quite a woman. Not still a child."

I thought it rather morbid, almost like a shroud, so I bought her some snazzy pyjamas and a smart wrap to go over the top. I can't tell if she likes them. She still won't speak. Occasionally she gets up from the chair and walks along the corridor behind the ward bays. I help her into her slippers and I walk with her and talk. I tell her about what's growing in my flowerpots. I tell her about Brenda's latest escapades and Janice's new recipes. I bring in magazines and read the problem pages for her. I think she's listening but I can't be certain. She draws her fingers into her palms and holds them in tight fists. Then she releases them. Open and close. Open and close, all the time as if she's trying to remember what she once held.

From time to time I come across Rob Carter in the visitors' room. We speak briefly. He never refers to the heart to heart we had and neither do I. I had hopes for a fresh beginning for them. They still have a lot of life left to live. What better time to put aside their differences and make a fresh start? They couldn't have a better reason, life beginning anew.

Sometimes it's possible to say *it's never too late.* Sometimes, we can convince ourselves that we can make a fresh start, that we can put everything behind us and wipe the slate clean. But each time I see him the defeated look he wears is further ingrained on his face. When I look into his tired eyes I can no more see a future with Wendy in that empty stare of his than I could have envisaged one for me that included Anthony. But I had been able to get away. Rob and Wendy Carter, it seemed to me, were trapped in a house they could not sell with a past that would not leave them alone.

Marcus believes she has retreated into a fantasy world. He says it's possible she may suffer from the same condition as her mother.

63

Did you think I'd gone away, my darlings? Disappeared forever? Not me. I'm always here somewhere. Always here for somebody. Even on the darkest days when you think all traces of me have been extinguished I'm waiting for your right time to reappear. So it's only right and proper that I should have the last word.

Listen. Mrs Wendy Carter is indisposed and will not speak for herself. She hasn't spoken for three weeks. Apart from afternoons when she sits in a chair or shuffles along in her slippers beside her friend Margaret she lies in her hospital bed and stares at the ceiling, or at the walls, or out of the window. Her doctors say she must have plenty of bed rest. She must conserve her energies. Her days pass to the tune of rattling medicine trolleys and the squeak of crepe soles against machine-polished floors.

"How are you feeling today?" the crepe-soled people say.

She will not answer. Only I know the reason. She dare not begin to express the way she feels. Cheated. Betrayed. Forgotten. Used. Angry. Very angry. If she were to let the first thing out she fears she would never be able to stop. The lid would explode away from the forbidden thought box and all hell would be let loose. One word out of that box would release a storm, a howling banshee of profanities screeching into eternity.

Her whole life has been the gathering of this epic storm. Her mother started it. Jenny Carter with all her ups and downs, taking to her bed for weeks of bad days when Dad did all he could until the day he died. More weeks of bad days when Wendy didn't go to school because she was afraid of what might happen if she wasn't at home to take care of things. At nine years old she began taking on adult duties. At fourteen she was still taking on all that responsibility with nobody to help her. Missing lessons. Missing exams. Not learning the things young people are supposed to learn. Learning instead how to stifle her own needs by closing herself down.

Ah, the storm clouds have been gathering a long time. And then there was Rob. Rob who was supposed to be her knight in shining armour. He who was supposed to understand. The two of them against the world. What a sick joke. But Wendy isn't laughing. People whose bodies and minds are beaten hollow cannot laugh.

And Rafe. Even Rafe. What was he doing collaborating with the manipulative Sophie? Riding in her car? Wendy had seen them together on the day her boys came home for Easter. *What secret girlfriend,* Wendy had asked. And Richie had stunned her with his reply. *Her name's Sophie, Mum. She's the doctor's daughter.* Wendy stares out the hospital window and thinks, *Rafe, oh Rafe. How could you?*

And Margaret. Wendy has grown to love Margaret even though she is a Harding. Wendy put aside the knowledge of whose grandmother, whose mother Margaret is. For Margaret's sake. To be a good friend to an old lady who had lost her only daughter. To enjoy the feeling of giving loving friendship. Revelling in receiving back the same nurturing care. It had been wonderful for a time. It felt like everything Wendy had ever wanted. But it couldn't work. Not when Sophie could turn up at any time. Did Margaret know what Sophie had done? Hadn't she realised who Sophie's boyfriend was?

There are greeting cards on Wendy's bedside cabinet. Get Well Soon and others with pretty pink flowers and plump cherubs. The one from Joan says she's sorry but she can't get away just yet to pay Wendy a visit. Her lump of a husband has been ill and now Joan's got it and it wouldn't be right to bring all those germs into hospital so she's sending a card and some flowers instead.

Wendy is waiting in silence for the storm to pass. She knows how to wait. She's good at it. She's had years of practice. She waits until the lid on the forbidden thought box is as good as nailed into place. Nurses bring her medicine. Auxiliaries bring her meals and coax her to eat a little more.

"It's not good for baby," they say. "Come along, Wendy. Baby needs you to be well."

Baby's not here yet. Baby has been hiding. That's why Wendy must have bed rest. Baby is undernourished and in some distress. Wendy is required to keep on giving of herself. Someone new is now more important than anything else.

Wendy called me the Sandman. She needed a name for the way she found to relieve her frustration. She chose a name familiar to her from a time when I had helped her before. It's understandable. You all have your coping mechanisms, my darlings. You may find your own name for whatever it is that keeps you going when the way seems insurmountable. And when you have found the means to press on and given it your choice of name you should not be surprised to learn that I am the reason you do it.

And now you need closure. You need all those loose ends tying up for you. Of course you do. It's human nature. I'm made of loose ends. I *am* loose ends. *Human nature* is a wonderful thing. It has as many faces as there are people in the world. Here's an example: I know how much some of you enjoy having someone to hate. Were you disappointed when Sophie confessed to Rafe and it seemed she had been misjudged? Didn't you have a little sinking feeling that the self-obsessed teenager wasn't going to get her comeuppance?

But how can we know she was telling Rafe the truth? She might have been telling more lies. When I told you there are no liars here did you think I meant *everybody?* I was referring to the narrators. Did I mislead you? Or did you put that together by yourself? *Human nature.* How do you know when anybody is telling you the truth? Would you be able to tell if Sophie was using Rafe to get to his brother, Richie who she fancied more? Richie would be more her type, wouldn't he? A little bit dangerous in his circus clothes and with his wacky haircut. Can you see Sophie being satisfied with good old Rafe in his boring jeans and with his gentle, caring ways? You must decide.

Here's the end of one of those loose ends: the bottle of sleeping pills in Wendy's handbag. Why did she always carry them with her? It's really very simple: to remind her of what she nearly did. What she was planning to do to herself. She found the strength not to do it. That's how much she loves *me*. When she came away from Doctor Marcus Harding's surgery with the prescription in her hand did you think, even perhaps for one fleeting moment, that she was planning something even more terrible? Working in the coffee shop it would have been a simple matter to crush those pills and sprinkle some onto Margaret's food to get her revenge on the Harding family. She had every opportunity to do just that when she was caring for her elderly friend. She hated the Hardings, after all. I bet it crossed your mind. You like mysteries. *Human nature.*

You think we are now coming to the end? I don't think so. My darlings, I'm still here for all of you. I'll always be here. I'm deathless. That's why I know everything about all of you. You can't know it for yourself because you can't always see beyond what's in front of you.

Remember when Wendy first went to see Doctor Marcus Harding? He knew she was agitated and uncomfortable in his presence but he had no idea why she could hardly look at him or why she sat in his surgery office twisting away at her wedding ring. Doctor Harding also sincerely believes his daughter is turning into a lovely young lady but you're not so sure about that, are you? He also believes his wife is honest to a fault. Ah, Marcus, how little you really know about what goes on in your own home. And Margaret believes Sarah is such a good mother. Does a good mother lie to her husband? Surely with all her perceptiveness Sarah would have seen through her daughter's explanation of what had happened in college?

But it's probably for the best you don't know everything about other people. How would Rafe have coped with the knowledge that the grandmother he'd loved as a child had called him and his brother ugly babies? Ah, Rafe. You have a lot to learn about me. We can forgive your little white lie about the minibus at Christmas. You only wanted to protect others. You pretended you were meeting friends at the pub. Another lie. See how one lie always leads to more even though you have other people's feelings at heart?

But there are lies intended to harm. Jenny Carter had a habit of using them often. She must have taken pleasure from hurting those closest to her. Maybe it was the clandestine medication that made her that way. Pharmaceuticals, as you all know, can alter people's behaviours. Maybe she was suffering the effects of her psychopathy and couldn't help her behaviour because her brain was wired differently from yours. That species of humankind feel no emotion: they are incapable of empathy or any of the finer feelings you associate with being human. Perhaps she was a narcissist who masked her true personality with a false persona designed to deceive and she deliberately chose to be cruel for the thrill it gave her. You'll never know. She is finished with me now but Wendy must live with the aftermath of the tragedy her mother brought upon herself. I am here to help you all but only up to a point. You have to want me.

You think I'm just a fantasy? Only a chemical imbalance in the brain? How can something that doesn't exist have a physical effect on a physical body? Ah, I'm an abstract noun then. Like Fear, you say, which has physical effects that can be measured. Like Hunger or Thirst. Jealousy and Greed. Pain and Suffering. I notice you do not mention Love. Without it there is such a void in people's lives that *something* will come in to fill the gap. The absence of real love in your relationships is like a welcome mat to me. The door to your house stands open and I *will* come in.

You can take your psychoactive drugs for an experience that approximates. You know the ones I mean: those that slip through the blood-brain barrier, the ones that come sometimes in a nasal spray and make people with autism behave in a more socially *acceptable* fashion. You can study the effects of serotonin and oxytocin and give them cute names like love-drug or make your ecstasy type recreational pharmaceuticals. But you will be pretending.

I'm the real thing. I'm like Tinkerbell. All my darlings have to do to keep me alive is *believe*.

Wendy's baby arrives in July. Rafe will give her one of my names. Conceived in a brew of one's lust and the other's disgust what chances will Hope Carter have? Born into a house of sorrow amid the ghosts of other people's terrible mistakes how will she grow? Will she be like her mother? Will she be like her grandmother? What child would choose to live in a home like that? You don't get to choose. You get what you're given. But, sometimes, what you see is not what you get. Hope Carter will be who she is either because of her upbringing or in spite of it. Whether she is aware of it or not she will have the choice. I see it so often my darlings. Just when you think you have everything bowling along nicely something unexpected makes the people you love behave out of character. Or maybe they were out of character all along and only now are you seeing the real person underneath the sham.

Yes, I confuse you. All of you want to know what my purpose is. You have wondered about that since the beginning of time. You like to have a purpose for everything. But everything changes. Nothing stays the same. You have to find your own ways of dealing with that. Some of you find it harder than others.

Before I go, here's a question for you. How can you ever understand what is going on in somebody else's mind when you know so little about the way your own mind works? Don't waste your time. There isn't an answer. You can't be in someone else's head. If you could, wouldn't that mean you'd have to be out of your own and where would that leave you?

I am your most precious gift though some of you don't know it. I am yours to do with as you choose but to many I'll always be a mystery. I never promised it was going to be easy. Were you hoping for a conclusion, my darlings? Ah, but real life has none because it has no narrative. You think this is The End? I know it isn't.

THE END

ABOUT THE AUTHOR

Celia Micklefield has worked in an accountant's office, a high street retail store, a textile mill and a shoe factory as well as short stints in a fish and chip shop, behind the bar in a pub and running a slimming club. She studied for a teaching degree and went into teaching at high school, became a partner in an import and wholesale business and ran a craft outlet at a country shopping experience. She returned to teaching where her last position was at a sixth form college.

She was born in West Yorkshire and has lived in Aberdeenshire and the south of France. She currently lives in Norfolk.

More books by Celia Micklefield

Patterns of Our Lives

Trobairitz - the Storyteller

Arse(d) Ends

Queer as Folk

All available in paperback and for Kindle. Visit Amazon's Celia Micklefield author page and join the conversations on her website www.celiamicklefield.com

You can follow Celia on Twitter @cmicklefield and on her Facebook author page.

Printed in Great Britain
by Amazon